Along Came Love

By Tracey Livesay

Along Came Love
Love On My Mind
Pretending with the Playboy
The Tycoon's Socialite Bride

Along Came Love

TRACEY LIVESAY

AVONIMPULSE
An Imprint of HarperCollinsPublishers

Excerpt from *Intercepting Daisy* copyright © 2016 by Julie Revell Benjamin.

Excerpt from *Mixing Temptation* copyright © 2016 by Sara Jane Stone.

Excerpt from *The Soldier's Scoundrel* copyright © 2016 by Cat Sebastian.

Excerpt from *Making the Play* copyright © 2016 by Tina Klinesmith.

EPub Edition OCTOBER 2016 ISBN: 9780062497758
Print Edition ISBN: 9780062497826

Avon, Avon Impulse, and the Avon Impulse logo are trademarks of HarperCollins Publishers.

10 9 8 7 6 5 4 3

*To my readers, who continue to
make this journey possible.
Thank you.*

Chapter One

INDIA SHAW'S STOMACH twisted into a Gordian knot. She pressed a hand to the still-flat surface, cursing the unfortunate mingling of nerves and nausea.

Settle down, Nugget. Please.

She lifted the starfish pendant that hung from the long silver chain around her neck and brought it to her nose. She inhaled, grateful when the sweet, bracing aroma of peppermint had the desired effect. Exhaling, she squinted against the bright San Francisco sun and watched the uniformed doorman assist the exiting man pushing twins in a top-of-the-line stroller, a leather messenger bag slung across his body. Sending them on their way with a wide smile, the doorman turned back to Indi and the indulgent expression melted from his countenance.

"Was there something else?" he asked, his tone managing to convey his disinterest in her response. He eased past her and reclaimed his post behind the chest high amber-colored glass cubicle.

Indi cleared her throat, choking on the *Asshole* that yearned to escape her lips. "About that list—"

"You're not on it."

"That's not possible." She took a deep breath, pushing back the panic that threatened to overwhelm her. "Can you check again?"

He ignored her and continued studying the large computer screen in front of him.

She braced her hands on the rich wood-grained counter and shifted her weight forward, trying to see the spellbinding monitor.

The man tightened his thin lips and shifted the screen, further obstructing her view of the list. "I don't need to check again. Your name isn't on the list of approved entrants for Penthouse A."

Her stomach churned again and she slid back to the ground, her boots knocking against the bag at her feet and echoing on the marble floors. This couldn't be happening. What was she going to do? Where was she going to stay? And how could she have forgotten that Chelsea and Adam wouldn't be home?

Because from the moment she'd seen those contrasting pink-toned, parallel lines, her brain had been as disordered as a greasy diner's breakfast scramble.

Sorry, Nugget. Bad analogy.

But how else to explain her sudden resignation from her job as a craft beer server at the brewery, her mad dash to the Seattle train station, and her having endured loud one-sided phone conversations and bone jarring bumps and rocking for the thirty-five-hour trip? She'd eschewed freshening up at the train station before heading to the apartment—preferring necessity over propriety—and assumed she'd sidestep her sister's interrogation, take a much-needed shower, grab food and a nap, *then* talk to Chelsea about her situation.

Not for one second had she thought gaining entrance to the apartment would be an issue.

Looking at the stack of brochures proclaiming the expanded hours of the restaurant off the lobby, she straightened them, making sure the edges lined up neatly and all the papers were facing in the same direction. "Clearly there's been a mistake—"

"This may be new to you, especially if you live in the Tenderloin," he said, scanning her braids, cable-knit sweater, long floral skirt, and leather ankle boots, "but here at the Hermitage at Avalon, we take pride in protecting the privacy of our homeowners."

Indi frowned. She didn't know what "live in the Tenderloin" meant—how could someone inhabit a piece of meat?—but his arched brow, curled lip, and eau de condescension was enough to clue her in to his opinion of her.

Did this man think he could intimidate her? She'd been thrown shade by people more elite and more proficient at it than him. She plastered on a bright smile.

"I'm sure Chelsea and Adam appreciate that, but it's not required in this case. You've met Chelsea, right?"

"Mrs. Bennett?"

Indi rolled her eyes. "Technically, but she's keeping

her last name. We used to talk about it when we were younger. She'd say she wasn't going to work hard to establish her career and name only to give it away when she got married. So, see? How would I know that if I didn't know Chelsea? We're sisters."

Lines creased his forehead. "Mrs. Bennett doesn't have siblings."

She swallowed. "Why would you say that?"

He narrowed his eyes. "Because I heard her mention it to Mr. Bennett."

Why would Chelsea tell Adam she didn't have family? Was it happening already? And if it was, could Indi blame Chelsea for wanting to embrace the happiness in her future and forget everything—and everyone—who reminded her of the past?

Indignation battled with anxiety and disappointment.

And nausea. These days there was always nausea.

"You were eavesdropping?" she challenged. "Is that part of the service the Hermitage at Avalon provides?"

"Maybe not," he said, his gaze darting away from her, "but a good concierge uses whatever tools are at his disposal to help him do his job. That's how I know you're not related to Mrs. Bennett."

"Your tools are a little dull. Chelsea and I aren't sisters by blood, we're sisters by circumstance. Foster sisters."

The doorman smirked and turned his back to her, but Indi reached across the desk and grabbed his arm. "Don't underestimate the bond we created. We're very close."

She couldn't imagine loving a biological sibling more.

Her chest tightened at the invisible wound created by that bond being severed.

He looked down at her hand on his arm and then back at her. She unclenched her fingers and removed her hand, holding both up in a gesture of peace.

"Look, I appreciate you're just doing your job, but Chelsea and Adam would want you to grant me access to their house."

"I'd have no problem doing so, despite my personal opinion, if they'd put you on the list. But they didn't, so . . ." He shrugged, not bothering to finish the sentence.

"So if Chelsea or Adam called and said it was okay, you'd put me on the list?"

His eyes remained glued to the screen as his fingers flew over the keyboard. "*If* they called *and* used their password, then yes, I'd put you on the list."

She couldn't even bask in the fleeting moment of satisfaction she'd experienced at his acquiescence. They wouldn't call because they were on their postponed honeymoon. She didn't remember where they'd gone, or even how long they'd be away, just that Chelsea had mentioned something about a resort in Fiji where Adam wouldn't be able to use his devices and they'd be free from any contact with the outside world for at least a week.

Dammit. She bit her lip and stared at the professionally garbed patrons dining next door. What if . . .

"Does it have to be Chelsea or Adam?"

That got his attention.

"Excuse me?"

"You said 'on the list,' so one must already exist for them. Is it fair to assume it contains other names?"

He crossed his arms tightly across his chest and stared down his nose at her. "Possibly," he said, drawing the word out into several syllables.

Indi nodded. If this list granted access to their house, it would be populated with the names of people they trusted. If Chelsea had set it up, Indi's name would've occupied the top slot. Their stint through the foster care system solidified their relationship. They'd experienced ordeals that either caused people to never speak again or bond for life.

Chelsea trusted her. Of course she did.

Are you sure?

Indi refused to take notice of the splinter of doubt that implanted itself just beneath her skin.

That meant Adam had probably established the list and moved on to his next task, not thinking Chelsea's input was necessary. To say the gorgeous genius and CEO possessed a single-minded focus understated his intensity. And suddenly, Indi was certain of who was on the list. Adam's two best friends, Jonathan Moran and Mike Black.

Sensation bobbed and weaved in her belly.

Oh, so you recognize the name, huh, Nugget?

Mike.

Memories she'd tried desperately to suppress came skipping to the fore of her mind. His brilliant blue eyes holding her gaze while his hands learned the contours of her body. His unruly blond curls clutched between her fingers, while his lips skimmed across her skin. His lean muscled body nestled between her thighs as he coaxed back-arching orgasms from her.

He was Adam's best friend and Chief Operating Officer of their immensely successful technology company, Computronix. He'd played an instrumental role in Chelsea and Adam meeting and almost losing each other forever. The man was tenacious, ruthless, and self-righteous. But after three tequila body shots, she found him charming, fascinating, and panty-meltingly sexy. Why hadn't she learned her lesson in five semesters of college?

Nothing good *ever* comes from tequila.

She refocused on the point she wanted to make. "If a person on the list called you, could they verify that I should be on the list?"

"No."

Crap. She twirled one of her long braids around her index finger. But—

"If a person on the list showed up and requested entrance, you'd have to let them in, right? Even if they were with a guest?"

His face contorted as if he'd swallowed something unappetizing.

Score! *It's your birthday, it's your birthday. Go Indi, go Indi.*

And yet, once again, she had to deny herself the taste of victory. Jonathan, a James Beard Award-winning chef wasn't in the city. At Chelsea and Adam's wedding he'd informed everyone that he'd be spending the next year in DC, opening a new restaurant.

That left Mike as her only option.

She couldn't call him. The last time she'd seen him, she'd been leaving his bed at the crack of dawn after a sex-filled—and -fueled—weekend. The last time she'd spoken to him had been the night before she'd crept away: she'd screamed his name and dissolved into an orgasm when his tongue pushed against her clit. She couldn't call him now and say, "Hey, I know I disappeared on you and ignored your calls and texts, but can you put that behind you and help me?"

And that would be the *easiest* part of their conversation.

No, she couldn't contact Mike. Not yet. So what was she going to do? Despite her travels, she'd never been to San Francisco. Besides Chelsea, Adam, and Mike, she didn't know anyone else in the city, and she'd spent most of her cash on the train ticket and the cab from the station. If she'd stayed in Seattle and worked in the brewery until the weekend, she could've made more than enough in tips to—

Her lips parted on a gasp.

Her stash.

Sporadically over the past few years, she'd entrusted some of her earnings to her sister. A personal savings account that earned no interest because Indi refused to let Chelsea deposit it in a bank. And Chelsea always had it, no matter where she'd been living. It was here. Indi could take some of that money and get a nice hotel room until Chelsea and Adam returned from their honeymoon.

"When does Barney's shift begin?" she asked, changing tactics. "He was on duty when I stayed here three months ago during the wedding."

The doorman blinked. "Barney is on indefinite leave."

"Oh no!" she gasped. "Is he okay? Was it his wife?"

The doorman's eyes bulged briefly before receding back into his face. "I cannot discuss his private information." He hesitated. "But how did you—"

"The last time we talked she'd just been diagnosed with Parkinson's. I volunteered at a hospital where they'd had successful trials using a cancer drug to treat some of the symptoms. I gave him some information so he could mention it to her doctor."

"Oh," he said, tapping his thumb against his bottom lip.

Was that a weakening in the levee? "How would I know that if I hadn't spoken to Barney? And I'd only have spoken to him if I was here and spent time with him and that would only have been possible if I actually knew Chelsea and Adam."

She waved her hand with a flourish. That had been a persuasive argument. Surely he couldn't refute that logic?

"If I recall it properly, we had really low temperatures a few months back. Maybe you stepped in from the cold, and Barney, being the nice guy he is, chatted with you while he let you thaw out. Maybe you *have* been here before, but to visit other people. Or maybe you're a stalker and that's how you know the information."

She frowned. *Come on.* She hopped up and down on her toes, attempting to hold off the encroaching exhaustion. "This is silly. I'll only be a second. You can come with me. There's something I need to get—"

"You're not on the list."

"Enough with that fucking list!"

The door to the restaurant opened and the overpowering odor of garlic wafted over and immediately snuffed out her ire. The assault to her senses was devastating. She placed a hand on the counter, bent over at the waist, and took several deep, cleansing breaths. She grabbed her scent necklace, willing the peppermint to assist Nugget and the nausea in chilling the hell out.

Most people would've shown her some compassion, some consideration. Not the doorman. He offered no assistance, just delivered his final poisonous barb.

"Did you ever consider that you're not on the Bennetts' list because they didn't want you to be?"

His words were more disruptive then the garlic. They snaked their way through her, winding their way around the handles and flinging open the doors behind which she'd hidden her deepest fear.

Indi was no longer the most important person in Chelsea's life. And she'd continue to tumble down that list as Adam's friends, family, and kids arrived on the scene.

Her muscles tightened and her belly fluttered. Indi straightened and pushed her shoulders back.

Don't worry, Nugget. I don't care what that asshat says. I'm getting into that apartment.

WITH A SATISFYING click the last tumbler settled into place. Indi removed the bent hair clip from the lock, dusted her hands together, and pushed to her feet. The fact that the lock was still an old-fashioned tumbler and key and nothing more high tech was her first clue that Chelsea and Adam still hadn't settled in.

People thought very little of expressing their opinions about her "frivolous" tendency to move from city to city, job to job. But she learned something important from each relocation experience, whether it was a clearer understanding of what she didn't want to do or a skill she could cultivate for later use. In this case, working with a private investigator in Greensboro yielded more than the money she'd needed to get to the next city.

She hefted her fringed backpack over her shoulder and edged open the door. She'd left the building after her encounter with the doorman only to sneak back inside when he'd provided assistance to a guy delivering several large packages. She paused, listening for the telltale beeping of an alarm system. Hearing none, she slipped inside, turning to quietly shut the door . . . and causing her backpack to crash against a pile of boxes stacked near the entrance. She cringed and watched as the box on top clattered to the marble floor in horrifyingly slow motion, the noise resounding throughout the cavernous foyer.

Dammit.

Had that been as loud as she feared or was the reverberated noise amplified by the pounding of her heart, the ringing in her ears? She stared at the mess she'd created and recognized the contents as accessories from Chelsea's apartment in LA. Working quickly, she stacked the gold-framed pictures and books back into the box. She rescued a lamp that dangled by its cord, frowning at the frosted glass bowl that lay in pieces on the floor.

"This is all the doorman's fault," she told Nugget, using her boot to sweep the pieces of the bowl into a pile. "If he'd just let me in like I'd asked, I wouldn't have had to stoop to these tactics."

Indi headed down the short hallway. The sun glinted off the bare beige walls and spotlighted another stash of boxes piled beneath the chair rails. In her LA condo, Chelsea had displayed her vibrant art collection. Their absence here was her second clue that the penthouse hadn't become their pent*home.*

The hallway opened into a large, bright room bracketed by two walls of floor to ceiling windows. Dropping her backpack on the caramel-colored sofa, she took a moment to soak in the majestic view. It was postcard quality: pale blue waters, cloud-capped mountains, a bridge in the distance. She was as enthralled with it now as she'd been when she'd first seen it before Chelsea and Adam's wedding. Unlike then, she didn't have time to sit on the wraparound balcony. She needed to locate her cash stash and get out of the building without the doorman's knowledge.

The burnt-orange area rug muffled the sound of her boots. Where to begin? More boxes populated this room, too. On the floor, on the large stuffed sofa, on the low coffee table made of some dark, thick wood. Some boxes were opened with bright accessories peeking out of the top. Some of the boxes were closed. Most were covered in Chelsea's familiar scrawl. Indi conducted a cursory examination of the boxes' labels, finding nothing more descriptive than the owner's name and the location.

Despite the clear disarray of the place, the tableau represented a harmonious merging of two households, two styles, two personalities. Her vision blurred. What would it feel like to belong? To know where you were supposed to be and who you were supposed to be with? The closest she'd ever come to that feeling was the eight months she and Chelsea had been foster sisters. She'd finally met someone who cared about her well-being. Someone who looked at her and saw a person, not a paycheck.

A lesson for you, Nugget. Self-pity is so unbecoming.

She wouldn't begrudge Chelsea her happiness, even as she dreaded the eventual change in their relationship. Pursing her lips, she headed across the large room, toward the master bedroom and the section of the house that led to Chelsea's office.

When Chelsea had given Indi the tour before the wedding, she'd shown Indi the room she'd claimed.

"It gets great light and the view of the bay is incredible. But most importantly, it's on the opposite end of the house from Adam's office and his workshop. When we both need to work, it's best if we stay away from each other."

Her features softened, one corner of her mouth quirked upward, and her eyelids lowered like window blinds covering a provocative scene.

It was the look of a woman recalling sheet-fisting, toe-curling sex.

"Ewww," Indi said, slapping her shoulder.

"Don't you 'ewww' me." Chelsea planted her hands on

her hips. "If I had to listen to you create odes about the showerhead in my old apartment, you can deal with a look while I think about the man I love."

Chelsea had managed to mount the big screen TV on the wall opposite her desk and assemble the ceiling high bookcase and shelving unit. But the stash of boxes labeled "Chelsea—Office" and the clutter of supplies on her desk indicated that she still had a ways to go before she was settled in.

Ugh! Indi clenched her teeth. There was no way she could go through all of these boxes. She let her head drop back and her gaze fly skyward. That's when she saw it. On the top shelf, a small blue sphere jutted from the bookcase. She'd found one.

She rolled her eyes. Of course it'd be at the top. Chelsea was an Amazonian goddess, several inches taller than Indi's own slightly above average height. But even she would've needed help getting it up there. These were ten-foot ceilings.

Indi grabbed the lightweight chair from the corner and carried it to the bookcase. Bracing herself against the unit, she climbed up and grabbed the blue ceramic penis from its "hiding" place.

There was a slit in the top—heh!—where money could be put, but unlike most piggy banks, no plug in the bottom to make accessing the money easy. If you wanted your cash back, you had to break this bad boy.

When Indi had aged out of the foster care system, she'd vowed to never be dependent on anyone else again. She'd go *where* she wanted, do *what* she wanted, and not let anyone dictate *how* she would live. For the first time ever, *she* was in control of her life. To that end, she got a job as quickly as possible and worked nonstop for six months. She saved up every penny she could until she had an amount she believed she could live off, for a month or so, if necessary. She'd sent that money, in a ceramic figurine, to Chelsea and asked her to hold on to it. Over the years, she'd sent her more and more cash-filled figurines until Chelsea could've operated her own tchotchke kiosk at the mall.

They were her cash stashes. Her "break only in case of an emergency" savings fund. And not an "I need this dress—it's on sale for only two hundred dollars" kind of emergency. This was for a "shit's going down and my options are limited" kind of emergency.

Pregnant. Alone in an unfamiliar city. No place to stay, no money at hand.

Yeah, this qualified.

She carried the earthenware phallus back into the great room and shoved it inside her backpack. She couldn't chance breaking it here. She needed to get out of the building unseen. She remembered there was a cute artisanal bakery up the street. She'd go there, use their restroom. She didn't know how much money was in this one, but there had to be enough to cover decent lodging for a week or so until Chelsea—

The door crashed open. Indi gasped, skidded back against the sofa, and sat down hard on the rolled arm.

The doorman frowned and pointed his arm, like a bad extra in an episode of *Law & Order*. "She— That's the woman who tried to talk me into letting her in here!"

Indi had difficulty catching her breath, the air around her selfishly deciding to remain free instead of trapped in her lungs.

"Wait, what?" she wheezed.

"I thought you'd left. You can't be in here. You're not on the list."

"Sir, please." An officer held up a hand, an imposing figure in dark blue attire displaying the San Francisco Police Department seal. "Let me handle this."

Indi blinked. "This is just a misunderstanding. My sister lives here."

"But you're not on the list," the doorman interrupted. "If you're not on the homeowner's list, I can't grant you access when the homeowner isn't home."

"Ma'am, he says he didn't let you in because you don't have the proper authority." The officer's voice was low and steady.

Think, Indi.

"Authority means different things. I'm not on the list, but—"

"Then how did you get in here? Do you have a key?"

"Well, no, but—"

"Can you produce a key?"

The cold fingers of inevitability skittered down her spine. She crossed her arms over her belly. "No."

"Then I'm afraid I have no choice." The officer strode over to her, magically whipping cuffs from some undisclosed location on his uniform. The creaking of his leather shoes and gun belt seemed loud in the sudden silence. "You're under arrest. You have the right to remain silent . . ."

Chapter Two

MIKE BLACK HELD his right hand up, letting it hover several inches away from the glass orb affixed to the wall. Alternating red-and-blue lights scanned his palm.

"Fingerprint identification not secure enough?" The distinguished male voice behind him carried a trace of amusement.

"For Adam Bennett? No," Mike said, responding to Franklin Thompson, Founder and Chairman of the Board of ThomTexteL, a media and telecommunications conglomerate based out of San Francisco. "Palm-vein identification is extremely accurate because of the complexity of vein patterns. It's difficult to counterfeit because vein patterns are internal to the body, and unlike fingerprint scanners, it's contactless, therefore hygienic."

The orb glowed green. Lowering his hand, he pulled a platinum security key card from the inner pocket of his jacket and pressed it against the card reader beneath the palm-vein scanner.

"Michael Black, Chief Operating Officer. Entrance granted to the Palo Alto campus at 1:42 p.m.," a computerized voice intoned.

Thompson stilled. "Two layers of security. Impressive."

"Adam designed it himself. He's nothing if not thorough," Mike said, referring to his best friend and CEO of Computronix.

The large steel doors slid open with a whoosh. Above them, lights flickered on, one section at a time until the entire space, about eight thousand square feet, was illuminated.

"This is our Industrial Design Lab."

The masculine curse and feminine gasp of his two guests made him smile. He resisted the urge to spread his arms wide and slowly turn in a circle, though there was nothing he could do about the satisfaction expanding in his chest. If the executive floor was the brain of their company, this was its heart. The Lab, and the extraordinary people who worked there, was a large reason why Computronix was the fastest growing tech company in the world.

"Any other time our design team would be here, but we've given them two weeks off while Adam is away on his honeymoon."

Thompson took it all in, shaking his head as if in a daze. "Even within TTL, there are people who would sell their soul to be in this room."

Mike slipped his hands into the pockets of his slacks.

"Access *is* limited. There are Computronix executives who've never been in here."

"Then why do we rate this honor?" This from the petite blonde woman standing to the right of Thompson.

Skylar Thompson, Senior Vice President and Chief Financial Officer of ThomTexteL, Thompson's daughter, and if everything went according to his plan—and why wouldn't it?—his future wife.

"Because I have an exciting proposal for TTL and I hoped seeing this would put you in the right frame of mind."

Frosted windows enclosed three-quarters of the room, transparent enough to allow in light, but opaque enough to prevent anyone seeing inside.

Mike pointed to a glass enclosed office on the left. "That's Adam's private workspace. He has an office in the main building near mine, but when he's on campus, he's mostly down here with the team."

He stopped before a large open area where black tarps covered long wooden tables. "That's the Shop. It's where we manufacture our prototypes. Just behind it is the snack area. And over on the far right are our designer workspaces."

"I've never seen anything like it," Thompson said.

"Good." Mike paused. "Then you agree it was worth signing the nondisclosure forms."

"It was," the other man said.

"So, what's this exciting proposal?" Skylar's voice was all business, like her expertly tailored suit and the cornflower blue eyes that assessed him. There was no teasing, no innuendo, no coquettish come-on.

Her directness was one of the traits he respected most about her. She valued her business as much as he valued his. Neither of them had the time or desire for an impetuous romance. Skylar understood that companies the size of Computronix and TTL required total dedication and commitment from those charged with running them. It was why they would make a great team. They were ambitious, disciplined. Appropriate for one another.

Unlike other people . . .

"Let's talk over here," he said, moving quickly. As if he could outrun the memories.

He led Thompson and Skylar to the Presentation Space where large acrylic tables—mainly used to display current prototypes—were set up, almost like a classroom. He'd had most of the tables pushed back several feet, leaving one table placed before the large flat screen TV mounted on the side wall.

Mike grabbed the black case, the size of a ring box, located in the table's center next to a chrome cube twice its size, and opened it.

Skylar looked up at him and smiled. "I love my HPC. I use it daily."

"We're beta testing a new version, one that will allow you to use it with a screen or monitor." He placed the Holographic Personal Computer behind his ear, adjusting it until it fit snugly, like a hearing aid.

Thompson frowned. "Like a projector? Isn't that a step backward?"

"The HPC itself wouldn't project the image. It would transmit the data digitally and stream it to a display of your choice, using one of those." He pointed to the chrome cube.

"What is it?" Skylar circled the table in her designer heels and picked up the object.

"We're still workshopping names. Right now, we're calling it OTTo, for Over the Top box."

"A tad on the nose," Thompson said.

"Over the Top doesn't describe its looks, Dad." Skylar exchanged a knowing look with Mike. "It refers to its method of delivering media over the internet without the involvement of a cable company's service."

Mike rewarded her assistance with a wink.

Thompson crossed his arms over his chest. "TTL owns quite a few cable channels. We wouldn't be interested in a device that devalues our contract with cable companies."

"But I think you should be." Mike pressed the power button on the HPC and his desktop screen materialized in the air in front of him. He pointed to his presentation program then reached out and grabbed the small keyboard icon from the lower right corner, tossing it upward to bring forth its virtual counterpart. His fingers moved across the air, typing in his request for the outline he'd prepared for this meeting. "We recently commissioned a report on the viewing habits of millennials."

Skylar's hair swept against her shoulder as she tilted her head to the side. "Why the interest in what young people are watching?"

"Not *what*. How."

Thompson rubbed his chin. "I don't understand."

With the first page of the report visible before him, Mike took the chrome cube from Skylar, pressed the recessed power button beneath it, and placed it back on the table. He pressed another button on the HPC and his presentation dissipated from in the air and reappeared on the mounted TV screen.

"That's fucking incredible," Thompson said.

Mike took a deep breath and savored the moment. This was going even better than he'd anticipated. "Most people watch TV through cable companies. They purchase a package of channels, but rarely watch all of them."

Skylar and Thompson looked at each other and nodded.

He continued. "The report stated that most people only watch seventeen channels regularly. But how many channels do most cable packages give you? Two hundred? Four hundred? Cable companies know which channels are most popular, so they spread them out, stocking the premium ones in the most expensive packages. The consumer can spend more than one hundred dollars a month for a handful of channels."

"What does this have to do with TTL?" Skylar asked.

"Millennials are the fastest growing group of people who consume products and they are the first generation to not feel bound by loyalty to cable companies. They are cord cutters, cord cobblers, or cord nevers," he said, using the industry jargon that referred to the growing number of viewers who either canceled cable services, downsized their service in conjunction with using the internet to watch TV or those who never subscribed to cable service in the first place. "They watch Netflix or Hulu. They don't feel the need to watch anything in real time."

"They like to binge," Skylar said.

"Exactly."

"So what are you proposing?" Thompson asked.

"It's time Computronix got into the TV-streaming business."

Thompson shrugged. "Good for you. But you still haven't said what any of this has to do with TTL."

Skylar pursed her lips. "I'm guessing Mike knows TTL has been steadily losing money in our cable broadband division."

Thompson's head swung sharply in her direction and Skylar held her palm upright. "Not so much that it's a worry now, but enough that it's a noticeable trend."

Grooves and divots appeared on Thompson's forehead. "You want a merger?"

"A merger?" Mike shook his head. "Computronix would like to purchase exclusive rights to your digital cable channels."

Skylar wrapped one arm around her waist and rested her other elbow on it, the knuckle of her index finger tapping her chin. "And what would you do with them?"

"Offer them to our customers via OTTo."

It was a bold move, one no other tech company had yet to execute. The success of the HPC had been a game changer for Computronix. They'd gone from a successful tech company to the fastest growing one in the world. Additionally, the name *Computronix* had become synonymous with cutting-edge chic. They'd managed to cultivate a lifestyle brand. Mike was certain their customer base would follow them from technology into entertainment.

The stratagem would work. Of that he harbored no doubt. He'd known it'd be successful the moment he'd come up with the idea. He'd experienced the same feeling two other times: when he'd thrown his lot in with Adam during the genesis of Computronix and when Adam had first explained his concept of the HPC. Each pivotal moment he'd been on the verge of making an important decision that would affect the rest of his life. And he *knew* the right thing to do.

Still, he always weighed the pros and cons, refusing to make those decisions based solely on his gut. He could hear his father's voice:

"Your worst battle is between what you know and what you feel. Choose knowledge."

"It's a great idea," Thompson conceded, "and it could be beneficial to TTL. But what's to stop me from declining your offer and suggesting this same idea to another tech company? Hell, what's to stop me from manufacturing my own OTTos?"

Skylar swung around. "Dammit, Dad—"

"The noncompete clause in the nondisclosure agreement you signed when you first arrived," Mike interrupted coolly, holding the other man's gaze, refusing to rise to the bait.

Thompson blinked first. "So you're more than a pretty face. Good. I wasn't sure how much of this company's success was due to Bennett's genius and how much was due to you."

"I'd say we both bring essential traits to the table."

"I can see that." The muscle in Thompson's jaw pulsed. "Did you start dating my daughter to get to me?"

Tension added starch to Mike's neck and shoulders. It was an offensive question that challenged his integrity and impugned Skylar's judgment. He glanced at her to see how she'd respond, but she just watched him, her eyes narrowed a fraction, her glossed pink lips barely parted.

He refocused on Thompson. "No, but our association gave me the idea. It was the perfect partnership between our two worlds."

Thompson scrutinized him for an intense moment before a smile broke across his face. He nodded. "I like that."

Skylar's eyes crinkled at the corners. "I do, too. And on that note, we have to be going. Dad has a meeting back in San Francisco in an hour."

"You've given us an intriguing offer to consider," Thompson said. "We'll need some time to discuss it."

"I don't want to wait too long on this," Mike warned.

"Skylar told you we're heading to New York the day after tomorrow?"

Mike nodded. "For two weeks."

It's the reason he'd insisted on meeting with them today.

"As soon as we return, we'll call and set up a meeting. You have my word."

Warmth flooded him. Everything was falling into place.

This deal would make both companies a lot of money and propel him closer to fulfilling his ten-year plan.

Mike clapped his hands together. "Great. Let me walk you out."

They left the Lab and traversed the covered walkways back to the main building. They took the elevator to the roof and within seconds the loud cadenced hum of the approaching helicopter filled the air. Mike allowed Thompson to walk ahead, using the slight pressure of his hand on the small of Skylar's back to communicate his wish to speak with her.

She turned to face him, the silk curtain of her hair fanning against her cheeks and carrying her customary rich floral fragrance.

Quite unlike the sugared vanilla scent of another woman, another time.

"Are we still on for tonight?" he asked. With the finish line so close, he struggled to check his impatience.

"I'm sorry I had to cancel last week, but I knew you'd understand. It was imperative that I participate in that conference call."

He did understand. There'd been occasions where pressing matters at work had required him to call off their plans.

She smoothed his lapel. "Pick me up at eight."

He smiled. "See you then."

When he bent to kiss her good-bye, the coolness of her lips against his was . . . nice. Like he'd told her father, the perfect partnership.

Chapter Three

"I HEAR THE lovely Skylar Thompson and her father paid us a visit."

Ryan Sullivan, Senior Vice President and General Counsel of Computronix, met Mike when he exited the elevator on the executive floor.

Mike pointed his thumb over his shoulder. "They just left."

"How'd the meeting go?" Sully asked, falling into step beside him.

"It went well. They listened to my pitch, asked questions, and promised to give me an answer in a couple of weeks."

Sully stopped him with a hand on his bicep. "Please tell me you made them sign the nondisclosure contract before letting them into the Lab?"

They'd been lucky to recruit Sully after Computronix's initial growth spurt had overwhelmed their first general counsel. Sully understood his job was more than drafting contracts. He not only advised the senior executives on legal matters, he kept them apprised of public policy issues and ethical considerations. He exerted a great amount of influence on the overall activities of the company.

Mike smiled. "I did."

"My man!" Sully said, clapping him on the back. "And Adam's on board with this strategic shift?"

"I wouldn't make this move without him. This isn't a shift as much as it's an expansion. He's content to remain in charge of tech research and development. This area interests me and I have his full support."

Sully nodded. "I wouldn't be doing my job if I didn't double-check."

"Feel free to verify with Adam."

"Oh, I did. Before he left." Ignoring Mike's excoriating glare, he said, "You're not wasting any time on this 'expansion.'"

"When I see what I want and I know it's right, there's no reason to wait."

"Is that your professional motto or your personal one?"

"Both."

"And is dating Skylar right for you personally or professionally?"

"Excuse me?" Mike frowned at Sully, sure he hadn't heard him right.

"This deal with TTL. Is that why you're dating her?"

The affront chafed. "I suggest you don't ask me that question again."

He'd prepared to defend the benefits of Computronix and TTL going into business together, but he'd never considered that anyone would assume those benefits were the reason for his involvement with Skylar. The poisonous thought appeared to be taking root faster than the fallout from a blown dandelion weed.

But why would anyone question his interest? Skylar Thompson was beautiful, intelligent, poised. The type of woman to make his family—his father—proud. They'd been dating consistently for just over a year, except for the two weeks around the holidays when they'd been on a break.

A vision of sleek brown skin, slim thighs, and soft lips swept into his mind. He forced the image away. He wouldn't think about that weekend or her.

It had been an aberration.

Thick-pile carpet muffled his steps when they entered his suite of offices.

His assistant, Evan, swiveled away from his computer and stood. "How did the meeting go?"

"We'll know in a couple of weeks."

"Anya's waiting for you in your office. Would you like some coffee?"

"That'd be great."

Evan headed to the outer office. "I'll bring it in when it's ready."

"I'll come back later—" Sully began.

"Stay. Whatever it is, it shouldn't take long."

Anya perched on one of the wood-and-leather chairs that graced the front of his desk, her khaki-clad legs crossed at the knee, a Converse-covered foot jangling. Her hair was such a flaming shade of red, he had a difficult time believing it was natural.

But she could color her hair turquoise as long as her work remained exceptional. Her outside-the-box promotional strategy for the HPC had gone so well, they'd given her a raise and a promotion to Coordinator of Brand Management.

At his approach she shifted on her hip to face him, while pressing a hand against the small wireless headset she wore nestled within her fiery strands. "He's here. I'll call you back." She nodded in his direction. "I've been looking for you."

"So I gathered." He settled behind his desk.

"Do you have a moment?" she asked, looking between him and Sully, who sat in the chair next to hers.

"Sure. What can I do for you?"

She reached for the large envelope on the edge of his desk. "*People* magazine sent over an advanced copy of next week's issue. They're running the spread from Adam and Chelsea's wedding. Isn't that a gorgeous cover?"

Mike stared at the picture of the glowing couple gazing into each other's eyes against the backdrop of the San Mateo Mountains beneath a headline proclaiming Adam "The Sexiest ~~Man~~ Husband Alive!"

Their relationship had been a PR bonanza ever since Adam had announced it during the HPC launch event. They'd wanted the wedding to be an intimate affair and had opted for a small ceremony at their mountain home, banning press. Anya had been the one to suggest giving the magazine exclusive photos, arguing they could take advantage of the publicity while maintaining their privacy.

"Chelsea will love this," he said.

Adam's wife was a partner at Beecher & Stowe, one of the top PR firms in the country. Though she hated being in the public eye, she'd often said the benefit to both of their careers was invaluable.

"I can't wait for her to see it," Anya said.

"Do you know when they'll be back?" Sully asked.

"In another two weeks, according to the itinerary Chelsea left with me."

Anya smiled, revealing the piercing beneath her bottom lip. "A year ago I never would've imagined Mr. Bennett on an off-the-grid honeymoon."

A year ago Adam never would've entertained the idea, let alone gone through with it.

But that was before Chelsea.

"Why do you call him Mr. Bennett?" Sully asked the younger woman, his face molded into lines of faux innocence. "You call us by our first names."

Heat flooded her cheeks. "I know! But he's so . . . intimidating."

"Has anyone heard from Adam since they left? A covert text or email?" Mike asked, taking pity on her. He directed a cease-and-desist look at Sully.

She shook her head. "Nothing."

"He's probably going out of his mind," Sully said.

Mike pointed to the stunning woman on the cover. "Have you seen his wife? I'm pretty sure he's managing to stay busy."

He turned the page, stopping when he spied the photo of the wedding party. Adam flanked by his father as well as Jonathan and Mike. Chelsea flanked by Adam's sisters, Amy and Sarah, and . . . Indi.

He stroked a finger over her picture. God, she was beautiful. Smooth tawny skin, big light brown eyes, and luscious lips made for kissing. After the wedding, they'd spent a glorious weekend together and, despite knowing the rules of casual sexual encounters, he'd allowed himself to harbor expectations that it could lead to something more.

So he appreciated that she'd left while he'd been asleep and spared him the awkwardness of asking to see her again. His gratitude increased exponentially when she didn't respond to his calls or texts. Especially since she was not the type of woman he could've brought home to his father. Indi was too quirky, too spontaneous. A relationship between the two of them wouldn't have worked.

Yeah, gratitude. *That's* what he'd felt.

"Mike?" Anya tapped the back of his hand. "Are you okay?"

Fuck. He leaned back in his chair and scrubbed a hand down his chin. Wave her picture in front of his face and he fell into his feelings like a hormonal teenager. "I'm good."

Anya sat forward and stared at the magazine. "That's Chelsea's sister, right? She has an unusual name—"

"India." He couldn't help himself.

"She's hot," Sully said, pulling the magazine toward him. "I'm sorry I missed the wedding."

Jealousy scorched a hole in his gut and his upper and lower molars became intimately acquainted.

"She looks like this fragile, delicate being, but man, could she put away some tequila," Anya ended on an awe-filled whisper.

He'd done a few of those tequila shots himself, their intoxicating warmth later overshadowed by the feel of Indi's body pressed against his while they slow danced in the corner.

As if Anya had morphed into a mind reader, she said, "You two looked like you were enjoying yourselves during the reception."

He wasn't about to indulge her curiosity. Not now, when he was hours away from proposing to another person. "It was a magical day where my best friend married the woman of his dreams. Everyone enjoyed themselves."

"Okaaay." She rapped her knuckles against the magazine and stood. "I'll write up a report on the initial impact of the magazine's spread after it comes out."

"Thanks."

Sully's phone beeped and he checked the screen. His blue eyes sharpened. "Looks like we may be filing our first HPC patent infringement suit. I'll walk out with you, Anya."

Mike had barely begun jotting down notes from his meeting with the Thompsons when Evan rang from his desk in the outer office. "Your mother's on line two."

He placed her on speaker. "Mom, I told you to call my cell. Then you don't have to go through my assistant."

He always gave his parents the latest phones from Computronix with his information preprogrammed.

"I pressed the handset symbol next to the first number." Barbara Black's voice had a direct line to his smile, something he did easily—and often—in her presence. "That dialed your office. If you weren't there, I would've gone to the next one. Either way, I'd get to talk to you."

He shook his head, but since his mother never used the camera-phone feature, he knew she couldn't see him. "Everything okay?"

"Of course. Why?"

"We talked a few days ago."

"A mother can't call her son more than once a week?"

"Sure. You usually don't."

"I know."

She sighed and the emotion-ladened sound triggered his protective instincts. If his mother had a problem, he'd do whatever was necessary to find the solution.

"What's wrong?"

"It's your sister."

"Morgan?" His baby sister was in her second year at Stanford.

Cold fingers scrambled his insides. Had something happened? Had she been in an accident? Was she ill? If Morgan was in trouble, why hadn't his mother led with that information, instead of forcing him to pull it from her?

Her next words assuaged that fear but incited a whole host of others. "She's threatening to take time off from college, starting next year." A hitch in her breathing and then she said, "How can she quit when she's barely started?"

Something was going on with Morgan. He'd noticed it over the past few months. His sweet little sister had transformed into a moody, distant contrarian.

No matter. There's no way he'd let her throw away her education. Take time off from school? That was one step away from dropping out and leeching off their parents for the rest of her life. A plight that had already befallen some of her high school friends. For Morgan it would be unacceptable, not when she was capable of so much more.

His fingers curled into his palm. "I'll talk to her, Mom."

"Good." Barbara's relief was palpable. "She'll be home next weekend. You can talk to her then."

Reason for call ascertained and crisis handled, he'd already directed his attention to papers on his desk. "Why would I wait a week and a half? I can call her right now."

"Wouldn't you rather talk to her in person? This is pretty important."

"In person? Next weekend?" It took several moments before he noticed his mother hadn't responded. "Mom?"

"You forgot."

The accusation stung. "I—"

"Michael Justin Black, I told you about this months ago." Her admonishment faded into hurt and it bruised his heart. "I even called your assistant, who promised he'd put it on your calendar."

Mike scrolled to the appropriate app, pulled up his schedule and, clearly and conspicuously, several days were blocked off and labeled "Weekend in Barton Point,

Dad's party." He inhaled through gritted teeth. "I'm sorry."

Now he remembered. The Barton Point Chamber of Commerce was honoring his father for his contribution to the small city. Mike had planned to attend. He couldn't believe he'd forgotten about it.

"I have to leave for a meeting with the Junior League." He heard a muffled voice in the background, and then his mother's faint response. "Yes. You can talk to him while I finish getting ready. Give me a moment to say good-bye." She came back on the line, although the volume of her speech remained low. "Your father wants to speak to you. I haven't told him about Morgan yet so don't mention it. He'd have a heart attack."

Forget heart attack. Robert Black would have a stroke.

Mike knew he'd had a charmed upbringing. His family hadn't been rich—not the way he was now—but they'd been comfortably well off. Instead of spoiling his kids, his father had always preached that education combined with an impeccable work ethic led to an auspicious life. There'd never been a question of *if* they were going to college and graduate school. The only question had been *where*. If his sister thought she'd be able to get away with not finishing her studies, she was due for a rude awakening.

The fact that Morgan even considered such a move was concerning. His sister had always done what she was supposed to do. Save a few notable lapses on Mike's part, they both had. Their father wouldn't tolerate anything less.

The last time he'd gone against his father's wishes had

been when he'd chosen to start Computronix with Adam instead of staying in Barton Point and going into the family's real-estate business. Most fathers would've been proud that their son was strong enough to forge his own path in life. Not Robert Black, who'd expected his son to show his gratitude for the life he'd been provided by following the footsteps his father had already tread.

Their relationship had been strained for years because of that decision.

"I was talking to the guys at the country club yesterday and they reminded me it's been a year since we launched the HPC. What's next?"

No greetings, no easing into the conversation. Robert Black's voice heralded his imposing presence, whether it was heard in person or buffered through electronic devices.

Mike's gaze flicked upward. In the past few years, every conversation with his father involved talk about Computronix. And not as it related to Mike's health, happiness, or sense of well-being, but rather, what Mike was doing to make the company bigger and better than its competitors. More like an investor—which he wasn't—and less like a parent.

Mike shouldn't complain. He understood his father's need to make sure his children were living up to their potential. It had contributed to his titanium-strong work ethic. But though he understood it, his mood today wouldn't allow him to passively tolerate it.

"Don't worry. Adam and I are working on new projects."

If Robert caught his correction, he didn't acknowledge it. "Be that as it may, you can't rest on your laurels."

Mike exhaled loudly. "We're not."

"Good. Your generation possesses a tiresome sense of entitlement, but you can't coast on the coattails of Adam's invention. 'Hard work beats talent when talent doesn't work hard.'"

Sense of entitlement?

Bullshit.

He and Adam hadn't built Computronix with handouts. They'd worked their asses off and created their own success, in spite of some in the tech industry who'd chafed at their ascendency and had constructed roadblocks to impede their efforts.

"If you're going to stay on top," Robert continued, "you need to keep moving forward, pushing new products, and as a shareholder, I have the right to question . . ."

Shareholder: Robert's favorite refrain. The one he'd trot out anytime he wanted behind-the-scenes information. Hard-to-attain knowledge and the access such possession implied to his peers, was a valuable currency and one in which Robert Black was a master at trading. If the shareholder card didn't get him what he sought, he'd employ the Father Maneuver.

Mike interrupted the other man's lengthy tirade on his rights and responsibilities as a shareholder. "There is a special project but we're keeping it under wraps for now."

"But I'm your father," Robert said, the displeasure crystal clear in his tone.

Check.

"And I'm not too keen on an SEC investigation for insider trading."

Deeming a verbal submission beneath him, Robert moved on. "The Chamber of Commerce gala is on a Sunday, but you're coming in a few days early, right? I've already booked a round of golf for us at the club."

The carpet absorbed the rapid tapping of his foot beneath the desk. "I haven't played golf in years."

Not since his last visit to Barton Point. He hated golf. The only time he played was when his father dragged him to the course during his visits.

"Not a problem. Most of us are scratch golfers. We'll balance out your high handicap."

Gee, thanks.

"Are you coming alone?"

Where was this going? "Yes."

"Oh. You've been seeing a lot of that Skylar Thompson. I thought you'd bring her with you."

He'd thought about it, especially considering the change about to occur in their relationship, but the timing wasn't right. She'd still be in the midst of her New York trip and this visit was about Robert. He didn't want to shift the focus from his father's achievements. There would be plenty of time for Skylar to meet his family, something he'd never allowed with any of the women he'd previously dated.

"You can't wait too long," Robert said. "Adam has already taken the plunge. Hell, I was married and we were expecting you when I was your age. It's time for you to be thinking along those same lines."

That had occurred to him, too, but again, his mood didn't appreciate Robert's like-minded reasoning.

"I'll see you next weekend," Mike said, ending the phone call with his father.

He was mindful of the load of work clamoring for his attention. He needed to finish the notes on his meeting with TTL, read last quarter's financial reports, and sign off on five new HR hires.

All before his date with Skylar.

His gaze landed on the magazine Anya had left behind. His strong sense of caution couldn't prevent his fingers from pulling it toward him, flipping it open to the picture of the bridal party. He focused on Indi. In it, her smile was wide, beatific. But her eyes were a poignant mixture of happiness, guilt, and heartache. It had been her quiet sadness in the midst of the cloying joy that had drawn him to her. She'd had a secret. And he'd needed to find out what it was.

No, no, no.

He shook his head. Forget about Indi. Tonight he would propose to Skylar. He was doing the right thing. Their relationship, this deal, was the smart play for both his personal and professional lives.

His cell phone vibrated against his chest and he pulled it from his inner pocket. The caller ID showed an unfamiliar number with "San Francisco, CA" beneath it, but no other identifying information.

His brows converged in the middle of his forehead. There weren't many people who had his private cell number. He'd just told his mom to call his cell instead of his office. Was she calling from a landline he didn't recognize? But wouldn't the description read "Barton Point, CA"? It was probably a wrong number. And yet his finger hovered and then pressed the green button.

"Hello?"

"Mike."

He straightened. Her photo had seized his attention, but her voice . . . Her voice stroked his hedonistic hotspots. The tingle caused by every whispered declaration, every lingering caress, hit him all at once.

"Indi."

"Long time, no hear."

Her forced gaiety jarred him loose from her vocal web and allowed his brain to function. Why had she left? Where had she been? What did she want? Why was she calling?

"I know I'm probably the last person you want to talk to and I understand, considering how I ended things and I—"

He remembered this about her, the stream of talking on an endless loop. His favorite remedy? A cock-stirring, toe-curling kiss.

"Indi, spit it out."

A thick silence, and then—

"Can you post bail for me? I've been arrested for burglary."

Chapter Four

WELL *THAT* HAPPENED.

The door to the precinct closed behind Indi. Exhaustion weighed her down, leaving her head throbbing and her sight unfocused. She shivered, her cable-knit sweater offering inadequate insulation from the chill. Since her arrest, the fog had rolled in, bringing cooler temperatures and an ominous atmosphere.

If she had a bucket list, she could confidently check off this experience: get yourself arrested in an unfamiliar city. It hadn't been anything like *Orange Is the New Black*—Thank God!—but she had met some interesting women while she'd been booked and processed. Turns out, her unstable living situations and various relocations had equipped her with the unique skill set needed to survive the city's holding cell.

But she didn't do bucket lists. They were created for people who scurried through life afraid to take chances, regretting their caution when faced with their mortality. Indi's life *was* a bucket list. Hence, her current predicament.

"Where's Ryan?"

The brusque voice wrapped itself around her heart and squeezed. She stilled and her breath went on strike.

Those words. That tone. This situation. It wasn't how she'd pictured their reunion.

Though their best friends were married to one another, careful planning on her part would've given her several years to let time and distance erode the memories and allow them to communicate without her recalling the way he'd made her body quake with ecstasy. She'd be cool, look polished, and possess the proper grace to put them both at ease.

That had been the fantasy BN . . . before Nugget. Now she'd settle for an encounter where she didn't look and smell like a cat lady's ashtray and where she possessed something other than an unplanned pregnancy and a felony charge.

Despite his harsh tone, the man leaning against the silver Porsche Panamera—new; the last time she'd seen him, he'd been driving a Jaguar—was as gorgeous, as powerful, and as autocratic as the luxury sedan he drove. He'd tamed his blond curls—what a shame—into a sleek mass that shone beneath the street lamps and his body looked trim and powerful in a dark tailored suit and crisp white collared shirt without a tie. He could've been waiting for his date to a society gala and not standing in the street in front of the sheriff's office after midnight, waiting for the state judicial system's newest enrollee.

Indi hefted her backpack onto her shoulder, ignored the dips, swerves, and inversions occurring in her belly and slowly descended the concrete steps. "He's finishing up the paperwork."

She'd forgotten how big he was. She was a tad taller than average and she knew from experience her eyes would be level with his chin, a chin now covered in downy blond fuzz. Experience also taught her the stubble would be a delicious abrasion against her skin.

"Do you have anything to say to me?"

She blinked. She had much to say to him. But here? Now?

She'd hated calling him. Truthfully, she would've hated calling anyone in this situation. Would rather have stayed behind bars and figured a way out of this mess. But this wasn't about her personal preferences. She needed to make decisions in Nugget's best interests. And *that* meant doing what was necessary to ensure she spent as little time in jail as possible.

She hadn't seen Mike in three months, since she'd awakened to see his face softened in sleep. Terrified of the feelings budding to life within her, she'd stealthily gathered up her belongings and left without looking back. And despite her behavior, when she'd called, he'd shown up. He deserved many things from her, starting with gratitude.

But did he have to be an arrogant ass about it?

She balled a fist in the folds of her skirt. "What else would you like me to say?"

He pushed away from the sexmobile. "How about 'Thank you for canceling your plans and coming to get me'?"

Crap. She'd pulled him away from something. Or someone.

Heat simmered in her chest. Had he been with Skylar Thompson? She of the Pantene-shiny pale blond hair and blue eyes? She'd seen pictures of the two of them online when she'd "accidentally" Googled Mike. The other woman looked stylish, dignified, and refined, the complete antithesis of Indi.

It was none of her business. She'd given up any say in who he spent time with the night she'd walked away.

"How in the hell did you get arrested for burglary?"

She swiped at the allegation. "Those are trumped-up charges."

"So you didn't do it?"

"Of course not. I mean, breaking and entering makes you think of a cat burglar or someone in a ski mask robbing the place. That's not how it happened."

Mike narrowed his eyes and subjected her to his self-righteous stare. "Then why don't you tell me what happened."

She shrugged off her backpack, let it rest at her feet, and squeezed her shoulder blades toward one another to alleviate the ache. "It's not that big of a deal. I wanted to get into Adam and Chelsea's apartment. That's all. And it wouldn't have been a problem except Barney, the doorman who knew me from when I was here for the wedding, was off. This new doorman, besides being a grade-A douchebag, didn't work the week of the wedding, so he wouldn't let me in. It was so ridiculous. I was like 'Hello, I'm her sister—'"

"Foster sister," he said, his lips quirking at the corners.

"Same diff." She huffed.

What was up with everyone's need to technically categorize their relationship? If she and Chelsea never brought it up, why did others feel the need to do so? Unless—

Was Chelsea making the distinction?

Stop being paranoid, Indi.

Mike flicked the single button on his suit jacket and her eyes tracked him while he removed the garment. His shirt clung to his upper body like a long-distance couple's farewell.

Lucky shirt.

Indi cleared her throat. "Anyway, if Chelsea was here, she totally would've wanted me to get into the apartment."

He drew near and placed the jacket over her shoulders and the chill in the air receded to be replaced with . . . him. Holy shit, he smelled good!

Focus!

"What was so important it couldn't have waited until she'd gotten back?" Mike slid his hands into his pockets. "And why are you here anyway? I'm sure she told you they'd be gone for a total of three weeks."

Indi looked away, not ready to share that piece of information. She dropped the hand that she'd instinctively brought up to pat her belly. She was going to tell him. Really. She'd always planned to. Just not right now.

"It's personal. But all of this could've been avoided if the doorman had let me in."

"You mean all of this could've been avoided if you hadn't tried to break into—"

"There you go using that word again! I did not 'break'"—she formed air quotes—"into their apartment." She bit her lip and let her gaze fall from his. "The door and lock still work."

"I don't remember you being this aggravating." The heat in his crystalline blue eyes intensified, his stare scorching her mouth. "But then, we didn't do much talking."

She shivered. Only this time, she couldn't blame the weather.

"Who eats linguini and clams after midnight? The whole damn place reeked." Ryan Sullivan, the handsome attorney who'd been there when she'd been released, strode down the steps. "Sorry to keep you waiting, India."

She clasped her hands together and placed them against her chest. "Thank you so much for your help, Mr. Sullivan."

"Him you thank," Mike muttered.

"It was my pleasure. And you can call me Sully," he said, his brows hovering near his sable hairline. His gaze bounced between the two of them.

Mike held out his hand. "I appreciate this."

"No problem. It was worth it for the shits and giggles alone." Sully backhanded Mike on the shoulder and lowered his voice. "You wouldn't believe what I heard. I was signing the paperwork and they kept talking about the weird things they found in the detainees' belongings. Then this one officer walked in and said she'd seen it all. She'd had to inventory a large blue ceramic penis."

Mike choked out a bark of laughter. "You're fucking with me?"

Sully shook his head, his eyes crinkled at the corners. "I couldn't make this stuff up."

Warmth flooded Indi's cheeks and her eyes fluttered shut. The owl. The turtle. The freakin' rainbow-colored ladybug. Those were the statuettes Chelsea should've displayed. Instead, she'd chosen the phallic figurine Indi had sent as a joke. The moment she was alone, she was going to break it into a million pieces. Overkill for the several thousand dollars it contained, but it'd make her feel better.

Sully pulled a business card from his pocket. "I called a criminal defense attorney I know. Vivian Sutton. She's amazing. She can squeeze you in tomorrow at 1:00 p.m. Uh, make that today. Can you be there?"

Mike plucked the card from Sully's fingers. "I'll make sure she's there."

His presumption pierced her bubble of embarrassment. "Excuse you. I believe he was talking to me."

"Actually, you both should be there. You," he said, nodding to Indi, "because you're the defendant and Mike because he posted your bail. Where are you staying?"

Good question.

She kneaded her forehead. "I don't know. I'd planned to stay at Chelsea and Adam's place—"

"That's out of the question now," Sully said.

"Well, I didn't have time to make any other arrangements. I used my one call on Mike, not a travel agent!" She'd never understood the phrase *bone weary* until Nugget. After the day she'd had, she was cloaked in fatigue. She sighed. "I'm sorry. Is there a hotel nearby?"

"I've got this, Sully. Thanks for coming out this time of night."

"Anytime. Now don't forget, Vivian's office at 1:00 p.m. She's doing me a favor, so don't be late." Sully raised his hand in a mock salute and headed off.

Mike opened the passenger side door of his car. "Come on."

"You'll take me to a hotel?" She slid off his jacket, grabbed her backpack—as aware of the ceramic penis inside as if it were promoted with a flashing neon sign—and climbed inside the spacious opulence of the vehicle where the butterscotch perforated leather seats molded to her body. After hours of sitting on an uncomfortable wooden slat bench, it was like a personal spa treatment.

Mike settled beside her and started the engine. "You're staying with me."

Shock temporarily whisked away her fatigue. "Don't be ridiculous."

She couldn't stay with him. In such close proximity, there was no way she'd be able to hide her pregnancy.

"The last thing I ever am is ridiculous. It's late and I'm tired. We can argue about this in the morning."

"Just take me to a hotel."

Mike shifted in his seat, draping one arm over the steering wheel, the other behind her headrest. His fresh, crisp, clean scent wafted across and teased her senses. "Either you come home with me or I take you back in that building and tell them I changed my mind and I can't guarantee your appearance for the court date. Your choice."

Maybe jail would be preferable. She didn't know if she could handle staying in a place filled with so many memories. Where they'd spent that unforgettable weekend. Where Nugget had been conceived.

He must've read the trepidation on her face because he said, "Not my house in Palo Alto. I have a condo here in the city, only ten minutes away."

A little better, but not by much. *He'd* still be there. And the idea that she'd lost control of her own movements bothered the hell out of her. *She* decided where she stayed, where she slept.

Always.

But she didn't doubt he'd go through with his threat. He was an ends-justify-the-means type. He'd lied to his best friend about the new woman in his life to force Adam to accept help with the HPC presentation. And he'd forbidden Chelsea from telling Adam who she was, making her job more difficult. That lie had almost ended them before they'd begun. Adam and Chelsea had managed to work it out, but Indi knew if a successful outcome required that same deceit, Mike would do it again.

She laid her hands on the folded jacket in her lap. "Your place it is."

MIKE PULLED INTO his underground parking spot and turned off the engine. Nighttime street work had stretched ten minutes into twenty-five. He leaned back and rolled his head to look at his passenger. Her brief foray into crime must have been exhausting. She'd fallen asleep.

He clenched his hands so tightly on the steering wheel his knuckles paled. He was so close. Ten years ago when he'd graduated from Stanford with his MBA, he'd laid out a plan to achieve his goals. With the HPC and Computronix, he'd managed to reach his professional target. And tonight, the personal one had been within his grasp.

Then she'd broken back into his life.

Pun intended.

If only he could travel back in time to the night of the wedding and stay in instead of venturing out . . .

He'd been watching her all evening.

A beautiful fairy in coral chiffon and flower-crowned waves. She talked to everyone, charming and animated, leaving smiles in her wake. He'd tried to ignore her, but no matter his position, he was acutely aware of her location in the room.

One time he looked up from a conversation with Adam and Jonathan and scanned the crowd only to find her missing. Craning his neck, he caught sight of her as she slipped down the stairs. Minutes later, he found her sitting alone on the stone bench in the front yard, her hands braced on either side of her, head tilted skyward.

"I thought Adam would be the first person to need a quiet moment."

She smiled at him over her shoulder. "A moment is all I can stand. We've lost the warm weather from earlier and I'm about to freeze."

He'd taken off his jacket long ago, but. . .

He held up two shots of Casa Noble tequila. "Maybe these will help."

A look of distaste marred her delicate features.

His smiled flattened. "Maybe not."

"No, I'm sorry. Bad memories from college. But I'm adventurous. How about we make some new ones?"

Adrenaline billowed through him. He sat next to her and handed her a glass. "Salut."

"Salut." Her voice was soft. Husky.

The alcohol burned going down before blossoming into a blanket of heat that settled on his chest.

Indi puckered her lips and blew a stream of air. It was sexy as hell.

"How was that?" he asked, bewilderingly enthralled by this woman.

She tossed her head back. "As good as I remember. Which can only be bad."

She was so different from the women he usually dated. So different from Skylar.

Which is what he wanted.

"It was a beautiful ceremony. I can't believe Adam wrote his vows."

"I know." She rolled the shot glass between her palms. "Are you worried?"

"About what?"

"Your relationship with Adam. Are you worried it'll change?"

He shrugged. "It can't help but change. But I don't see that as a negative. Do you?"

"Maybe. I don't know. For years it's just been Chelsea and me and now I'll have to share her." She let her chin fall to her chest. "That probably sounds selfish."

"It does—"

Her head swung in his direction, but when she saw the smile on his lips, she slapped his arm. "You jerk!"

"But it's understandable," he continued. "Don't worry. I know how much she loves you. You two will be okay."

"Thanks."

The smile she gave him lit up their small part of the mountain. Made him want to do whatever was necessary to see it brighten her face again.

They sat together, listening to the conversation and laughter that flowed through the open windows. When the beginning notes of a song joined the cacophony, Indi clapped her hands. "Chelsea requested that, I'm sure of it. An oldie but goodie."

She sang the words and swayed to the beat. "'. . . You make me feel so brand-new, I want to spend my whole life with you . . .'"

Her eyes were closed and a rapt expression settled on her face. He yearned to share the moment with her. He stood and held out his hand. "Would you care to dance?"

She tilted her head and rich dark waves flowed over her shoulder, the ends brushing the top of her cleavage. She stared up at him, her wide, light brown eyes guarded but curious. His heart pounded the rhythm of his longing. He'd been waiting for this all evening, the opportunity to touch her, to hold her, to try and understand this need to be close to her.

Without breaking visual contact, she placed her hand in his. His palm tingled like he'd accidentally brushed it against a live wire, and he was struck by the simple beauty of their contrasting skin tones. He closed his fingers around hers and pulled her from the chair and into his arms.

The scent of warm sweet vanilla swirled around him, making his head dizzy . . . and his cock hard. She smelled so good he wanted to nibble that tantalizing spot where her shoulder met her neck. He settled for flexing his hand against the small of her back and drawing her closer. She inhaled audibly and stiffened and he held his breath, praying she wouldn't reject his touch. Surely, this attraction wasn't one-sided? It was too potent. But she exhaled and her body softened against him.

They moved like that, her temple against his cheek as the song melded into the next one. She leaned back and stared at him with eyes that burned bright with the reflection of the stars. And when her lips parted, he could no more resist than he could deny his name. He lowered his head and captured her mouth with his own. . .

Mike scraped his fingers through his hair. Why couldn't she have stayed away? From the moment he'd met her he'd been consumed by this powerful and unexplained attraction. And until Adam's wedding, he'd been intent on fighting it.

Until he couldn't.

When he'd awakened that morning to find her gone, he'd been blinded by a rage he'd never known. A rage so overwhelming it threatened to destroy everything in its path. He hadn't cared about work, his friends, or his obligations. Only her. He'd been surprised and unnerved by the strength of his reaction. It had taken several days for reason to take hold of him again. And he'd fortified that reason with resolve. Her leaving was the best outcome of their fling. Indi was quirky, impulsive, easygoing. Not to mention so sexy it was distracting. Those weren't the traits he needed in the other half of his power couple.

But that didn't make him want her any less.

She was turned to face him, one hand resting beneath her cheek, the other lying on her stomach. Even the harsh fluorescent lighting couldn't detract from her beauty, the smooth richness of her skin calling out to be touched.

He shook her shoulder. "Indi, we're here."

She jerked awake, her lashes fluttering, a flush settling on her high cheekbones. She straightened and smoothed a hand down her sweater. "Sorry. I didn't realize how tired I was."

A sudden protective instinct surged through him—one he quickly quashed.

No, it wasn't happening. He wasn't getting involved with her. Not again. She was his best friend's wife's foster sister. Practically family. He'd help her through this mess she'd gotten herself into until Adam and Chelsea got home.

Then he'd be the one to walk away.

Several minutes later, he flipped the lights on in his condo and tossed his jacket on the marble countertop. Before him, the floor-to-ceiling windows allowed in the glittering vista of the city at night.

"That view is breathtaking." Indi came to stand beside him.

Now, under the recessed lights in his house and not the lighting of the garage or the city's street lamps, without the filter of his unchecked emotions, he could see her exhaustion. The slight bruises beneath her eyes, the droop of her shoulders, the dimming of her inner light.

"This has been a long day for you. Your room is down here." He gestured for her to precede him down the hallway. "It's the second door on the left. The first door is the bathroom."

She fingered the strap of her backpack. "I know I didn't say it before, but thank you. You really came through for me. I . . . I had no one else to call."

She placed a hand on his shoulder and leaned up to kiss his cheek. When she pulled back, their eyes met . . . and locked. A teaser trailer of their weekend together premiered in his mind. Tequila body shots and dancing until dawn, a movie double feature of *Four Weddings and a Funeral* followed by *Boomerang*, sex on the picnic table under the stars.

What was wrong with him? He was on the verge of closing the biggest deal of his career and starting his life with the right woman on his arm. He'd lost a weekend to the headiness of Indi's charms. He couldn't lose his life.

He broke eye contact and put some space between them. "You're welcome. Get some rest. We have an appointment with the attorney this afternoon."

She nodded, turned into her room, but hesitated. "Can I have some water?"

"Of course."

He handed her a bottle from the refrigerator. She took it and went into the bedroom, closing the door quietly behind her.

He exhaled deeply.

If only Chelsea had been home. Unfortunately, Adam had been in the midst of working on OTTo when he and Chelsea had married on New Year's Eve, so they'd agreed to put off their honeymoon for several months. Their venue choices ended up being as unique as the couple. Chelsea was interested in a spa resort. Being a gamer and a technology geek, Adam wanted to go to the American Classic Arcade Museum in New Hampshire. In the end they'd compromised and spent a week in London, with several trips to the London Science Museum before heading to Fiji for two weeks to stay at a technology-free resort with no internet access.

Mike tugged his shirt out of his pants and walked into his room. Despite what he'd threatened, it was a mistake to keep her close. He'd accompany her to the attorney's office, get clear on his responsibilities regarding her bail, then pay for a hotel for her until Adam and Chelsea could get home to clear this up. That's what Adam would want him to do. He'd also email his friend, so when he finally left the resort and regained internet access, he'd be apprised of the situation at home.

He'd taken off his shirt and unbuttoned his pants when he heard a commotion in the hallway.

What the hell?

The door to the guest bedroom swung on its hinges and the bathroom door rebounded against the tub, evidence of the force with which it had been shoved open. The grating sound of retching blared out into the hallway.

Indi.

The acrid tang of fear coated his tongue and his protective instincts ballooned to life, ramming through his earlier erected barriers. He hurried into the bathroom and found her bent over the toilet on all fours in her bra and panties.

"No, don't come in." Her protest was feeble and she could barely lift her hand to fend him off.

He knelt beside her and rubbed her back, his heart breaking at the never-ending spasms that bowed her body.

Goddammit! He managed the day-to-day operations of a billion-dollar tech company, consorted with some of the most powerful people in the country: businessmen, celebrities, and politicians. He had more money than he could ever spend in a lifetime.

And yet he'd never felt so useless.

Finally, the convulsions subsided and she quieted. He grabbed a washcloth, wet it, and gently cleaned her mouth. Beads of sweat dotted her brow, clung to her clammy skin and she didn't object when he lifted her in his arms and carried her into the bedroom. Laying her gently on the bed, he covered her with a light blanket.

"What happened?" he asked, smoothing her braids away from her face.

"I didn't have anything to sleep in, so I was going to ask you for a T-shirt." Her voice was drowsy.

During their weekend together, when she hadn't been naked, she'd been in one of his shirts.

"I opened my bag, and got a big whiff of the clam sauce . . ."

Her lashes never stirred, resting beneath closed eyes.

"Do you have a bug or something?" Maybe he should take her to the hospital . . .

"No, it's Nugget. He doesn't like garlic," she said, in a whispered slur.

Had she said *nugget*?

"What's a nugget?" Could she have the flu? Did dehydration cause hallucinations?

"Not what. Who." She exhaled and succumbed to sleep's siren song. "Nugget's our baby. I'm pregnant."

Chapter Five

HE WAS GOING to be a father.

Mike stood in the living room and stared out the window. The midmorning sun burned through the fog of the evening before, its rays cascading onto his polished hardwood floors. He'd barely slept last night, his mind unable to quiet after Indi's announcement.

Pride expanded in his chest, filling every inch of the cavity until he could barely breathe. A baby. A son or a daughter. An image of Indi holding their newborn tantalized him, offering a glimpse of a future he'd always assumed he'd have, but now he couldn't help wanting. Still, he couldn't allow himself to get excited about the news. He had no proof Indi was pregnant or, if she was, that the baby was his.

His own father's exasperated tones. *Be smart, Mike.*

He took a sip of coffee, hoping the steaming hot beverage would eliminate the stupor impairing his ability to function rationally. Why had she come to San Francisco? Was she looking to get money from him? What did he really know about her apart from the way she made him feel? And wasn't that enough for him to distrust her?

He hadn't been able to get much information from her last night. Attempts to rouse her after she'd fallen asleep had failed. But staring down at her, knowing she might be pregnant, had filled him with the primitive desire to protect her and the life growing inside of her. One thing was certain, if the baby turned out to be his, he'd make sure his child was taken care of. How he'd go about doing that, he had no idea.

His cell phone rang and he pulled it from his pocket.

"Skylar." His presentation and plans for dinner with the other woman seemed like a lifetime ago.

"Is everything okay?" Concern threaded Skylar's brisk tone.

His gaze slid to the hallway. Indi's door was still closed. "Why would you ask that?"

"You abruptly canceled our plans last night without a reason."

His jaw tightened. He didn't appreciate having to explain himself to anyone.

"When I called with my regrets, I explained I had some old business that came up."

"I know. It's just"—she paused—"you're usually so even-keeled and composed, but last night you were harsh. Ill-tempered. You've never been that way with me before."

He sighed. "I apologize. I didn't want to break our date, but it couldn't be helped."

"I understand. Mostly, I was disappointed because it was our last opportunity to see one another before I leave for New York."

He set his mug down on the coffee table and pinched the bridge of his nose. Last night he'd intended to propose to Skylar. Instead he'd learned he might have fathered a child with another woman.

His father would be suitably scandalized.

"I promise it won't happen again," he said, injecting a silky warmth into his tone in an attempt to mollify her.

It worked.

"You can make it up to me when I return in two weeks."

"I'm looking forward to it," he said, disconnecting the call.

"Good morning."

Indi stood in the doorway, looking fresh and natural in the plain white T-shirt he'd left on her bed, her bare toes peeking beneath the hem of the skirt she'd worn the night before.

His chest tightened and contrition thickened the back of his throat.

He battled through it.

There was no reason to feel guilty about talking to Skylar. *She* was the woman he was dating, the woman he'd planned to marry. He and Indi didn't have a relationship.

Yeah, you only have a child together.

Maybe.

"Thank you for the toothbrush and shirt." She pulled on the hem.

He set his phone on the coffee table. "How are you feeling?"

She grimaced. "Like an alien invaded my body and proceeded to veto anything I wanted to eat."

"Can I get you anything?"

"Do you have peppermint tea?"

The corner of his mouth ascended. "Do I look like a man who'd stock peppermint tea?"

"You asked." She twined her fingers until they resembled sweet licorice ropes. "I'll take some water for now."

He took his mug into the kitchen, placed it in the sink, and grabbed a bottle of water from the refrigerator. He unscrewed the top and handed it to her.

"Thank you."

The tension in the room hovered like a low-lying cloud, easy to maneuver around, but difficult to ignore.

"You got back together with your girlfriend."

A statement not a question. He arched a brow.

"You mentioned her before," she elaborated. "That first night, during the tequila shots."

"Right." Heat slithered up the back of his neck and he cleared his throat. "Yes, for a few months now."

"Good. I'm happy for you." She bit her lip.

Fascinate, he lasered in on the plump, erogenous organ as it reemerged dewy and pink.

Fuck!

He wrested his focus away from her mouth and on their predicament where it belonged. "How far along are you?"

Her glide into the living room devolved into a stumble before she righted herself and sank down onto his sofa, pulling her legs up under her. "We were together around three months ago, so . . ."

"So what?" he asked, his fingers burrowing through his hair. "We used protection."

"Always, except—"

Except the time he'd surprised her in the shower. He hadn't believed his dick could handle another back-to-back session, but when he'd strolled into the bathroom and seen her leisurely soaping up her breasts . . . he'd been unable to call upon his well-exercised control.

He cursed softly and closed his eyes. "And that was all it took?"

"Apparently."

"I haven't seen or heard from you since then but I'm supposed to believe you?"

She blinked up at him. "I have no reason to lie to you."

He scratched his jaw. "Really? The last time I checked I'm part owner of a company that brought in twenty-six billion dollars in revenue the last fiscal quarter. By my rough estimate that's at least twenty-six billion reasons to lie."

She wrinkled her nose. "I wouldn't lie to you about being the father to get your money."

"Says the alleged felon."

She leaned back, crossed her arms, and scowled at him. "That's a low blow."

He exhaled through his nose. It was. But as foolish as it made him seem, he believed her. Still, he had to be sure. If Indi was carrying his baby, it would crimp the smooth flow of his plans. Plans ten years in the making.

"I'm going to need confirmation the baby is mine."

She shrugged. "I expected as much."

Asking for validation of her claim was the prudent thing to do, but she made it sound like an insult. "What does that mean?"

"That I knew you would be suspicious."

"I call it being smart."

"Whatever you call it, I knew you'd want proof. I'm going to make an appointment with Chelsea's doctor. You can come with me."

Shrewd move. Her invitation lent credence to her belief that he was the father. If she wasn't pregnant, or he wasn't the father, she'd be warning him away instead of encouraging him along.

He pulled the coffee table out and sat on its edge, facing her. "How do you know Chelsea's doctor?"

"You've never moved with a woman, have you?"

And that had *what* to do with his question? "No."

"When a woman moves to a new city, one of the first things she does is get recommendations for a hairstylist and an ob-gyn. We only trust those body parts to exceptional practitioners." She smiled. "Chelsea told me she'd found one in San Francisco. Said it'd be easier to make appointments closer to her office."

He touched the back of her hand and fire grazed along his nerve endings. He raised his gaze to hers and her eyes shimmered as if lit from within. Her hand clenched briefly before she pulled it from his.

"I'd appreciate going to the appointment with you," he said, sitting back. "If this is my baby, I will take care of him."

She rubbed the back of her hand. "I know."

"I don't have personal experience, but I imagine it's quite expensive to raise a child."

"That's what I've heard. But it won't be a problem. That's why your money isn't an issue. I'm not planning to raise our baby."

Blood iced over in his veins. He shot to a stand, planted his feet. "Are you having an abortion?"

"God, Mike," she yelled, flinging her hands upward. "Is everything black-and-white for you?"

Her words echoed through the space and she surprised him by laughing.

He scowled. What was so fucking funny?

"Black-and-white? Us?" She motioned between them.

He crossed his arms over his chest and narrowed his eyes. There was nothing amusing about this situation. He thought she agreed, as her merriment tinged on hysteria. When her laughter subsided, she exhaled shakily and pressed fingertips to her eyelids.

"I'm not having an abortion. There's another option for people who choose not to raise their children. An option I know well." She blinked. "I'm putting him up for adoption."

As THE ASSISTANT showed them into the attorney's office, Mike struggled to smother his outrage. Over the past few hours he'd careened from pride to confusion, from guilt to anger. And all of those emotions were intensified by an ever-present layer of lust. His feelings were extending past his usual comfort zone, veering close to a diagnosis of emotional whiplash.

Adoption?

Sure, it was a viable choice. Hell, Morgan had come to his family by way of the legal process. It would certainly solve one of the ever-growing problems in his personal life.

Still, everything in him rejected the idea of giving his child away. It might work for others, but not for him. Even under these less-than-honorable circumstances, he couldn't imagine his father ever choosing that resolution.

Remember, you don't know if it's yours.

That one fact is what stopped him from going the fuck off. One problem at a time. She'd called the doctor and managed to get an appointment tomorrow morning. Today, they needed to deal with her pending criminal charges.

Criminal charges. He shook his head. The state of California had charged the mother of his child with a felony. A foreign notion his brain processed with distaste.

"Will you sit down?" He aimed an icy stare at Indi, who'd stood to straighten the "Top Lawyers under Thirty-Five" and "Law Digest Criminal Lawyer of the Year" plaques fastened to the wall. She was currently neatening her way through the scales of justice and paperweights loading the bookcase. "Your pacing is making me dizzy."

She bestowed a glaring side-eye upon him. "I had enough in the car. I need a break."

"Enough of what?"

"Your silent treatment. Stop brooding."

"I do not brood."

"Oh, please. You've had an attitude since we left your place."

"You told me you're giving our baby away!"

"And you told me you didn't believe it was 'our' baby."

He wouldn't let her distract him. "Is it money?"

Her head jerked back. "I don't need your money—I work."

"Do you?"

"Yes."

"What type of job do you have that allows you to travel whenever it strikes your fancy?"

"I don't have one job. I do a lot of things."

"What does that mean?"

"It means I don't live to work. I work to live."

"Spare me the internet meme."

"Of course that's all it is to you"—she lowered her voice—"Mr. My Company Made a Bajillion Dollars Last Year—"

"*Bajillion* isn't a word," he muttered, annoyed at the accuracy of her mimicry.

"Look, I get that your job is a key part of your identity, but my jobs allow me to have fun. To pay my bills. When I'm ready for a new adventure, I give notice and move to the next place. That's why I work and I'm happy. I spent three months with a mentalist in Vegas, I've been a purser on a luxury cruise ship, and I have the opportunity to travel for a year with a renowned, international photographer. I'd never have those experiences working in a cubicle."

"You can't build a life if you're constantly wandering. There's no stability."

Her elevated chin and starched posture clued him in to his lack of persuasiveness.

He shifted tactics.

"Don't you get tired of roaming the country?" He moved to stand behind her. "I'm sure Chelsea would love to have you close by. She's the only family you have. Wouldn't you like to be near her?"

Her shoulders loosened and for a second, he thought he'd gotten through to her. But like a folded umbrella being hauled back into service, she stiffened.

"Chelsea is busy with her own life. Opening the new San Francisco office of Beecher & Stowe, getting married to Adam . . . She'll have a lot on her plate." Her voice lowered to a hush and if he hadn't been close, her words would've been lost to the void. "She won't be worried about me."

He opened his mouth to respond but the door to the office swept open and a tall woman, resplendent in diamonds and pearls and a pin-striped sheath, strode in. Her reddish-brown hair was pulled into a knot at the crown of her head, a pair of stylish frames perched on her nose.

"So you're Ryan's friends. I'm Viv Sutton."

Her firm handshake soothed him and her cool, confident bearing screamed this woman was exceptional at her job.

In case one hadn't noticed the plaques.

"I'm Mike Black and this is India Shaw."

"A pleasure. Please, have a seat." Viv motioned to the red leather chairs situated in front of her desk. "I was pleased when I heard Ryan had taken a position with Computronix. He's a brilliant attorney. Your company couldn't be in better hands."

He straightened, appreciating her sincerity. "We're very happy to have him."

Indi strode forward and took the indicated chair. "You call him Ryan and not Sully?"

Viv looked away from them, placing a file on the corner of her desk. "He doesn't . . . feel like a 'Sully' to me."

Mike narrowed his eyes, hearing something in the attorney's voice.

Indi scooted to the edge of her seat. "Thank you for seeing us. I'm sure you're very busy."

"A favor I was delighted to grant. Ryan called last night and explained the situation. It's better that your arrest occurred when it did. If you'd been taken into custody tomorrow, you might have been held over the weekend." Viv opened another manila folder on her desk. "This morning, I had one of my clerks go over to the courthouse and pull the paperwork. There wasn't much there: just the arrest warrant, police report, and the bail information sheet." She swung her steely gaze to India. "You were arrested on suspicion of burglary—"

"That's ridiculous. I did not break into their home."

"I see." Viv made notes on a legal pad. "That might come in handy. The district attorney's office has three business days to determine whether or not they want to file charges. If this has been a misunderstanding, the case may not go any further."

"What do we need to do to nudge them toward the not-filing-charges side?" Indi asked, with a smug *I told you so* look at Mike.

Viv sat back. "Let me ask you a few questions. The charge is burglary in the first degree. The police report says they responded to a call at the Hermitage at Avalon building and when they entered the Bennett residence they found you. Are you a registered owner of the unit?"

"No."

"The doorman said they keep a list of authorized entrants. Are you on that list?"

"No. But I promise you, Chelsea and Adam wouldn't have minded if I were in the apartment."

"Then why aren't you on the list?"

"Because Chelsea probably didn't have the time to put me on it," Indi said through clenched pearly whites.

Indi's frustration coated them both, like softly falling mist. He stepped in. "I assure you, Chelsea wouldn't object to Indi's presence."

Viv's gaze never wavered. "Unfortunately, I can't take your . . . affirmation to the DA."

"But he's on the list," Indi said, pointing at him. "If he'd been there and I'd been with him, this wouldn't even be a problem."

"If only you'd taken the time to consider that *before* your little crime spree," he muttered.

Viv's pen tapped a rapid, repetitive beat on her desk.

"The *prima facie* case for burglary is entering someone's property with the intent of committing a felony or petty theft once inside." She flipped through the documents in the folder. "There's no evidence, at this point, that you took anything from the residence. That's information they'd get from the Bennetts. So, how did you enter their property? Do you have a key?"

"I picked the lock."

He'd misheard that, right? She didn't say—"You picked the lock? Jesus, Indi!"

She crossed her legs, primly repositioned her skirt. "I learned it on the job."

"Who were you working for? The crew of *Ocean's Eleven*?"

She was the mother of his unborn child? He didn't believe Indi possessed a malicious bone in that gorgeous body . . . still, her impetuousness worried him as much as any malevolence.

You loved her spontaneity when she took your cock in her mouth while you ordered pizza.

Oh, shut up, he snapped at the unwelcome remembrance.

The lawyer cleared her throat. "Let's focus on the other part of the statute. Why did you need access to their home?"

"At first, I'd planned to stay there. When the doorman made it clear that wouldn't be possible, I went in to retrieve something of mine that Chelsea had."

"What?"

Indi's chin fell. "I'd rather not say."

Mike barely resisted the urge to fling his arms upward. What kind of bullshit response was that? Was he the only one interested in her remaining out of prison?

Viv pursed her lips and widened her eyes in a look that cried out, *Okaaay...*

"Look, as soon as Chelsea gets home, this will all be cleared up." Indi's tone said that it was a foregone conclusion.

Viv nodded. "Having the Bennetts contact the DA directly and explain that you had permission to be in their home is the easiest way to convince them not to file charges."

"But you said we have three days?" Mike asked.

"Yes."

"Then that's going to be a problem. Adam and Chelsea are on their honeymoon and are out of contact for the next two weeks."

Viv's arched a perfectly shaped brow. "What does that mean: 'out of contact'? No one is out of contact these days."

"They're at a resort in Fiji with no internet access and no cell phone service."

The lawyer's head jerked back. "Voluntarily? Okay, no contact." She squinted her eyes, pondering. "Even in an emergency?"

Indi shook her head. "This doesn't count as an emergency."

Mike exhaled audibly. "Indi—"

"They put off their honeymoon for months. I'm not going to be the reason they have to come back earlier than they planned."

Viv clasped her hands together, steepled her arms on her desk. "What is your relationship to the Bennetts?"

"Chelsea *Grant* is my sister."

Mike eyed Indi at her emphasis of Chelsea's maiden name.

"Really?" Viv's brown eyes brightened. "And you're close?"

"Of course. I was her maid of honor."

"The pictures will be in *People* magazine next week," he added. "I can have my office send over the advance copy, if that will help."

Excitement tinted Indi's features. She shifted in her seat, her knees brushing his. "Really? I hadn't seen the pictures. Were they beautiful?"

He tightened his jaw. "Not important at this moment."

Indi rolled her eyes but didn't comment further.

"Do your parents live here?" Viv inquired. "Again, none of this explicitly negates the *prima facie* case, but if we put enough before the prosecutors to paint a picture, they may decide it's not worth moving forward."

"Parents aren't an option. My bond with Chelsea isn't biological. She's my foster sister."

"Uh-huh." Viv pursed her lips. "You should prepare yourself for the DA to file charges against you."

Fuck! This wasn't happening.

Viv massaged her temple and glanced back down at the documentation. "Ms. Shaw, your bail was set at one hundred thousand dollars, and Mr. Black posted bond for you. Since you're out of custody, you'll probably get an arraignment date three weeks out."

"What's an arraignment date?" Indi asked.

"It's the hearing where you'll be formally charged. At that time you'll enter a plea of either guilty or not guilty. If you plead guilty, the court will set a date for sentencing. If you plead not guilty, they'll set a date for your preliminary hearing. If you decide to retain me, I'd file notice with the court that I'm your attorney, and the notice of arraignment or sentencing, and all further correspondence, will come directly to me."

Mike spoke up. "Consider yourself retained."

The lawyer looked at Indi, whose lips tightened, but she nodded.

"Perfect." Viv picked up the phone on her desk and pressed a button. "Jocelyn, can you bring in the Shaw retainer agreement?" Hanging up, she eyed them. "I'll schedule a prehearing conference with the DA and present what we have, including a statement from Mr. Black and the pictures from the wedding, and maybe they'll decline to get involved. It's a long shot. With victims as high profile as the Bennetts, the DA will want to err on the side of caution. And barring any contact with them, the state will want to press charges."

A few minutes later, a young woman entered with a file. "The clerk just called. The judge in the Collins case wants to see you and the prosecutor in his chambers in half an hour."

Viv looked at her watch and nodded. She slid the agreement across the desk. "Please read it over before you sign. It sets out—among other things—our retainer, my hourly fee, how you'll be billed and the scope of my representation. I'll give you two a moment."

Indi waited until the attorney left the room before grabbing the contract. "Ten thousand dollars! I don't have that kind of money right now."

"I'll take care of it."

"I told you, I don't want your charity."

"It's not charity. Think of it as a loan."

"What are the terms?"

He didn't expect Indi to pay him back, but he threw out some conditions.

"Are you serious? I can get better on the street."

Why did she know that?!

"Maybe, but you wouldn't. With your work ethic, it would take you years to pay them back." He shrugged. "But to me, you're a good risk. I know where Chelsea and Adam live."

"Don't you dare ask Chelsea for it! It's my debt. I'll pay it."

He started at her vehement tone. He'd meant it as a joke.

Viv reentered the office. "I'm sorry, but I'm due back in court. If you need more time, feel free to take it with you—"

"No, it's good." Indi looked at him then signed her name in an illegible flourish.

Viv scanned the documents. "I want to quickly go over the terms of your bail. This money was paid as a surety for your promise to make all of your court dates. Mr. Black paid it, so your failure to appear means he'll lose the money he posted for your release."

"Reason enough to forget a court date," Indi said under her breath.

Viv's gaze volleyed between the two of them. "Maybe, but the warrant issued for your arrest is not. And in case you're wondering, you'd stay in jail until your hearing."

"For a host of reasons, Ms. Shaw won't be far from my side," Mike promised.

"I'll send Jocelyn in to take your payment and I'll be in touch early next week."

"What did that mean, I won't be 'far from your side'?" Indi asked as they stood outside the law office, waiting for the elevator. "You can't hold me hostage."

"I just paid one hundred and ten thousand dollars on your behalf to an attorney and the state of California!"

"What? You think that means you *own* me?"

"Ye—" He narrowed his eyes. That was dirty and she knew it.

The corner of her mouth quirked, but she took pity on him. "By the time the court date rolls around, Chelsea will be back. She'll tell the judge who I am and that I wasn't trying to steal from them. Problem solved. Case over. You'll get your money back. It's not a big deal."

She was unbelievable! Did she really think their involvement would end with a thank-you and a handshake? If only that were true.

"You're right, it's not a big deal. It's enormous. You wander from place to place, you might be pregnant with my child, and you keep talking about giving him up for adoption. So, for the time being, consider my name Ruth." At her confused look, he elaborated. "From the Bible. 'Whither thou goest, I will go.'"

Chapter Six

"Pregnant?"

Mike's HD monitor showed every forehead crease and brow depression on Jonathan's shocked face.

"Yes."

"Is it yours?" Jonathan leaned forward.

"She says it is."

"Do you believe her?"

The twenty-six-billion-dollar question: had Indi lied to him when she'd said he was the father of her unborn child?

In any other situation, he'd be the embodiment of skepticism. The pregnancy scam—where women claimed to be pregnant by wealthy men to either live off the child support or take a payoff to go away—was well-known and discussed among men of a certain tax bracket, and Mike had always endeavored to avoid situations where he'd be vulnerable. And he'd succeeded.

Until Indi.

But besides the incident of unprotected sex, he knew her regard for Chelsea. And he didn't believe Indi would risk that relationship, a possibility if she lied to Chelsea's husband's best friend. Not for any amount of money.

"I do, but I'm accompanying her to a doctor's appointment tomorrow. I'll inquire about a paternity test, just to be certain."

"Trust but verify, huh?" Jonathan's brown eyes crinkled at their corners. "I guess that's the smart thing to do."

Mike smiled. "I'm not a genius like Adam, but I have my moments."

Jonathan settled back in his chair, his white chef's jacket unbuttoned at the neck. His office rocked a utilitarian vibe: white walls, wood-and-steel desk, gray filing cabinets. Not the digs one imagined for a chef, save the colorful drawing of a hectic kitchen at work on the wall above his head. "Speaking of Adam, does he know?"

"About the pregnancy?"

"That you even slept with India in the first place?"

"No. But I did email him with a heads-up that she was in San Francisco." Among other things. Mike raked his fingers through his hair. "I would've told him if I thought it was going anywhere, but she left after our weekend together."

"Not something you're used to," Jonathan said, his tone soft.

Mike thought he detected a vestige of amusement in his friend's voice, but he ignored it. "She never took my calls, didn't answer my texts. I'd assumed we were done. And then I got back together with Skylar—"

"I'd forgotten about Skylar. Man, you're fucked."

"I know."

"What are you going to do?"

"My first priority is the baby." His chest tightened. "Indi doesn't want to keep it."

Jonathan shook his head. "I hate to say it, but an abortion *would* solve your problem."

"She's not getting an abortion. The other *A*— adoption."

He experienced a fun-house mirror sense of déjà vu. He'd had this same conversation with Indi yesterday, speaking roles inverted.

"Adoption? Well, that's something you're familiar with. Your parents adopted Morgan when you were how old?"

"Fourteen."

"And it turned out well for her. The same thing could happen with Indi's baby." But Jonathan's tone belied the optimism of his words.

As someone whose family benefited from the adoption process, Mike knew this could be a rewarding and positive experience for both the baby and the family fortunate enough to adopt him. The baby would grow up in a stable environment with people committed to loving and providing for him. The family who wanted him would benefit from the blessing of adding to their family and the ability to fulfill their dreams of raising a child. And Indi could take comfort in knowing she'd placed her baby in a safe and attentive home.

And yet, he still couldn't muster the strength to

form the supportive words this choice—and situation—warranted.

"Has she said why she wants to give the baby away?" Jonathan asked.

"No! And that's what's frustrating. She won't talk about her reasoning."

"This is crazy," Jonathan said, stroking his jaw. "I'm not saying I know India well, but . . ."

Mike reached for a pencil on his desk, concentrated on not breaking it in half. "I wasn't aware familiarity was a prerequisite for your sexual affairs."

Jonathan may not know Indi well, but that day—the day Adam proposed to Chelsea at their house in the San Mateo Mountains—the two appeared to get on like a rock star and his groupie.

Shame thickened his throat. He hadn't been on his best behavior, had done a first-rate impression of an asshole. People who knew him would agree he was an even-keeled sort of guy, and yet the first time he'd met Indi, he'd been unable to process his attraction to the enigmatic beauty.

Jonathan swallowed. "Dude, if I'd known—"

Mike waved a hand. "Forget it. There was nothing to know. We weren't involved at that time."

"I know, but I don't want you to misconstrue our interaction. She's a beautiful woman, but we both knew our interest was only in friendship."

He couldn't relate. There was nothing amiable about his feelings toward Indi.

"I find it hard to believe she would give away her

child," Jonathan continued, "for no validly stated reason. Especially considering her upbringing."

"There's Morgan's situation and there's her own. Indi spent years in the foster care system. Isn't she curious about her own parents? About why they gave her up? And yet she's considering the possibility of sentencing her child to the same life of questioning and self-blame."

Jonathan nodded. "Something's going on."

"And I intend to find out what it is." He set his jaw. "There's no scenario where I know I have a child out there in the world and I'm not involved in his life."

What kind of man abdicated his responsibility to others, especially when he had the resources to shoulder it himself? Those weren't the values his parents instilled in him and that didn't describe the type of man he wanted to be.

But he'd back burner his predicament for now. Of the three best friends, Jonathan usually possessed a fixed affability, one that was restrained today, despite his best efforts to appear engaged.

"How are things going in DC? I got the pics you sent. That's an incredible location."

"Yeah, I'm really psyched about the space." The words warred with the turbulent expression on Jonathan's face.

Mike crossed his arms over his chest. "Dude, what's going on? You've talked about opening this restaurant in your hometown for almost a year. You look like *you* just got disturbing news."

"I'm thrilled about the restaurant. Determining the concept, the long hours acquiring and training staff, designing the menu and interior . . . it's exhausting. Still, I've never been more certain about a move in my life."

Mike sensed there was more. "But—"

"Remember last year when I told you Thomas had met someone?"

Jonathan and his brother weren't close. In fact, in all the years he'd been friends with the talented chef, he'd only met his brother once.

"Yes."

"Well, I've met the special woman."

Mike hefted a shoulder. "Okay, and—"

"And she's a piece of work," Jonathan said, his words rushing together and ending in a huff.

"Really? Care to share some details?"

"Her name is Leighton Clarke and she's a political lobbyist," he said, imbuing the title with viscous disgust.

Curious about the strength of Jonathan's response, Mike pulled out his phone and quickly Googled the woman. His eyes widened. Smooth dark skin, dagger sharp cheekbones, and thickly lashed, tilted eyes the color of espresso. Leighton Clarke was a stunning woman, though she possessed an aura of hardness that slightly diminished her appeal.

"Lobbyists aren't well regarded," he said, in an understatement of epic proportions, "but you're not the one marrying her. It's likely you won't have to spend more than the occasional family dinner with the two of them."

Jonathan sighed and lifted a hand to knead the nape of his neck. "You're right. It's none of my business."

But the vexation on his face bolstered the fact that a resolution wouldn't be that easy.

A brisk tap on the door and Sully peered around the frame.

"Is this a good time?"

Mike motioned him in. "Yeah, I'm just talking to Jonathan."

"Yo, J, what's up?" Sully asked, maneuvering around the desk and perching on the corner.

"Nothing much compared to what's going on around there." Jonathan slipped back into his jovial manner with enviable ease.

"I took a date to Quartet last week," Sully said, referring to Jonathan's three Michelin-starred restaurant in San Francisco. "It was incredible."

Jonathan pointed at them through the screen. "That's what I like to hear. Even in my absence, the place should run smoothly."

"Did you hear the news about India?" Sully asked.

"Yeah. I can't believe she's pregnant."

"India's pregnant?" Sully's head whipped in Mike's direction.

Mike scrubbed a hand over his face.

"You didn't know?" Jonathan narrowed his eyes. "What were *you* talking about?"

"I was talking about her arrest for burglary and Prince Charming over here"—Sully jerked a thumb in Mike's direction—"bailing her out."

"What the hell?"

This situation was a prime example of the problem with his continued attraction to, and relationship with, India Shaw. He would never have this conversation about Skylar.

"India's pregnant." Sully looked stunned. "Are you the father? How is that going to affect your relationship with Skylar? What about the TTL deal?"

Jonathan failed to hide a wide grin behind his fist. "So it seems worrying about the restaurant was wasted energy. You're the one who's gone to pieces since I left."

"Fuck you."

"Yeah, fucking *me* isn't what got you into this situation. You talk about being involved in this child's life, if it's yours. How? If India wants to put the baby up for adoption, it means she doesn't want to raise him. Or her. Are you prepared to raise a baby?"

"She's putting the baby up for adoption?" Sully's gaze bounced between the monitor and Mike.

He clenched his jaw. "Keep up, Sullivan."

He needed to take his own advice. His life had spiraled out of control in the past twenty-four hours. He was having difficulty keeping abreast of the new developments.

Was he prepared to raise a child?

He had a wonderful life, but it was hectic. He was in charge of the day-to-day operations of a multi-billion-dollar company. He worked long hours and at least once a week he spent the night in his office, showering and changing in the en suite bathroom.

"Why would she do that?" Sully asked.

"I can't imagine it's an easy decision to make," Jonathan allowed. "Maybe she feels it's the right thing for the baby."

Mike couldn't hold his tongue. "Better than the baby being raised by its father?"

Sully pulled his ear. "How would she know you're interested in having a baby? I wouldn't intuitively think of you as the family type."

"But I am. At least, I will be if it's my kid we're talking about."

"So you *would* be willing to adopt the baby?" Jonathan pressed him.

"You'll need to talk to an attorney who specializes in family law," Sully said. "But we're skipping over a lot of current problems. What about Skylar? Putting aside the possibility of a negative effect on your personal relationship with her, you were very excited about moving forward with the digital entertainment branch of Computronix. An end to your relationship with her will affect those goals."

What *about* Skylar? He didn't know if she was interested in having children, let alone raising someone else's child. He knew from experience her schedule was just as demanding as his.

Sully shook his head. "You have a lot to consider. I don't envy you."

Jonathan clapped his hands together. "As entertaining as this soap opera is, I've got to turn the channel. I have a meeting with an organic hand soap vendor about an order for the restaurant. You guys will fly out for the grand opening in a few months, right?"

"Wouldn't miss it for the world," Sully said.

"Excellent. Oh and, Mike?"

"What?" He practically growled.

"Have you told your father?"

Jonathan's humorous expression blacked out before the pencil bounced off the monitor.

"Bastard," Mike muttered.

Sully's laugh turned into a serious throat-clearing session. Mike glanced at him. "What do you want?"

"Checking to see if you and India made it to Viv Sutton's office."

"We did. Thanks for the referral. We retained her services."

"Excellent." Sully remained seated.

He shot his friend a prompting look. "Is there anything else?"

Sully ran his palms down the front of his pants. "Did she, uh, mention me?"

Mike's gaze narrowed on the other man.

Ryan Sullivan was a shark, the kind of attorney who made other lawyers nervous when they discovered he was their opposition on a case. And yet that man was sitting here bouncing his knee and scraping the back of his neck raw, torturing Mike with the verbal equivalent of passing notes in homeroom?

He recalled Viv's odd demeanor when Indi had questioned her about Sully. "Something going on between the two of you?"

"No. Not yet," Sully said, his jaw set, his tone a guarantee their not being together was just the jumping off point to start negotiations. He stood.

Mike held out a hand. "Before you go, what can you tell me about adoption?"

Sully shifted his weight onto his back foot. "Not much. Although I know a little about family law, it's not my practice area."

Shit.

"Are you wondering about the process in general or your rights in relation to it?"

"The latter."

Sully sat in the chair he'd just vacated. "I asked if you were considering adopting the baby yourself. Are you?"

YES!

The word wanted to vault from his throat and burst into the room like fireworks during a summer celebration.

Again, his father's voice urged caution. *"Your worst battle is between what you know and what you feel. Choose knowledge."*

"Maybe."

"I'm not comfortable giving advice on a legal matter outside my expertise. So use this for informational purposes only. If India lists you as the father on the birth certificate, you're automatically imbued with rights to your child. You won't need to adopt him."

"The court would allow that?"

"Courts don't get involved in family matters until someone gets them involved. If she truly has no interest in raising this baby, this could be as simple as her giving him to you—the father—and leaving."

He wasn't an attorney, but he could connect the dots to see the picture that was forming.

"But where's my protection in that arrangement? If she could give him to me without legal intervention, what's to stop her from coming back one day and staking a claim to him?"

The woman had bypassed security and picked a lock to gain entry into a premises she knew she was forbidden to access. Despite her reasons, that level of impulsivity proved she could change her mind at any time.

"She could do that anyway," Sully said, "whether she signed legal documents or not."

"But if she'd signed the documents, she'd be starting from a weaker bargaining position."

"True."

That wasn't his only concern.

"Once these criminal charges are sorted out, could she go to another state and put the baby up for adoption without my knowledge?"

Sully shrugged both shoulders. "You're going further into an area I'm not familiar with. But I do know this: courts will not terminate your rights without hearing from you. If India wants to give the baby up for adoption, she'll need your consent. Unless she lies and says she doesn't know who the father is or that she's exhausted all avenues to contact the father and was unable to."

"She wouldn't do that," Mike said, without hesitation.

"Then I'll find you a referral for the best family law attorney in the bay area."

After Sully left, Mike called on years of experience to shelve the concerns in his personal life and focus on his duties. He drafted a memo requiring Human Resources to revise and resubmit their training module for new hires in the finance department and reviewed a proposal from their head of Marketing about opening brick and mortar retail spaces.

He loved his work, aware that he was one of a fortunate few to be successful pursuing an enterprise that nourished the many facets of his personality. Being COO fed his need for order, as every department touched base with his office. The internal workings of Computronix were his responsibility and Mike ensured the company ran like an Olympic athlete.

On the opposite end of the spectrum, he was challenged creatively, as he possessed the ability to devise products and services that could grow their brand and their company. That freedom nursed his muse with regards to OTTo and digital entertainment, and he truly believed the idea would take off.

Evan beeped him. "Ms. Thompson is here to see you."

His assistant had barely uttered the words before Skylar sauntered into his office, smartly attired in a black business suit and a light gray blouse.

He stood, unsettled by her presence in his changed environment, and shrugged into his jacket. "What are you doing here? You should be preparing for your trip to New York."

She offered her cheek for his kiss and he complied, her familiar, expensive floral scent grounding him. This was the life he'd planned to lead. This was the woman who'd be by his side.

"I decided to stop by before I left. You sounded odd during our phone call this morning. I wanted to make sure you were okay."

It was a thoughtful gesture from a woman who was successful in her own right. The other half of his power couple.

And quite unlike the hippie chick now carrying his baby.

He guided her over to the seating area. "Can I get you something to drink?"

"San Pellegrino," she said, placing her expensive handbag on the coffee table and shifting toward him, crossing her legs at the ankle.

He placed the order.

Yesterday his life was progressing as planned, and he'd assumed this smart, beautiful woman would play a prominent part in his future. However, a minor subplot was angling for major attention, leaving him unsure of how to interact with her.

Somewhere Fate was laughing her ass off.

"So, New York. Are you excited?"

Smooth, Mike. Not awkward at all.

She laughed. "I spend several months a year there. You know I keep a penthouse on the Upper East Side?"

"I didn't."

She leaned toward him and brushed the back of his

hand. "Maybe the next time I go for business, you can come with me to see it?"

He straightened—breaking the contact—and nodded, noncommittally. "I thought our meeting went well yesterday."

She pursed glossy pink lips. "It did. Dad was very impressed with your thinking and your strategy."

"I hope he was impressed because it's an innovative idea and not because we're dating," he said, still smarting from the insults to his integrity.

"It's a first-class idea, but it's also true your connection to me gives you an advantage. You know we're very particular about our business associations."

Evan knocked briefly and entered, carrying the requested beverage. He sat a glass on the table in front of Skylar and filled it halfway with the sparkling mineral water before leaving.

She tilted her head, assessing Mike.

"Something's off," she finally said. "It's funny—I was certain you were going to propose last night. But then you canceled our date and acted irritated when I questioned you about it. Are we still on the same page?"

"Of course we are." Hadn't he praised her directness the day before? "Canceling our date couldn't be avoided, but I have been thinking about us and where we're going."

"Me, too," she said. "And I think I've been clear that I see us together."

So had he. But he wouldn't act until he settled the issue of whether or not Indi was carrying his child.

She trailed her finger around the lip of the glass. "Are you still angry because of our breakup last year?"

Anger didn't best describe his feelings about their split. He'd been annoyed. Her announcement had left him temporarily adrift, causing him to question the certainty of a plan ten years in the making.

And then he'd spent the weekend with Indi.

"I've known I was going to run TTL from the time I was a little girl. My father groomed me for it. Meeting you and having everything fall into place the way it did . . . I needed to make sure this was the right step to take," she said, appearing to carefully choose her words. "After some time apart, I realized my mistake. We want the same things. We're invested in our careers and we understand the importance of societal networking. We make a great team."

Valid points he'd made himself.

"And while we're not in love, our time together has been pleasurable." She squeezed his arm. "I'm just thankful you forgave my momentary crisis of faith. We can put all of that behind us and focus on this deal that will take our companies to the next level."

It was exactly what he'd wanted to hear.

Yesterday.

"Does a family figure into your plans?"

Her countenance shifted from persuasive to perplexed.

"You mean children?" At his nod, she responded, "I don't know. I guess I always thought about having a child, but sometime in the future. Definitely no time soon. We'll be too busy becoming one of San Francisco's top power couples. And that reminds me . . ."

She reached into her bag and pulled out her tablet.

"I had my assistant pull the society calendar for the next few months and I've picked out three events we should attend."

That was the type of thinking and planning he wanted from his life partner.

" . . . The Ribbon Legacy gala is being held at the San Francisco Museum of Modern Art at the end of the month . . ."

Someone who knew he'd be investing the majority of his time, effort, and passion into building Computronix's brand and market share.

" . . . We'll definitely need to make an appearance at the Gala under the Stars at the California Academy of Sciences in May, although, seriously, it's like a large aquarium . . ."

Who appreciated that the work he did off Computronix's campus could be just as vital as the work he did while on it.

" . . . The Benefit for Our Bridges isn't the most prestigious, but it's an up and comer, so being one of the first to recognize it will make us appear innovative and at the forefront of trends, which can only be good for both of our businesses . . ."

Not a woman whose idea of networking involved an emoticon-filled group text to her previous coworkers around the country regarding the latest Hollywood scandal.

Skylar closed the cover of her tablet. "Those were from the spring and summer functions. The fall and winter invitations will go out starting in July." A buzzing sound pierced the ensuing silence, startling Skylar. "Oh. That's the alarm I set on my phone. I only had a few minutes; I've got to get going."

She grabbed her purse and stood, and he followed suit. She'd left her drink untouched. Resting a hand against his chest, she pressed her lips to his. In her heels, she was almost as tall as Indi.

Dammit.

He slipped an arm around Skylar's waist and pulled her close, sweeping his tongue into her mouth.

Disappointed, he pulled away. Nice, but no comparison.

"I'll be back in a couple of weeks. We can continue this conversation then."

A short time ago, two weeks had seemed an interminable waiting period to find out if TTL was interested in his business proposal. Now, he could use that time to learn the status of his parenthood. If he wasn't the father, he'd follow through with his original plan to ask Skylar to marry him.

But if he was . . .

His pounding heart stole the moisture from his mouth.

His life was about to veer wildly off course and venture into uncharted territory.

Chapter Seven

IF THERE WASN'T a good possibility that she'd end up back in the county jail, Indi would've left San Francisco the moment Mike dropped her off after their meeting with Viv and headed back to his office.

She swung her legs against the examination table, nibbling on a thumbnail.

"Whither thou goest, I will go."

The Bible? Really? She was surprised both of them hadn't been struck by lightning.

The nerve of that man. She'd done the right thing. She was pregnant with his child and she thought he had the right to know. And for her honesty, he held her hostage.

Okay, so maybe the nausea had forced her hand. She would've waited much later to tell him about her pregnancy.

And there was the slight possibility that he wasn't

holding her hostage. She had to stay in the city, which is what she'd planned to do anyway.

But when she thought she'd be staying to spend time with Chelsea, she'd imagined being independent, free to remain or leave at her leisure. Because of the baby and the money Mike had put up for her, he was acting like her own personal ankle monitoring system. She hadn't been forced to stay anywhere since she left her last foster home at sixteen, and the confinement made her itchy beneath her skin.

She should've told him it was the flu.

"You're poking your lips out and scrunching your face," Mike reported from his seat next to the door. "Are you in pain?"

Oh, she had his pain, but she was saved from answering by a short knock. A woman wearing green scrubs entered, her dark hair pulled into a ponytail.

"Sorry for the delay, but I had an emergency C-section. I'm Dr. Kimball. And you're India?"

Indi held out her hand. "India Shaw, yes. It's a pleasure to meet you. This is Mike Black. Thank you for seeing us on such short notice."

"When my receptionist told me of your request, I was happy to accommodate you." Dr. Kimball rolled the stool from the corner and sat on it, positioning herself near the foot of the exam table. "Your sister mentioned you several times during our consult."

"You made quite an impression on her as well. When I found myself in San Francisco and in need of an ob-gyn, I knew who to call."

"You don't have to butter me up, you already have the appointment," Dr. Kimball said, her blue eyes kind. She glanced at Mike and then back to Indi. "Now, how can I help you?"

"I'm pregnant."

Dr. Kimball smiled. "I figured."

Heat bloomed beneath her skin. "I mean, I haven't seen a doctor yet, so it hasn't been confirmed, but I've been sick for the past couple of months, so I'm either pregnant or it's a fourteen-hundred-hour stomach bug."

The doctor laughed. "You do not have a stomach bug. When my nurse triaged you, she asked for a urine sample. We used it to run a pregnancy test and the result was positive. So, congratulations, you *are* pregnant."

She'd known it—had taken half a dozen pregnancy tests on her own—but hearing the doctor verify it . . . She looked at Mike, his image blurry through the shimmer of her unshed tears.

"It says on your chart that your last menstrual cycle was mid-December. That would make you fourteen weeks pregnant with a conception date around the first of January." Dr. Kimball stood and inched around the side of the exam table. "Lie back and relax."

"That's what he said." Indi's eyes widened. *Had she said that aloud?*

Dr. Kimball's smirk and Mike's furrowed brow indicated that Indi had indeed made the inappropriate joke. Thankfully, it was ignored and the doctor continued her exam, pressing on areas of Indi's lower stomach. "You've made it through your first trimester. If your pregnancy is like most, the nausea should settle down and you'll start to get your appetite back."

Mike rose to stand against the opposite wall, powerfully gorgeous in a charcoal-gray suit, his blue shirt accentuating his opalescent eyes. "Isn't that when it's safe to tell people because the chances of miscarrying are reduced?"

Indi looked at him in surprise. Had he been doing his research? She found it difficult to believe information about pregnancy viability had been hanging out in his mental vault. It wasn't the kind of knowledge single men usually possessed, like which person won the World Series last year and Michael Jordan's batting average.

Dr. Kimball nodded. "Yes, that's right. Many pregnancies are lost early, before a woman even realizes she conceived. After the third month, the chance of having a miscarriage drops to less than five percent."

Buoyancy dispelled the heaviness she hadn't known she was toting. What was her problem? She wasn't raising this child. In fact, were she honest, an early term miscarriage would've rescued this situation. And yet there was no denying the relief that streamed through her at hearing the odds of the baby's continued existence.

"I'll need to get a Pap smear." Dr. Kimball went to the door and asked for assistance. Once the nurse entered, the doctor engaged the stirrups at the end of the table and helped Indi place her feet in the metal holders. Dr. Kimball pulled a tray of instruments closer. "Slide down and let your knees fall open."

Mike started, pushing away from the wall. "Wait, what's that?"

"This?" Dr. Kimball held up the familiar steel tool that looked like a duckbill attached to a hand grip. "It's called a speculum."

He swallowed. "You're putting that in her?"

The doctor's voice was amused. "That's typically how it's done."

"Will it hurt her?"

His concern warmed her.

"I'll be fine," Indi said, offering him a gentle smile.

After a few minutes, Dr. Kimball tapped her knee. "All done. You can sit up."

Mike collapsed into his seat. "I would like to never see that again."

Dr. Kimball stripped off her gloves and threw them away. "You won't." She paused. "Not until baby number two."

"Then he won't," Indi injected into the awkward stillness.

The nurse took the tray with the tools and samples and left the room. Dr. Kimball washed her hands. "Since this is your first doctor's visit after conception, I'm assuming you haven't been taking prenatal vitamins?"

Indi shook her head.

"You'll need to remedy that immediately. And for future reference, waiting fourteen weeks before you see a doctor is not advised." Dr. Kimball made a note on the chart then named a brand of vitamin. "That's what we usually recommend, but any over-the-counter brand will do. Just make sure it has 1,000 mcg of folic acid per dose."

"We'll get some immediately," Mike said.

"Good. Do you have an exercise routine?"

Indi nodded. "I've practiced yoga for years."

"Yoga can be extremely beneficial during pregnancy, but you'll have to take precautions, especially since you're in your second trimester. My nurse will give you a brochure that spells out the adjustments you'll need to make."

Indi had taken her first yoga class in college, believing it to be an easy, undemanding way to fulfill her physical education requirement. Instead, she'd discovered a mental, physical, and spiritual practice that kept her sane, fit, and grounded in the transitory nature of her life. Over the years, her workouts evolved from gentle and meditative to fast-paced and intense, and she'd worried she'd have to give it up during her pregnancy. She was grateful to learn she wouldn't lose the ability to call on her center of focus, especially when she'd need it now more than ever.

"Before you leave," Dr. Kimball was saying, "we'll draw some blood so we can run tests to identify your blood type, check for anemia, and rule out HIV and sexually transmitted infections."

Mike leaned forward and rested his elbows on his knees. "What about a paternity test?"

A knot of embarrassment burned in her chest. If it wouldn't totally expose her naked bottom half, she'd raise the lap sheet to cover her face. God, she was a freaking stereotype. Unwed pregnant woman tricking wealthy man by claiming he's the father. She knew that wasn't the situation, but she wasn't blinded to the optics, either.

The doctor stilled. "If you need a paternity test, one can be performed after the baby is born."

"What if we need to know before the birth?"

Dr. Kimball took a deep breath. "Then you have two options, both invasive. The first is an amniocentesis. I would use an ultrasound as a guide to insert a thin needle into your uterus, through your abdomen. The needle draws out a small amount of amniotic fluid, which is tested. Risks include a small chance of harming the baby and miscarriage."

Indi gasped and placed her hands on her belly. There was no way in hell she was doing that if it wasn't medically necessary.

Mike's jaw tightened. "What's the second option?"

"The second is CVS or chorionic villus sampling. Again, guided by an ultrasound, I'd insert a thin tube into the vagina, through the cervix, to collect chorionic villi, which has the same genetic makeup as the fetus. This testing also creates a risk of miscarriage."

She wouldn't do it and there was no way he could force it upon her. She wasn't angry with Mike for wanting to know if the baby was his, but in the end it didn't matter. She didn't need anything from him, not his money, his support, or his permission. She'd told him because it was the right thing to do, but this wasn't a discussion or a debate. It was her body and she'd made her decision.

She was putting Nugget up for adoption.

And maybe, without concrete proof of Nugget's paternity, Mike's tenuous connection to the baby would fade and he'd leave them both alone.

"If you want the amniocentesis, we'd need to wait at least a couple of weeks. I prefer to perform that procedure after the sixteen-week mark. We could do the CVS as soon as you can schedule the appointment. Again, based on the sparse medical history you provided, these tests aren't necessary, and they can cause a quantifiable risk to you and the baby, including the loss of pregnancy. Unless learning the paternity will benefit the essential health of the baby, I strongly suggest you wait until the baby is born." Dr. Kimball braced her hands on her thighs. "Do you have any other questions for me?"

"I'm still trying to process everything you've told us," Indi said.

"When you check out, the receptionist will give you my card. If you have any questions between now and your next appointment, don't hesitate to call." She smiled, her blue eyes revived from their earlier somberness. "Would you like to hear the baby's heartbeat?"

Nugget fluttered in her belly.

Is that what you want? You want us to hear you?

Indi clasped a hand to her chest. "We can do that?"

"Absolutely. Lean back. No stirrups this time."

The paper sheet crinkling beneath her, Indi reclined on the exam table and placed her head on her bent arm. Mike came to stand next to her. She looked up at him and some emotion she couldn't define swirled in the arctic depths of his eyes.

Dr. Kimball parted the gown and squirted jelly from a tube onto her stomach just beneath her belly button.

The coldness startled Indi. "Ooh!"

"Sorry about that." Dr. Kimball grabbed a device that resembled a microphone for a toddler. "This is a fetal Doppler. It can detect a baby's heartbeat as early as eight weeks."

She placed the microphone in the dab of goo and swirled it around on her belly. The jarring noise of wind roaring through a tunnel erupted from the Doppler and was the occasion's only accompaniment for at least a minute. Worry vacuumed the moisture from her mouth. Was everything okay? Should it take this long? Then—

Whub whub whub whub whub whub whub whub whub whub whub whub whub whub.

The fast, hectic sound echoed throughout the small room. Tears stung her eyes and fell out the sides to wet the paper beneath her head. When Mike's hand swallowed hers in a solid, comforting grip, she realized she'd reached out to him. She looked up and the same awe, wonder, and amazement that filled her soul, colored his features.

"That's our baby," he told her, squeezing her hand.

Indi whispered, "Hey, Nugget."

"Everything sounds good. Your baby's heart rate is one hundred fifty-five beats per minute, which is right on target for fourteen weeks."

Dr. Kimball quieted the machine and the sudden silence was deafening. She got a tissue and wiped the goo off Indi's stomach. "Most couples hesitate to ask during their first visit, but, in case you were wondering, it's completely safe for you to have sex during your pregnancy. Your baby is not watching you and will not know what's going on, so don't let that worry you. In fact, during your second trimester, increased blood flow to your pelvis may make it easier for you to achieve an orgasm."

Oh. My. God.

Indi squeezed her eyes shut and prayed this had all been a super realistic dream. She wasn't pregnant, she hadn't been arrested, and she hadn't called Mike to bail her out of jail. There was no possibility of pending criminal charges, she wasn't in debt to the tune of one hundred and ten thousand dollars, and she wasn't in a doctor's office crying over the beauty of her unwanted baby's heartbeat and listening to her doctor calmly advise her about easily obtained orgasms.

Shit, that didn't sound like a dream. It was a meat lover's deluxe pizza at 2:00 a.m.–induced nightmare.

No matter. She'd wake up and find herself back in her loft in Seattle after a long night sampling the brewery's latest blend.

She'd be the same Indi as before: carefree, independent, and in control of her life. Able to keep everyone at a distance and protect herself from the hurt that came when people got close enough to realize the charm, humor, and amiability she exuded camouflaged a person who was, at her core, unlovable.

She pinched her arms, counted to three and opened her eyes to the "Ob-gyn Kenobi: May the Forceps Be with You" poster on the ceiling.

Nope. This was happening. All of it.

Mike cleared his throat. "Umm, good to know."

"Your next appointment will be in four weeks and we'll schedule you for an ultrasound. It'll be your first picture of the baby and we may be able to determine the sex. Again, congratulations, to both of you."

"Can you turn around?" Indi asked when they were left alone in the room, aching for the tiniest bit of space she could manufacture.

Could anything be closer than a baby growing inside of her and its father determined to keep her glued to his side?

His gaze flicked upward. "I've already seen it."

"That was then, this is now. Turn around, please."

He narrowed his eyes, but gave her his back, offering her a modicum of privacy to clothe her bottom half. The long, floral skirt—once a favorite—would now be relegated to the burn-this-I-never-want-to-see-it-again pile, after being called into service three days in a row.

She needed to go shopping.

She'd planned to go yesterday, having finally broken the ceramic penis and freed her savings. But exhaustion stole her opportunity to get out and see the city.

Sitting down, she slid her feet into her boots. "I'm done."

"I'll give you a ride back to the condo."

"No." The adamant shake of her head disturbed her braids. "I can find my way back."

He frowned. "You don't know this city. You need to be careful."

"I've been responsible for myself since I was sixteen years old. I'll be fine."

"Apparently not," he said, his meaning evident in his smug, self-righteous tone.

"I didn't get pregnant by myself. This wasn't the immaculate conception."

"You're right. But can't I be concerned about where you're going—"

She exploded. "Where do you imagine I'll go, Mike? You've got me fucking low jacked! I just need some space."

She turned to leave and he was behind her between one breath and the next. He braced a hand against the door, preventing her departure.

"This is the opposite of space," she gritted out.

"I'm sorry," he said, brushing her braids over her shoulder.

The unexpected tenderness was her undoing. She caved like a roof with insufficient support.

"I'm not making this easy on you, am I?" He stroked her back.

She didn't respond, couldn't as the power of his presence slowly encircled her, pushing out any alternative other than the one to melt into him, let him take care of everything.

"I want to, Indi. I really do," he said, his voice low and hypnotic. "But I can't. You've had time to come to terms with this. I've only had a day."

Yeah, well, she'd only had three.

She focused on the door in front of her, scrutinizing the minutia of the wooden grain, trying to focus on anything but the feel of his chest against her back and the crisp, fresh smell of his cologne.

"Don't you love him?"

His painful question was the barrier she needed

against the encroaching lethargy. She placed a hand against her belly. "Nugget?"

"Why do you call him Nugget?"

She recalled the grainy black-and-white images she'd seen when she'd Googled three-month fetus. Her throat tightened, making it difficult to speak. She struggled to form the words.

"When I searched online, that's what he looked like."

"You looked it up online? You named him? That doesn't sound like someone unattached to the baby growing inside her."

She trembled. "You don't understand."

"Then help me. Don't you love Nugget?"

Anguished, she faced him, certain her heart would burst from her chest, the pain was so intolerable.

"I love him more than I ever thought possible. That's why I *have* to give him away."

Chapter Eight

HE'D LET HER go.

Or had she taken her leave?

Either way, Indi walked down the shaded street, grateful for the freedom to determine her own movements for the next few hours.

How had she gotten entangled in a situation where she'd abdicated her autonomy to others? Her plan had been simple. Come to San Francisco, hang out until the baby was born, give him up for adoption, and get on with her life. Instead, she had found her sister gone, gotten herself arrested, and been charged with a felony, and now she was tied, legally and biologically, to a man who overrode her hard-won common sense and had her fantasizing about an existence she could never lead.

He wasn't even her type. She liked party boys. Guys who took her to exclusive clubs where she danced all night and drank for free because they knew everyone who mattered. Guys who invited her to the Hamptons for all-night raves, who were spontaneous and liked to have fun. Guys who didn't take themselves too seriously.

Mike was as formal as a Southern cotillion. He was proper, confident, disciplined. The only time she'd seen him dressed casually was when he was half-naked, having thrown on slacks to answer the door for the pizza delivery guy. He was more likely to take a date to the opera than to jet off on a moment's notice to some exotic locale.

But their differences didn't seem to matter when it came to the potent attraction between them. From the moment they'd met at Chelsea and Adam's engagement party, sparks had flared to life, simmering unattended until he'd approached her at their wedding. And then . . . fireworks.

And that baby she'd planned to give away? The moment she'd heard his heartbeat, emotions she hadn't known she'd possessed roared to life within her, creating rifts in her certainty that a better life awaited him elsewhere.

What in the hell was she going to do?

She knew what she wouldn't do. She wouldn't make the mistake of growing used to their presence or—heaven forbid—depending on them. They would leave: Nugget to his new family, Mike to his old girlfriend.

Chelsea to her new life.

And she'd be alone again. With the only person she could ever really trust to have her back.

"Indi?" A friendly, feminine voice. "What are you doing here?"

She froze. She could count the number of people she knew in San Francisco on one hand, and only one of them was a woman. Who was currently out of the country. She turned around to stare at the blonde standing a few feet away.

"Jill." Pleasure blossomed at the improbable sight of Chelsea's assistant. They'd gotten to know one another during Indi's many stopovers in LA before Chelsea had met Adam. "How are you? Congratulations on the promotion."

"Thank you. Chelsea's rise to partner at Beecher & Stowe meant I was upgraded from a cubicle to my own office. Name etched in glass and everything."

"Are you splitting time between the San Francisco and LA offices?"

"No. I relocated with Chelsea after the holidays."

"What are you doing here?"

"I asked you first."

"I'm taking in the scenery."

Jill's brown eyes widened at Indi's sparse reply but she answered in kind. "Our office is a block away."

Ahhh . . . Chelsea said she'd wanted to find a doctor near her job. Indi had believed that meant San Francisco versus San Mateo. She hadn't considered that Chelsea meant the proximity to her actual office.

Jill placed a hand on her shoulder. "I'm heading over to Union Square for coffee. Want to join?"

The chance to spend time with someone who didn't know her situation seemed like the greatest indulgence. From the moment she'd taken the pregnancy test, she'd been defined by the life growing inside her. Every decision she made, every action she took, every opportunity she turned down, all because of Nugget's presence. Coming to San Francisco, getting arrested, calling Mike . . .

Hell, being around Mike was akin to existing next to a walking billboard of her mistake.

"Sure. Thanks."

Even the weather cooperated, bestowing upon them cool temperatures and a pleasant breeze that stirred the fronds on the lush fan-shaped palm trees. The sun blazed brightly, as if gracing them with its presence, bringing to life the beautiful architecture of the city and glinting off the enormous, colorful metal heart that sat atop a stone pillar, surrounded by a throng of people.

"What's with the heart?" Indi asked.

"That's the Tony Bennett heart. It's a thing here, part of a fundraiser. I haven't been in the city long, but most days when I walk over to grab lunch, I see a queue of people lined up for selfies. Someone told me you can do a walking tour and see several others in buildings, gardens, or parks around the city."

When they reached the charming patisserie, Jill held open the door for her and the mouthwatering smell of baked items and coffee overwhelmed Indi. She paused just inside, waiting to see if Nugget would accept this assortment of aromas. When no physical indication of his displeasure was forthcoming, she sighed in relief.

"Does Chelsea know you're here?" Jill asked after they'd received their drinks and had chosen to sit at one of the wrought iron cafe tables on the patio.

"Not yet. It was a spur of the moment decision."

People strolled past in various states of dress, from those shivering in shorts, sweatshirts, and flip-flops to others clad in jeans, boots, and thick jackets. With only her cable-knit sweater for coverage, Indi was glad they'd chosen to forego a table beneath the large green canvas umbrellas. They needed the sun's warmth.

Jill gestured toward Indi's mug of steamed milk. "Not a coffee person?"

When she realized she'd have to give up caffeine—another decision dictated by Nugget!—she'd ordered the beverage she used to make for children when she worked at an Arlington, Texas, coffeehouse. "I am. I just—not right now."

Jill's brown eyes scanned her, from the top of her braids to her dangling foot. "Are you pregnant?"

Indi sputtered and her vanilla-flavored drink dotted the tabletop. "What?"

"Are you pregnant? That's the only reason anyone gives up caffeine. Or alcohol. And don't try to tell me you don't drink. I was at the wedding reception and I have two words for you." She held up her index and middle fingers. "*Tequila. Shots.* It was amazing."

Indi rolled her eyes and wiped her hands on her skirt. Christ, if she'd known everyone would be watching her and Mike instead of the bride and the groom, she would've sold tickets and used the proceeds to fund her next getaway. Since when had she shed the invisibility cloak that allowed her to operate beneath the radar?

That had always been a useful part of her survival kit,

knowing when to kick up her persona and when to fade into the background. Bartending, waitressing, trying to stand out during Children Services' annual adoption fair: sparkle, sparkle, sparkle.

Receptionist, data entry clerk, not making trouble when the social worker checked on you at your latest foster home: keep your head down and your mouth closed. Somehow, instead of her and Mike going unnoticed, their coupling had sparked the hell out of the party.

She opened her mouth, intending to wrap herself in indignation and—if luck decided to throw her a frickin' bone—divert attention away from her lack of verbal response. Instead, the telltale prickling of heat behind her eyes and—

Oh no, oh no, oh no.

—she was crying.

Deep, gut wrenching sobs. Pent-up, mournful sobs. Ugly, blotchy sobs that drew attention from their fellow customers and inquisitive passersby.

Dawning remorse reversed the trajectory of Jill's smile. She put her cup on the table and scooted her chair forward, taking Indi's hands in her own. "Hey, hey. It's okay. I'm sorry. Truly. It's none of my business."

Indi reached into her backpack and pulled a tissue from a travel-sized pack. "It's these damn hormones. They're driving me insane. I'm days away from ordering a cropped maternity straight jacket."

She wiped away the physical manifestation of her weakness and blew her nose.

"So you *are* pregnant. Congratulations?" Jill's tone

suggested she wasn't sure if the news warranted celebration or not.

"Thank you. I'm just a little overwhelmed."

"I can imagine. I have two older sisters, both married with children. You have that same wild-eyed, deer-in-the-headlights look they each had when they found out they were pregnant."

"Did they figure it all out?"

Jill slowly nodded. "I think they'd say yes, but my oldest sister swears enlightenment came after she had her second one. She says she never realized how easy having one was until number two's arrival."

It appeared Indi was destined to go through this pregnancy as clueless and confused as she was now. And she'd never gain sureness or confidence in her choices because she didn't plan on having another child. Still, admitting the truth to Jill lightened her in a way she hadn't imagined.

"Do you want to talk about it?" Jill picked up her cup, took a sip.

Indi traced the intricate scrollwork on the table with her finger. To discuss how she was feeling—with a person who had no personal stake in the outcome—was a comfort, but . . .

"You probably have to get back to work . . ."

"With Chelsea on her honeymoon, I've actually had some time off, but I wanted to come into the office and start preparing it for her return. Speaking of Chelsea . . . does she know you're pregnant?"

"No. I came to tell her, but my hormones . . ." She

stroked her braids. "I forgot she wouldn't be home for another couple of weeks."

"How far along are you?"

"Fourteen weeks."

Jill's precisely plucked brows strained toward one another. "And you just found out?" She held up a hand as soon as the words passed her lips. "Never mind. You don't have to answer that."

"It's okay. I've always had irregular periods. Missing one month wasn't unusual, but when it didn't start the second month, I prayed I was wrong. The third month Aunt Flo boycotted . . . well, there was no more living in denial."

Terror had driven the breath from her body and she'd collapsed onto the closest available surface, her legs unable to support her weight. She was pregnant. She couldn't imagine a circumstance she wanted to endure less. Twelve years of being jostled around the foster care system had convinced Indi she'd be a dreadful mother. She had no role model, no real-life behavior to duplicate. The only good mothers she knew were fictional. Okay, she knew there were real mothers who loved and cared for their children. But that reality wasn't part of her experience. Her day-to-day had been filled with women who didn't care to know what her needs were, never mind attempting to put those needs before their own.

And love? Indi's own mother hadn't wanted her, had dropped her off—when she was four years old—at an emergency room and walked away. She'd cycled through so many foster homes she'd lost count after twenty, and yet none of those families had ever come forth to adopt her. Other than Chelsea, Indi couldn't name a single person who ever cared about her. Unlovable and with no notion of how to care for and raise a child. And society wanted to entrust her to mold and shape a new life because her eggs had played Match.com with some sperm?

Her anguish had been exacerbated by the fact that the confirmation had come on the heels of an exciting offer to work with a renowned, international photographer. The referral had come from a man she'd met while working at a luxury resort in Charleston, South Carolina. The photographer was getting ready to begin a year-long project that included photographing the indigenous people of Cape York Peninsula in Australia and was having a difficult time finding assistants who'd consent to being away from family for that amount of time. It'd been an ideal find for Indi. With Chelsea starting a new life and no other family to speak of, she was uniquely qualified for the post and looked forward to indulging her love of travel and adventure.

Again, that had been BN: before Nugget.

"And the father?"

A pixelated image of Mike came into focus, one feature at a time. His pale blue eyes, able to transform from glacial to scorching between one blink and the next. His wheat-colored blond hair, sexy whether combed to perfection or stylishly tousled and curled. His strong, chiseled jaw, telegraphing his honorable intent and his determination to bring pleasure. His firm lips, convincing others of his judgment or kissing her senseless.

"I told him."

"Is he going to support you and the baby?"

"He says he will, but it's a moot point. I'm giving the baby away." Her gaze fell. "Adoption."

"Oh." Jill took another sip.

Indi wiped her suddenly damp palms on her skirt. "Do you think— Am I— Does that make me a bad person?"

The idea that doing the right thing—and giving her baby the opportunity to live a life with people who would shower him with the love and affection she'd never received—would make her the villain of her own child's story, riddled her with guilt and heartache. Although it shouldn't. It's not like she was dropping him off at the nearest fire station. Indi planned to use an adoption agency and personally pick the family lucky enough to raise him. She tried to swallow past the mass of unease lodged in her throat.

"Of course not. You have to make the choice that's best for you and your situation." Jill pursed her lips. "Chelsea doesn't really talk about it, but she's mentioned her past before and how the two of you met. I imagine it's difficult to think about raising a baby considering your own childhood."

"I wouldn't know where to start. And there's so much I want to do in the world. So much I want to see." Indi shook her head. "I can't be tied down."

She pressed both hands to her stomach. Maybe if she said it often enough, she'd start to believe it.

"Have you seen a doctor?"

"Yes, that's why I was in the area. I just left an appointment with Dr. Kimball."

Jill laughed. "Dr. Kimball should be named the official ob-gyn of Beecher & Stowe's San Francisco office. All of the women who made the move here from LA, or from any of our offices back east, go to her."

"Uh-huh. That's what I told Mike."

"Mike." Jill's eyes widened. "As in Michael Black, Adam's best friend?"

Shit! Coffee had morphed into an intimate confession session and she'd confided a lot in the other woman, but she hadn't planned on exposing *that* piece of information.

Jill's face brightened as she connected the dots. "He's the father. You're fourteen weeks, and the wedding was about three months ago . . . the tequila shots!" She slapped her hands against the table.

Damn, she was sharp. Whatever Chelsea was paying her, it wasn't enough.

"He's gorgeous," Jill continued. "But isn't he dating Skylar Thompson?"

"Yeah. Another fragment in the one-thousand-piece puzzle that is my frustrating life."

"Wow." Jill paused. "What are you going to do?"

"Continue with my original plans. Nothing has occurred to make me change them."

Liar.

"I understand," Jill said, reaching out to squeeze Indi's hand. "I just want you to know that I'm here if you ever need to talk, and I'd never betray your trust or confidence. Chelsea has become a dear friend to me and I know how much she loves you. After spending time in your company, I think I can see why."

"I appreciate your offer. Thank you," Indi said, energized by the notion that after all the people she'd met on her travels and the thousands she'd connected with on social media, in a small coffee shop in San Francisco, she may have made a true friend.

"Can I give you a lift back to your hotel? Or are you staying at Chelsea and Adam's place?"

She stood and gathered up her trash. "No, but if you have some free time, I'd love your company while I do some shopping. Chelsea may have mentioned my spontaneity?"

A wry smile crossed Jill's pretty face. "I believe she used another word for it."

Considering her more prudent sister, Indi said, "I don't want to know. Anyway, I told you how this visit was spur of the moment. I meant that phrase literally. This outfit is all I have to wear. I'm not showing yet, but I'm going to need some new clothes. And you have great taste. I've been eying that purse. That's a Torcano bag, right?"

Jill hefted the navy blue embossed satchel. "Yes. I treated myself after the promotion. I'm impressed. Most people wouldn't recognize the designer."

"I worked as an assistant stylist to Kate Crenshaw in New York several years back, when she was acting in that big budget romantic comedy. Anthony Torcano named a bag after her in his spring collection."

Jill's mouth dropped open. "You mean the Crenshaw?"

Indi nodded. "A little gaudy for my taste, but Kate loved it."

"Yup, we're going to be fabulous friends." Jill linked her arm through Indi's. "Now, most of the major department stores are close by, but let's skip those. I've found some great little boutiques I think you'll like."

"Cool. Let's go." Jill didn't know it, but her recently expressed feels regarding Indi's character were about to be tested. "So, about my staying at Chelsea and Adam's place . . ."

Chapter Nine

HE'D HEARD HIS child's heartbeat.

Yesterday as Mike stood in the examination room
clutching Indi's hand, hearing the cadence of life growing within her, his vision had expanded, allowing him
to see saturated colors and crisp detail. Just as quickly, it
narrowed until he was focused on one tiny point.

Protecting his baby.

The paternity test wasn't necessary. Between the doctor's confirmation of the timing of conception and the
knowledge that Indi wouldn't jeopardize her relationship
with Chelsea by scamming him, he had all the additional
verification he needed.

Indi was pregnant with his child.

There was no quibbling with the notion that it was
Indi's body and her choice. She'd chosen to give birth
to the baby, but give it up for adoption. That's where his
compliance ended. He could no more give away his child

than he could choose to stop breathing. Something had to be done. He couldn't allow Indi to go through with the adoption. Hence, his plans for the rest of the day.

He knew his decision would have a marked effect on his relationship with Skylar and his proffered deal between Computronix and TTL. Skylar had made it clear that his proposition had a better chance of approval if they were personally involved and Mike knew this deal meant amazing growth for Computronix. But at what cost?

Skylar had stated she wasn't ready for children—let alone a child borne by another woman—but they'd been speaking hypothetically. She'd agreed they made a good match, and if he stressed that he and the baby were a package deal, he hoped she'd reconsider. If not, so be it. Computronix offering OTTo and their own digital entertainment was another industry first. If Franklin Thompson turned him down because he and Skylar had called it quits, it'd be a decision the other man would regret for years into the future.

He checked his watch. Where was Indi? He'd asked her to meet him after lunch. Though it went against his burgeoning protective instinct, he hadn't stood in her way when she'd finally left the doctor's office. He'd given her the space she'd requested. That didn't mean he endorsed the idea of her wandering alone in an unfamiliar city. He pulled out his cell and sent a quick text to Evan.

Call our corporate car provider and have them send over a list of drivers available for a long-term hire.

He'd make sure she'd get where she needed to be—

promptly and safely—for the remainder of her pregnancy.

"Hey." A low, wary voice behind him.

His pulse throbbed in anticipation. He turned and found Indi with her arms crossed over a dark blue denim jacket, her head bent with braids spilling over one shoulder.

Despite her mood, she did not disappoint.

"Thanks for coming." He scanned the bright multicolored dress that showcased her slender curves and ended just below her knee. "You look great."

Her lashes flew upward and her gaze collided with his.

He swallowed. She had the most amazing eyes. They weren't hazel; no flecks of green would dare mar the translucent brown. Instead, the rich amber color of pure honey stared back at him and like the sticky substance, it threatened to bind him to her.

He blinked and severed their connection. The potency of their pairing was staggering. Guess there was truth to the idea that having a baby bonded two people.

Then how did he explain their connection *before* the baby was conceived?

"I went shopping yesterday." That explained the new clothes.

"I know I didn't make it home last night. After the doctor's office and your needing space . . ."

"I appreciated it. Really." She gestured to the fourstory warehouse blocking the sun and contributing to the cool afternoon. "What are we doing here?"

Last night, sitting in his office, a tumbler of whiskey

in his hand and starring into the inky black sky, he'd realized he'd been going about this all wrong. He'd been trying to force her into doing what he wanted, thinking he knew best. Although he did, that strategy wasn't working with Indi. She was different from any other woman he'd known. He'd needed to find another way to shift the circumstances and achieve the outcome he desired.

"We've been caught up in the trauma and confusion of the situation and ignoring the miracle. You're pregnant. We're having a baby."

She shook her head. "Mike, I can't—"

"I know you feel that way now, but I don't want you to look back and regret that you didn't do more to document the occasion. You told me you weren't making this decision lightly. That you truly believe it's in Nugget's best interests."

Her lips twitched when he said *Nugget*.

"Then it bears celebration. Whatever happens, our lives have been changed. Forever."

She dropped her head. Unable to keep his distance, to resist the need to touch her, he grasped her shoulders.

"I took the rest of the day off. Spend it with me."

Her response wasn't immediate. Damn, but she was obstinate. With everyone else she was easygoing, malleable. With him, unyielding as granite. He held his breath.

She gave a barely perceptible nod. Satisfaction sped through him. He took her hand, his body bracing for the jolt it experienced each time he touched her. Being in her proximity caused his being to hum with a vibrancy only she could arouse. It'd been that way from the moment they'd met. It'd unnerved him, disturbed him, taken him by surprise.

She had taken him by surprise.

He guided her through the metal door. An emergency stairwell—framed by the rectangular slice of glass in a beige nondescript door—was situated on their left. Fluorescent lighting ushered them down the long, cinder-blocked corridor to a swinging glass door. Entering the new space, they were greeted by a bright blue half wall with *Carrie Holland Photography* written in a crisp white script.

Indi blinked. "A photography studio?"

"I read online that some mothers like to get pictures of their bodies—"

"Seriously, you need to step away from Google."

"—as it changes. So you can remember."

She pulled her hand from his. "Are you being this dense on purpose? I'm giving Nugget away. I don't want to remember this."

"Now. You don't want to remember it *now*. But that might change. And if it does, I'll have the pictures."

The bulletproof shield of her crossed arms ascended back into place. He gave a mental sigh. One step forward, two steps back.

"Carrie Holland, huh? You just called up one of the world's most respected photographers and got an appointment? On a day's notice?"

"You know her work?"

"Everyone knows her work. You can find it on anything from T-shirts to calendars to coffee mugs. It's iconic."

He shoved his hands into the pockets of his slacks. "I

wanted the best. I've worked hard. Made a lot of contacts, made even more money. I can't think of a better way to spend it than on my child."

Her mouth tightened. "We didn't get the paternity test. How do you know Nugget is yours?"

"Because you said he was. And that's enough for me."

That connection zinged between them again. This time, she was the first to look away.

"Mr. Black? Is that you?" A raspy, female voice reached out to them from behind the wall. "Please, come on back."

They walked around the barrier and into a large open space divided by floor-to-ceiling white fabric, the bottoms pooling against the light hardwood floors. Both sides were set up with items he'd expect to see in a photography studio: large illuminated umbrellas, cameras on tripods, chairs, benches, and cubes. The only difference between the two spaces was the one on the left was helped by the addition of natural light coming from the large arched and gridded windows whereas the light in the space on the right originated from lamps.

"Hello." A short stocky woman in cargo pants with a camera around her neck strode forward, her hand extended. "I'm Carrie Holland."

"Mike Black." He admired her strong eye contact and firm grip. "Thank you for agreeing to see us."

"Yes, thank you. I'm a huge fan of your work," India said. "I love how you've made art accessible."

There it was. That warm, charming nature she shared with everyone but him.

A pleased expression glazed Carrie's face and she

smiled. "You're a dear. That was my intention when I first started. There's great beauty in the pregnant form."

Indi strode over to the framed portraits on the far wall. Pictures of all sizes, in differing tones—color, black-and-white, sepia—captured women in the later stages of their pregnancies, exuding an aura of sublime rapture visible to even the most jaded eye.

She tapped an espresso-colored wooden frame. "I'm not that far along."

Carrie narrowed her eyes. "What are you, three or four months?"

"Fourteen weeks."

Carrie nodded. "Your first pregnancy?"

"How did you know?"

"I've been doing this a long time. One, you're here for pictures and you haven't started showing. Classic give-away. Two, once a woman has a baby, it's like muscle memory. As soon as her body recognizes she's pregnant, her belly pops out." She nodded at Indi's midsection. "Too flat."

Mike flashed on a vision of Indi, her belly rounded with his child. He couldn't wait until the reality supplanted his imagining.

"I usually recommend pregnant women wait until they are thirty-two to thirty-six weeks along before being photographed," Carrie said.

He nodded. "I understand. But I wanted more than one photograph. I wanted the entire journey. We can come back every month or so throughout the preg-nancy."

Indi turned on him. "Excuse me?"

Carrie's eyes brightened. "Yes! A progression. You know, it would be a good idea to wear the same outfit for each session, to better highlight the changes in your body. What clothes did you bring? We'll want something that will accommodate your belly as it grows."

Shit. He raked a hand through his hair. He hadn't thought to bring a change of clothes.

Indi crossed her arms and jutted one hip. "Don't look at me. I didn't know we were coming here today."

Reading the consternation on his face, Carrie waved her hand. "It's fine. I have several pieces in the changing room and they're all freshly laundered. Look through them and pick what you like. Remember, you'll want a garment that'll adjust over the coming months."

Indi followed Carrie across the space, pausing to spear him with a look over her shoulder. He winked then exhaled a snort of amusement when she stuck out her tongue then sped to catch up to the photographer.

Carrie came back a few minutes later and began arranging the area. "We'll do two different setups. Let's start next to the window. Natural light is something I can't control and we lose more of it each second."

Mike mentally ran through the afternoon's itinerary. He didn't expect a miracle, but he hoped to generate the beginning of a thaw in Indi's steadfast notion of giving their baby up for adoption. His chest vibrated an instant before his cell phone rang.

Carrie ceased adjusting the height of the umbrella's stand and lifted a brow.

"I'll silence the ringer." He checked the caller ID. "After this call."

"The visual aids for your presentation just arrived," his assistant, Evan, said, the clacking of keys prominent in the background.

"Finally! It's been two weeks."

"I'm going to call the team together. I can set the meeting for an hour from now. How's three o'clock?" Evan's voice was brisk, the question pro forma, Mike's consent a foregone conclusion.

This meeting with the department heads on moving into the digital entertainment space was important. He needed to have a strategy in place by the time TTL agreed to his proposal. Under normal circumstances, nothing would've delayed this discussion.

Mike swung his gaze toward the changing room. But for the first time ever, there was something more important than business.

More important than Computronix.

"Set it for first thing Monday morning, 9:00 a.m."

"Sir?" Bewilderment clouded Evan's tone, as if Mike had informed the younger man that Thursday didn't follow Wednesday or money did in fact grow on trees.

"Set the meeting for Monday. It's the weekend."

"I know. I'm surprised *you* noticed."

"Well, I did. We already worked this morning. After you send out notices for the meeting on Monday, go home."

He held up the phone, made a production of silencing the ringer, and slid it back into his pocket.

Carrie smiled, nodded her thanks, and asked, "What's her favorite color?"

"Excuse me?"

"Indi. What's her favorite color?"

"I don't know." He crossed his arms over his chest. "Why?"

She shrugged. "Just mulling over possibilities for her backdrop."

As the other woman pulled down an assortment of textured and themed screens, Mike pondered the ramifications of her question. Why should he know her favorite color? Those little details emerged as people spent time together: they learned each other's favorite food, what kind of music they liked, their favorite movie. It's not like he and Indi had been in a relationship. Hell, conversation hadn't been top of mind during that weekend . . .

"This is your house?" she'd asked, her head thrown back, her eyes scanning their surroundings.

"Yes," he'd said, his eyes fixated on the graceful curve of her neck, the lean smoothness of her torso.

She'd straddled his lap, her frothy bridesmaid's dress gathered around her waist, her bare thighs bracketing his trouser-covered hips. He shifted, the hardwood floors beneath him softer than the erection he'd ceased trying to rein in.

"Yours personally? Not the company's?"

He loved watching her mouth form words. "No, it's mine."

"Did you just move in?"

"Hey, what's with all the questions?" He gave in to the

longing that had plagued him from the moment he'd first set eyes on her and stroked his thumb along her plump, kissable bottom lip. "I have other plans for that pretty mouth."

Her lashes dropped to half-mast and her glistening pink tongue darted out to lave the pad of his finger.

When he growled and leaned in to taste her, she angled away from him and tilted her head to the side, the wavy strands of her hair tickling the part of his chest bared by his opened dress shirt.

"It's a nice house, very neat and tidy. But it doesn't look lived in. The walls are still the generic builder-grade cream."

Teasing could go both ways and he wasn't the only one smarting from the attraction sizzling between them. He hadn't imagined her hands tracing the length of his cock during their earlier make-out session.

He pulled her close and bit her earlobe, sucking it into his mouth to soothe the sting. "What's your favorite color?"

She shivered. "Why?"

"Because I'll paint the walls any goddamn color you want if we can stop discussing my woeful skills as an interior designer and get back to what we were just doing."

"Poor baby." She laughed, the sound so sexy the hair on his arms stood at attention. "I don't have one."

His tongue traced the delicate shell of her inner ear. "One what?"

She pushed against his shoulders. "A favorite color! There are an infinite number of colors in the world. Why limit myself to one?"

He found her healthy appetite for life heady as it was so different from his deliberate, measured approach.

She wiggled her ass against him. "Are you ready?"

His fingers dug into her hips and he pressed her down on his rock-hard erection. "All day, every day."

Palming his face, she slid her fingers through the hair curling above his ears and slanted his head to the side. His eyes closed as her tongue stroked the side of his neck, the wet caress an arousing abrasion against his skin and the perfect adhesion for the cool sprinkle of salt.

He grabbed a slice of lemon from the pile on the coffee table—next to the shot glasses brimming with tequila—and placed it in his mouth, the flesh of the fruit facing her.

She stared into his eyes and his heart expanded in his chest. She rubbed her nose against his once, twice, then parted her lips, bent her head, and licked the salt away from his skin. His cock heaved against his pants, hating the barriers keeping it from its target.

She reached for a small glass, pounded the shot, and sucked the lemon from between his lips, tossing the debauched rind over her shoulder.

Fucking yeah, that was hot!

He was in so much trouble...

Okay, so he knew she didn't have a favorite color. No big deal. It didn't negate any of his earlier thoughts because he also knew Skylar's favorite color. It was ... um ...

He exhaled loudly. Shit.

The changing room door opened and Indi emerged.

His breath abandoned his body.

Carrie clasped her hands together and pressed her

joined index fingers against her lower lip. "Great choice. I love that ivory organza skirt. It sparkles against your complexion."

Indi had taken the skirt and pulled it up so it resembled a strapless dress. A slit parted the fabric right above her navel and she held it closed with one hand. Her braids fell in a cascade around her shoulders to trail along her breasts.

Beautiful.

"Let's start with some natural shots. Nothing too difficult, nothing too pose-y. The position you like the best will be the one we'll use each time you come in. That'll make the progression more pronounced, more noticeable. And trust me, as you get bigger, your center of gravity will shift. We'll save the contortions for the stand-alone pictures, okay?"

Indi nodded, her hand tightening in the semi-sheer fabric until her knuckles blended with the material.

"Good." Carrie led her to the area she'd set up on the left. "I want you to stand here with your profile to me."

Indi released the dress and it flowed around her to end at her calves. She shrugged her shoulders and shuffled her feet, bright pink toes winking up at him with the movement.

A muffled click of the shutter.

"Nice. Give me a soft smile."

Indi's cheeks twitched.

Whirr. Click.

"Now, look down and touch your belly."

Indi's chin dropped to her chest and she slapped a hand on her stomach.

He winced. He was sure that wasn't what Carrie wanted. Indi looked less like an expectant mother and more like someone in digestive distress.

"You're so tense," Carrie told her. "Loosen up. Relax your shoulders. This is supposed to be fun."

Whirr. Click.

"Your stomach doesn't have cooties. Touch it. Caress it."

If he didn't know better, he'd think she didn't like having her picture taken, but during the photo shoot at the wedding, she'd laughed and danced, her body swaying to music only she could hear. "Okay, let's go with serious. Solemn."

Whirr. Click.

"Come on, relax. There's life in there. Show me the wonder, the awe."

The more Carrie talked, the tenser Indi became until she resembled a statue one fissure away from crumbling. Still the photographer persisted.

"You've created something beautiful. She'll love you and depend on you—"

Indi's lips trembled and her skin took on an ashen pallor.

This wasn't working.

He interrupted. "Can you give us a moment?"

Carrie sighed. "Take your time. You paid for it."

She took her camera and exited through another door, leaving them alone.

"What's wrong?"

"I can't do this," Indi whispered, her shoulders slumping forward, her body caving in.

He resisted the urge to bare his teeth and snarl her into submission. Why was convincing this one woman to do what he wanted so difficult?

"Yes you can. You just need to—"

Her eyes flashed. "If you tell me to relax I will fucking stab you!"

He stiffened. Whoa. Those sites weren't kidding about the surging hormones.

She brought her thumbs up to massage her temples. "I appreciate what you're trying to do. But I'm not them," she said, flinging a hand to indicate the portraits on the wall. "Those women were excited about their condition. They probably had nurseries and wardrobes and couldn't wait until they brought their babies home. That's not what's happening here. I have to give Nugget away and nothing you do will change that. Going through this charade will only make it harder when the time comes."

Nothing he did would change the situation? This wasn't the first time he'd heard that particular sentiment. It didn't stop him then, it wouldn't stop him now.

"Indi, look at me." When her defeated gaze met his, he continued. "You had choices. You chose to give him life. Honor that decision. Are you going to spend the next five and half months shuffling through the world, pushing your friends and family away? Do you think that's healthy for him? For you? Be happy. And when he's born, you'll know you've done everything you can to start him on the path to a good life. As for these pictures"—he cupped her shoulders and squeezed—"you don't ever have to see them, but I'll want them." His chest tightened as he placed a hand on her belly. "I want to remember this."

She looked up at him, tears pooling in her eyes. A surge of tenderness rippled through his body, overwhelming him.

He trailed a finger down her dewy smooth cheek and kissed her forehead. "No matter what happens, I'll take care of both of you."

Whirr. Click.

"Beautiful." Carrie's voice was filled with reverence.

They both looked up.

"I don't know what you were thinking," Carrie said, camera resting against the side of her neck, lens facing skyward, "but that look on your face, his hand touching . . . It was perfect. That's it. That's the pose."

Chapter Ten

MIKE OPENED THE door of the car and held out his hand to help Indi emerge. She stood and stretched, needing the exertion after the thirty-mile drive from the city to suburbia.

Compared to the urban photography studio, the banality of the shopping center with its mix of upscale and traditional retail stores was a bit underwhelming.

"So this is our destination?"

She'd been furious with Mike, annoyed that he'd put her in a position of memorializing the thing she was barely tolerating, but he'd made an interesting point. She'd been acting as if Nugget was consigned to a prison. She had decided to give him life. Was it his fault she couldn't be a mother to him? Should he be made to suffer the poison of her bad feelings?

She wasn't sure she'd ever get to the point of celebrating, but she could try to be positive, to give Nugget the good vibes he needed. And since Mike appeared to be making an effort, she would, too. It was the least she could do considering what he'd done for her over the past few days.

The corner of his mouth quirked. "My life isn't all glitz and glamour. I can do regular people, too."

Indi glanced at the Towne Center's directory, helpfully provided on a digital kiosk. bebe. L'OCCITANE. Athleta. "If you think 'regular people' shop at these stores, we need to have a serious talk."

"What about the bookstore? Bookstores are 'regular people.'"

Say what now? "We came all this way to go to a bookstore?"

"Do you have a problem with bookstores?"

Was he kidding? Her smile expired before it could fully form. No, he looked serious. Actually, worried was more accurate, tiny lines forming between his blond brows. If he felt this strongly about them, he probably wouldn't like her answer.

"In theory? No. But in practice? I travel too much to purchase books in print." She held up her basic smartphone. "I have about a hundred books on here."

He took her phone and gawked at it like it was an ancient artifact. "I didn't know people still carried these. Can you text with this? Take pictures?"

She snatched it back. "Yes."

"Remind me to get you a Computronix phone tomorrow."

"I don't need a new phone. This one is just fine." A

whiff of a thought. "You're not buying me a bookstore, are you?"

"Hell, no. What would give you that idea?"

"I don't know. I never claimed to understand the buying habits of people who make twenty-six billion dollars in three months."

His features tightened. "Will you ever let me live that down?"

She tilted her head. "Maybe. But no time soon."

"Come on." He pressed a hand to the small of her back and led her into the store.

Dark wooden bookshelves, colorful covers, and table displays dotted the landscape. Bright fluorescent lighting bounced off fixtures, only to be absorbed into the navy blue carpet and the smell of coffee and baked goods both tempted and repulsed her. Considering the late afternoon hour on a weekend, the store was teeming with bodies, surprising Indi. What didn't surprise her was the customers' reactions to Mike. Necks twisted as they passed, like dominoes in motion.

The regular people knew gorgeous when it graced them with its presence.

A navy suit hugged his body like an affectionate lover. He'd removed his tie at the photography studio; now his white shirt lay open at the throat, giving him a coolly elegant air. Seriously, he could be a walking brand ambassador for Tom Ford.

"So, we're buying books?" she asked, wincing at her strangled tone. Notwithstanding everything going on around them, she was keenly aware of his touch. Heat flowed from the tips of his fingers to the sensitive spot between her thighs.

"Possibly."

Except there was no effort to browse the offerings. Mystery. Manga. Romance. Nonfiction. Test Prep . . . Surely the store had to end at some point?

Mike stopped at the entrance of a faux jungle. Tall "trees" towered above them, the leaves offering canopied access into a section strewn with multicolored beanbags, miniature tables and chairs, and cutout cartoon characters.

A massive pressure settled on her chest, making breathing difficult. She pushed against his hand. "No. The pictures were one thing. I don't want to read to little kids, or see a kid's reading group—"

"That's not why we're here." He pulled her to stand in front of a wooden bookcase labeled "Pregnancy & Childbirth."

Her heartbeat slowed and she inhaled shakily, the panic receding. "I don't understand."

"Even if you're giving the baby away, you still have to go through the pregnancy. I've done a little research. Have you?"

"Not really." She'd been afraid to, convinced that delving into the subject would make it a reality. It's why she'd postponed taking the pregnancy test, but at a certain point there'd been no mistaking the symptoms.

"So I thought we could learn about it together."

Just when she thought she had him figured out, he flipped the script on her. It was unsettling.

"Why are you doing all of this?"

"Because this is my child, too. And we both want to make sure you have a healthy pregnancy, right? To give Nugget the best start?"

She rubbed her belly. "Of course."

"Good." He smiled and she got a little light-headed.

She could shield herself from his sexiness when he was being all arrogant and overbearing. How was she supposed to resist him in sweet and protective mode?

He pulled a book off the shelf and read the title. "*So You're Expecting. Now What?* This appears to be the bible for pregnancy." He leaned a shoulder against the bookcase and started flipping through the pages. A few minutes later, he was still reading quietly to himself.

She trailed her fingers along the base of her neck. "Uh, Mike?"

"Hmmm?" He didn't look up.

"Is this supposed to be fun?"

That got his attention. "I don't know about fun, but we need to do it."

"But we could do what you're doing on the computer. Let's try something different. Close your eyes."

"Why?"

"Oh my God! You're so suspicious. Just do it."

He did.

"I'd forgotten how bossy you can be." His voice dipped an octave, sending ripples of pleasures through her. "I like it."

"I'm taking your hand—" She did. He had great hands.

She shivered. Magical hands. "And holding it up to the books. Now pick one."

He hesitated before hooking a finger in the spine of a book and pulling it from the stack.

"Okay, open your eyes."

He held up the book. *It's Coming in Nine Months.*

"Sounds like a horror movie."

She laughed. "Pick a page and read a random piece of advice."

"'Every belly button will pop out at some point,'" he recited. "'Just look on the bright side: you can clean out all your navel lint.'"

"Eww, gross."

"I get the feeling we'll encounter fouler things than that."

"My turn."

Those great hands covered hers. In the blackness tinged with red, she could feel the heat radiating from his body and discern the faint trace of his crisp cologne blended with him in a unique scent she'd know anywhere. Her nostrils flared.

Her fingers tripped over ridges and pointed edges until it landed on a wide expanse of grainy smoothness. She pulled. *There's a Baby in There, Bruh!* "'Its nine months up, nine months down. It took a while for her to put the weight on. It'll take her that long to lose it. And her body will never be the same. Hang in there. And be sensitive.'" She closed it and wrinkled her nose. "Wow, I can't tell if he's offering wise words or being an asshole."

Mike picked again. *The Nature-all Mother.* "Oh, I get it. Nature-all—"

"Natural . . ." Indi bobbed her head.

"'Don't let the doctor throw away your placenta,'" he said, his forehead wrinkling more with each word until it resembled a shar-pei. "'Take it home and plant it. Grow roses to commemorate your baby's birth.'"

Her eyes widened. "Is she for real? How am I supposed to ask the doctor for that?"

Mike shook his head. "Don't look at me. I'm not doing it."

Indi pulled a book written by a celebrity mom. *Fabulous & Fertile.* She rolled her eyes.

"'Girlfriend, get used to the sex dreams. They'll be vivid, realistic and they *will* give you the best orgasms of your life.'"

Hey now. . .

"Game over," Mike grumbled, taking the book from her. "Everyone's a fucking critic."

ON THE EDGE of the Towne Center—across from an old brick building bordered by an abandoned lot—they sat on an outdoor patio and ate frozen yogurt as the late afternoon sun warmed the surrounding environs. Another bite and Indi closed her eyes in appreciation, the cool, yummy treat a soothing balm to the emotional hurricane that hurled her back and forth all day.

"It's so good," she said, wincing as the cold dessert froze her teeth.

Mike pointed to her waffle bowl with his neon-green plastic spoon. "How can you tell? You have so many toppings in there, I'm surprised you even taste the yogurt."

"What? Everything melds. I have peanut butter, milk chocolate, and white chocolate frozen yogurt, topped with peanuts and toffee bits with caramel and milk chocolate fudge sauce. It. All. Melds."

"You make my teeth ache just listening to your description."

"My point is I'm not trying to taste the separate elements. It's the taste of all the flavors blended together that interests me." She waved her vibrant purple spoon like a royal scepter. "Don't worry about me. Enjoy your boring creation."

"Strawberry cheesecake is not boring. It's a classic." He scraped his last bite from the cup then set it down on the table. "And not worrying about you isn't an option anymore."

And just like that she was propelled back into the fray. She scrunched her eyes and stared at the building across the street, a colorful mural depicting people of different ethnicities sitting at a table holding hands, a bounty of fruit and vegetables spread before them, covering one side.

"Who knows you're pregnant?"

"You. And I ran into Chelsea's assistant, Jill, and she guessed. Other than that . . ."

"You haven't told Chelsea?"

A white delivery truck pulled into the empty lot next to the building. A man jumped down from the bright red cab, a clipboard in his hand.

"It's not something I wanted to tell her over the phone. Have you told anyone?"

"Only Jonathan and Ryan."

She tried to swallow past the knot in her throat. "Have you told *her*?"

"No."

She appreciated that he didn't feign ignorance. She leaned back in the chair and crossed her arms. "Are you going to?

"Dr. Kimball said we might be able to find out the sex at the next ultrasound. Do you want to know?"

It shouldn't matter that he didn't answer. They weren't a couple. They weren't even going to raise this child together. They were essentially strangers brought together by circumstance, like two college students who rode together to the same town during vacation, and went their separate ways when they reached their destination. How he lived his life—and the people he invited into in it—was none of her business.

She shook her head. "I don't want to find out."

"Why not?"

"I like the idea of being surprised that day. Truly surprised. And it's not like knowing changes anything. 'You get what you get and you don't throw a fit,'" she finished in a sing-song tone.

"Excuse me?" Confusion was sexy as hell on him. Everything was sexy as hell on him.

"Something I heard a mother tell her kid. I worked at this resort in Charleston and one day, they assigned me to the nursery. This woman came in and dropped her son off so she could make her spa appointment. He started fussing because she gave him a baggie of animal crackers instead of goldfish, and she told him—"

" 'You get what you get and you don't throw a fit,' " he repeated.

"Exactly."

Indi had given her notice at the end of her shift. She'd never been a kid person, and the idea of watching children while their parents enjoyed their lives, wasn't on her top ten list of ways she wanted to spend her time.

"You're basing your decision to discover the sex of our baby on a children's adage?"

"Seems to fit." She bent her head, but peered at him through her lashes. "Would you find out?"

"Of course. To plan. To think of names and decorate the nursery."

As the delivery guy unlocked the back of the truck and climbed into the cargo area, the wide wooden doors of the building opened and people attired in blue T-shirts with yellow lettering streamed out. From this distance she couldn't see their faces, but their swinging arms and energetic steps telegraphed a jubilation and purpose she envied.

"That won't be my concern."

"Possibly." He tapped a finger against the table. "But you're not raising the baby, so your concerns don't matter. The couple you're giving the baby to may want to know."

It was difficult not to wallow in her indignation at his stark statement, but he was right. Some of the decisions she'd make if she were keeping Nugget wouldn't apply in this circumstance. She'd probably need to consider that . . . later. The commotion across the street was a suitable distraction. "I wonder what's going on over there?"

The delivery guy hefted a box from the back of the truck and handed it to one of the assembled volunteers, who carried it into the building. He repeated the handoff, forming an assembly line, and giving Indi the opportunity to see the distinctive calligraphic *C* on the side of the packages.

She turned to Mike. "Are those boxes from Computronix?"

"Come on." He took her hand and cut across the street, against the light. She looked around for a police cruiser, certain there would be serious repercussions for another crime committed while on bail. Even if the crime was only jaywalking.

A big guy with curly red hair and a full beard broke away from the activity and strode over to meet them. "Mike, what a wonderful surprise! We didn't expect you to personally supervise the delivery."

He was dressed like the others—jeans, sneakers, and the blue shirt. Up close, she could read the yellow writing.

The Youth Alliance.

"Griffin." Mike shook the other man's hand.

Griffin squeezed Mike's forearm with his free hand. "This is unbelievably generous of you and Computronix. Our kids will flip."

Indi's gaze followed another large box as two volunteers transferred it from the truck to the building.

Flip for what?

Mike curved an arm around her waist and shepherded her forward. "Meet my friend, India Shaw. Indi, Griffin Adorno is the head of the Youth Alliance, a program for the city's homeless youth. They provide a temporary place for kids to stay while finishing school and undergoing job-placement training."

"That's wonderful!" She knew how much a program like that was needed. While her various foster providers—she'd never make the mistake of calling them families—could be accused of gross emotional neglect, she hadn't been subjected to physical or sexual abuse. Others weren't as lucky.

One of the reasons a place like the one offered by the Youth Alliance could literally be the difference between life and death.

"Thanks." Griffin shoved his hands into his back pockets. "We're funded from a collection of sources: state and city grants, foundations, and donations. But 75 percent of our budget comes from federal money. This year we learned we're losing the bulk of that federal funding."

"Why?"

"Federal monies for the homeless are limited and they want to funnel it toward areas that are shown to be the most effective. And according to them, that's permanent housing. Which is great for the adult homeless population, but not so much for the youth. We thought we'd have to close our doors." A smile brightened his face and he slapped a hand on Mike's shoulder. "But then we got a call from Mike. Computronix is providing us enough funding for the next five years."

Her jaw dropped. "How many beds?"

"Thirty-seven."

She pressed splayed fingers against her chest and turned shocked eyes on Mike. She had a rough idea of how much money it took to fund these types of programs. That was close to a million dollars.

"That's not all. He's donated the equipment for a new computer lab and gaming room."

Say hello to a million.

"Just remember our deal," he told Griffin.

"I will. No press." Griffin's eyes darted to a spot behind them. "However, it looks like I won't be able to prevent this. We were going to record a message and send it to you, but now that you're here . . ."

A group of teenagers stood at the base of the steps that led into the building. A soft count of three and they broke into an a cappella arrangement. Their voices blended beautifully and the harmonious sound washed over her, raising goose bumps on her arms. The spectacle was moving. These kids were so grateful they were expressing themselves through song. Mike moved closer to her and reached for her hand, entwining their fingers.

A crowd formed behind them, people holding up their phones to capture the moment.

"'I want to thank you for giving me the best day of my life
Oh, just to be with you is having the best day of my life.'"

The crowd burst into applause when the kids finished. Mike went forward and shook hands, bumped fists, and even received a few hugs and kisses on his cheek. Afterward, people stayed and gave of their time, helping to unload the truck—which had to be like one of those clown cars with infinite space inside.

"This is why you brought me out here today? So I could see this?"

He nodded.

"You're amazing," she said. "That has to be the most generous thing I've ever heard of."

"We were in a position to help, so we did."

She'd been around her fair share of people with money. They either spent it like water or refused to part with it. But if they gave it away, they all wanted the credit for doing so. And yet Mike didn't.

"You could've given to lots of charities. Why this one?"

One that was so close to her and what she'd gone through.

"I wanted you to see another side of me. To know that I care and can do good for the world." He placed a hand on her belly. "But mainly, I hoped to convince you to not give Nugget up."

"Mike, I can't raise him."

"Don't give him up for adoption." He looked deeply into her eyes. "Give him to me."

Chapter Eleven

INDI STARED AT the TV and snuggled further into the cashmere throw she'd found on the comfy sectional.

Mike wanted to raise Nugget. How? He worked long hours. Who was going to take care of the baby? A nanny? His family? Or was he assuming he could slot Skylar Thompson into the role? Indi would've laughed if her constricted throat had allowed it. He was an idiot if he thought Skylar was the type of woman who'd happily sign on to raise his biracial baby from a one-weekend stand. And Indi didn't intend to place Nugget in a situation where the parents resented his presence.

She should go along with her initial reaction to his request. Tell him no. She'd be doing him a favor.

A character's reaction on the screen clued her in to her disinterest. Reaching for the remote, she paused the DVR, aware that she'd failed to comprehend anything that had happened on the edgy sitcom for the past five minutes.

The lack of light from the screen rendered the room dark, the only illumination provided by the city lights shining in through the large windows.

She hadn't seen Mike since he'd made his request this past weekend. She'd needed the two days apart. There was too much exposure. To him, to Nugget, to projections of a future they'd share together. She was susceptible to thoughts she didn't want to think, feelings she didn't want to feel.

As if conjured by the strength and frequency of her thoughts, the door opened.

Indi froze.

Steps on the hardwood floor, the jingle of keys, and then the door closing. A sigh, and a world of weariness encompassed the sound.

That moment of vulnerability touched her more than all the bombast, charisma, and swagger. She'd spent a lot of time concerned about how this pregnancy was affecting her—rightfully so. But hers wasn't the only life disturbed by her unexpected condition. And yet he was willing to take responsibility in a way she would—could—not.

She peered over the back of the sofa and watched while he laid his keys, phone, and briefcase on the entry table and loosened his tie. Even after what had to have been an exhausting day, he looked sexily disheveled, in an I've-worked-fifteen-hours-but-I-can-still-ravage-you way.

She sat upright, ready to make her presence known. "It's after midnight. You didn't drive here from Palo Alto, did you?"

He started, turning wide eyes to her. "You should be asleep. You need to rest."

His deep, sluggish tone stroked her senses.

"I was. I crashed late this afternoon and woke up an hour ago."

"Couldn't go back to sleep?"

Not with her mind racing like the lead car at Daytona. She shook her head. "Sometimes watching TV helps."

He nodded toward the black screen. "Except you're not."

She pressed a button on the remote and the LED screen gleamed to life. She muted the volume.

"Oh." He scrubbed a hand over his face. His fatigue was obvious.

"I'm not the only one who should be resting. Why did you come here tonight instead of staying at the office?"

"Because you're here."

What did he mean by *that*? Was he concerned that she was alone in his home with his belongings? Was he reminding her that he was her keeper while she was out on bail, pending charges? Or, more disturbing, was he implying that he wanted to be where she was because . . . he missed her?

Impossible. But speaking of bail and her case—

"Viv called earlier today. The DA has decided to press charges. She said they'll probably set the arraignment for two weeks from today. She'll let me know when she gets the official notice."

"Fuck."

She'd used that exact same word after she'd gotten off the phone with the attorney. Along with a few choice variations. This whole criminal case was being blown out of proportion. Everyone was acting like she was an elusive jewel thief and not a woman who'd had to get resourceful to get into a residence she had permission to enter.

Jeez.

"We can talk about it after I've grabbed a few hours of sleep."

"Do you always work this late?" she asked.

"Not always."

"Way to dodge the question."

He hunched his shoulders. "Are you saying I'm lying?"

"I'm saying this probably isn't the first time you've come through that door at midnight."

"You'd be correct."

She studied him, thrusting her tongue into the pocket of her inner cheek, before she set aside the blanket and stood, yanking her T-shirt down to cover her leggings. "Did you eat dinner?"

He narrowed his eyes as he considered her question. "No," he finally said, "I couldn't spare the time."

"You didn't *take* the time."

She padded into his gourmet kitchen, trailing her fingers against the coolness of his soapstone countertops. She turned on the pendant lights—brightening the room with their gentle glow—and opened the refrigerator.

"You've got to go grocery shopping. This is a top-of-the-line appliance. You insult it with the paltry ingredients you store in here."

He laughed and the invigorating sound warmed her. "I don't spend much time eating here."

"Obviously." She parsed the contents. "These eggs still have a few days left and there's some cheese. An omelet?"

He lounged on one of the bar stools, so sexy she didn't think she could handle it. "You can cook?"

"I've been cooking most of my meals since I was eight years old. I think I mastered the omelet around age ten."

The words were lightly said, and she prayed he'd take them in the manner they were given instead of delving deeper.

He didn't.

"Were you in foster care at that time?"

"Yup."

She hoped she was successful in molding her face into calm lines, though her heart pounded against her ribs like a trapped being seeking freedom. She placed the ingredients on the counter and began searching his espresso-colored cabinets for the tools she needed.

"What about you?" he asked. "Have you eaten?"

She shrugged as she sliced cheese on the cutting board that still held a small orange price sticker. "I tried, but after a few bites I knew it was pointless. I've been drinking water, though. Staying hydrated."

"Good."

He walked over to his briefcase—a black leather and steel-gray tweed piece too stylish and modern to simulate the old-school image—and pulled out a brown paper bag.

She paused and held the knife aloft. "What's that?"

"From my research I've learned that tea and crackers is a go-to for nausea." His fingers tightened on the sack. "Does it work for you?"

She swallowed. "Yes."

"Excellent."

She tapped an egg on the counter. "During your hectic day, you took the time to go out and buy me some tea?"

"No. I had my assistant call down to the cafeteria and have them bring it to me."

He was charm personified. She licked her parched bottom lip. "Still, it was extremely thoughtful. Thank you."

"You're welcome."

He brushed past her to grab a mug down from the cabinet and the hair on her arms stood at attention and saluted. His closeness drew her like a magnet and the effort it took to fight it was overwhelming. She resumed her tasks, still aware of him moving around the space. He reached into the bag and extracted two boxes of tea. "What will it be: ginger, ginger, ginger? Peppermint, peppermint, peppermint?"

He held a box in each hand, bouncing both up and down.

She laughed. She'd forgotten about this part of his personality. His secret zaniness had delighted her during their weekend together, and she hadn't seen it once during their recent reintroduction. Though to be fair, their circumstances didn't scream "time to par-tay."

"Peppermint, definitely."

He nodded and tossed the other box over his shoulder. "I had a feeling you'd pick that one."

"How?"

Could she be any more obvious with this perma-smile creasing her face?

"The necklace you wear. It gives off a faint minty odor and you always hold it up to your nose when you look queasy."

Surprised that he'd noticed, she lifted the aromatic starfish suspended from the chain. "It was a gift from one of my coworkers in Seattle."

"A male coworker?"

Why did it matter who gave her the necklace? She could receive gifts from men. He had a girlfriend.

That's right, Indi. A girlfriend. Remember that the next time his nearness causes your nether regions to go all warm and gooey.

"No. A woman who recognized some of my symptoms before I did."

They moved about the space in a semi-companionable silence. She whisked the eggs with a fork, while Mike dropped a peppermint tea bag into the mug.

Turning his back to the counter, he crossed his legs at the ankle and treated her to an intense gaze from his cerulean-blue eyes. "So, how long were you in the foster care system?"

Dammit. She thought he'd abandoned that train of thought. "Do you have a skillet?"

"A what?"

Was he kidding? Her gaze flew to his slack expression. He wasn't.

"A pan to make the omelet."

"Oh, a frypan."

"Skillet, frypan, same diff."

He raised his brows, indicating he didn't agree, but he

reached beneath the island and brought out a pan, which he sat on the stove for her.

Except stove didn't seem adequate to describe the appliance. A stove was a dingy white range with four electric, circular grates—though only two ever worked consistently—surrounded by burned crud that resisted all efforts at removal. Not this . . . war machine, with six gas burners, ceramic grates, a griddle, *and* a double oven.

She ran her fingers over the chunky knobs—not one missing!—in appreciation. "Has Jonathan ever cooked on this thing?"

Grooves appeared on either side of Mike's mouth. "Why?"

"This looks like the type of stove you'd see in a restaurant, not in a kitchen. And of course, thinking about restaurants made me think of Jonathan. He's opening up his newest one in DC, right?"

"Right." She felt the blaze of his stare. "You've kept in contact with him since the wedding?"

An innocuous question, if one didn't notice the tone of voice. Indi not only noticed it, she recognized it as one meant to convey shame and judgment to anyone close enough to hear it loudly expressed. But to hear it from Mike? She patched the tear on her heart before the hurt could seep through. Why was she shocked that he'd asked? They'd only made a baby together. It's not like he really knew her.

Her hands shook, but she clenched the edge of the counter and kept her voice calm. "You're asking if after a weekend spent fucking my new brother-in-law's best friend, I'd set my sights on the other one?"

He had the sense to recognize his error. "Fuck! Indi, I didn't mean—"

She held up a hand, shook her head.

He pried the fingers of her other hand off the counter and took both of them in his. "I know you well enough to realize that was a stupid, unfair question. Allow me to blame it on exhaustion, confusion and"—he gently squeezed her hands—"a tiny bit of jealousy."

"You don't have the right to be jealous."

"Whether or not I have the right to be doesn't mean the feeling ceases to exist."

"Whoa. For a second there, you channeled Adam."

"That, more than anything else, proves how tired I am."

Maybe, but she was still in her feelings and not willing to forgive him so easily. Pulling her hands from his, she picked up the bowl and gave the fork a final flick of her wrist. She checked the temperature of the pan, added a pat of butter and poured in the eggs, watching the mixture cover the bottom until it resembled an expressionless emoji.

He settled his hip against the counter. "When you were in the foster homes—"

She expelled a forceful breath. "You're determined to talk about it, aren't you?"

"Just as determined as you are not to."

"If you know I don't want to talk about it, why do you keep asking me questions? Why do you feel it's any of your business?"

"Because I'm curious. Because you're the mother of my child. Because I'm intent on convincing you to give Nugget to me and I want to understand why you'd be willing to give him up."

She tilted the skillet and used the tip of a spatula to lift the omelet, checking it for doneness. She shook her head. "I don't want to talk about it."

"Okay. For now." He took the mug with the tea bag, filled it with water, and placed it in the microwave. He pushed several buttons then busied himself going back and forth between the kitchen and the eating area.

He wasn't going to stop asking questions and she had no intention of giving him any answers, so where did that leave them?

Finding the once semi-companionable silence now sour, she focused on finishing his omelet. Because she couldn't help herself, and to show that she wasn't bothered by his thoughts about her or their conversation, she lifted the skillet from the burner and with a jab she watched the fluffy omelet complete a somersault in the air and land with the slightly browned side on the top.

"Impressive."

"Thanks." She sprinkled on the cheese she'd sliced and folded the omelet in half. "I worked for a few months as a short order cook in Atlanta, Georgia."

"Of course you did."

"Sarcasm isn't attractive."

"You move around a lot."

What was this: midnight confessions with Michael Black? She was starting to regret her offer to feed him. "I do."

"Why?" He handed her a plate.

She took it and slid the omelet on it. "Never found a place I liked enough to stay."

"Will you join me?"

He carried his food to the table where he'd set two place settings. Next to hers was a steaming cup of tea and a bowl filled with saltines. Sensation fluttered in her belly.

Don't get any ideas, Nugget.

"Sure."

He held her chair out and waited for her to be seated. He had impeccable manners. He often held the door open for her, ushered her into places. She remembered the heated imprint of his hand pressing into the small of her back. She'd never thought of herself as some damsel who required an offered coat to traverse a puddle, but she liked the little gestures. They showed he thought of her, cared about her well-being.

He probably did the same things for his girlfriend, too.

"How did you two meet?" she blurted out.

She'd caught him taking a drink of water. He started choking.

"Mike!"

Heart racing, she jumped up and hurried to the kitchen to get some paper towels.

He coughed, his eyes watering.

"Raise your right arm over your head!"

He still managed to give her an are-you-an-absolute-loon look, even as his face turned varying shades of red.

"Do it!" When he didn't comply, she lifted it herself. "There was an old lady in my neighborhood, and if a kid started choking she'd tell them to raise their arm over their head. Said it opened the airways, making it easier to breathe."

After an interminably long moment, he got himself under control. She lowered his arm then wiped up the spewed water, throwing the paper towels away. She took her seat, relief making her light-headed. This was way too much emotional upheaval for this time of night.

"I don't think that's true," he wheezed.

Talk about gratitude. "You stopped coughing, didn't you?"

He wiped his mouth with a napkin and took a tentative sip of water. He inhaled and released it shakily. "How did I meet who?"

He knew who. "Your girlfriend? Cortland? Sawyer?"

"Skylar," he supplied with a wry tilt of his lips.

Why was she being such a bitch?

Hormones. Yeah, that's it. Pregnancy hormones.

And didn't that show she'd be a terrible mother? She was already shifting the blame to Nugget.

"I met her at a fundraiser. She's a Senior VP and CFO of ThomTexteL."

She'd whistle . . . if she could. She'd never been able to, another childhood embarrassment. "The one owned by Franklin Thompson?"

"Yes."

She made the connection. "She's his daughter."

He nodded.

Good lord, there had never been any competition. That's the type of woman he should be with. Someone classy and cultured, someone comfortable with sharing his life, attending fundraisers and balls and the ballet and other rich-people society things.

"If anyone wanted you, do you think you'd be here? You're only worth the paycheck we get every month."

Her mouth dry, she forced out her next words. "Is it serious?"

"Do you really want to know?"

She didn't. "You're the one who keeps saying we should get to know one another."

He leaned back in his chair. "She and I have a lot in common. We socialize in the same circles, enjoy doing the same activities. She's the type of woman I've always imagined myself marrying."

Unlike you.

He didn't say the words, but that's what she heard.

She nodded, took one last sip of her tea, then carried the cup and bowl into the kitchen.

"Are you angry?"

An emotion, like the man, she had no right to claim. He wasn't hers, had never been. Their time together was like a vacation she'd won: sweet while there, but eventually, she'd have to go home.

She rinsed out her dishes, put them away, and settled on the sofa, wrapping the soft blanket around her.

"Why did you leave?"

Like she was going to sit across from him and pretend nothing had just been said or proclaimed? "I was done eating."

"Not the table. That weekend."

Heat suffused her body and she stared at the muted television. A woman was rubbing cream on her face and, beneath her image, there was a split screen with a before picture—which showed her skin looking like a page from a connect-the-dot workbook—and after—where it was miraculously smooth and unblemished.

"What about it?"

"Really?" She heard the angry scrape of the chair against the hardwood floors. "What happened? I thought we'd had a great time. Why did you leave?"

She'd had no other option. Even though it'd only been two days, she'd gotten comfortable with him, lowered her guard, begun imagining what life would be like come Monday morning. In the real world. "We both knew it was temporary."

"Temporary or not, it was rude," he said, standing before her, all masculine anger and frustration.

Clearly she had the willpower of the gods to have been able to walk away from this man.

"No one cares about manners anymore."

"I do. I invite you into my home and then you sneak out like a common criminal."

She tensed. "I'm not a thief. I didn't take anything from you."

He frowned and some of the stiffness leeched from his posture. "I didn't say you were. It's an expression."

"An expression I don't like."

"All right, all right. It's probably too late for this conversation."

When Mike came to sit next to her on the sectional,

she drew her feet closer to her body, trying to keep some distance between them.

"Just as well you left when you did." He slid her a side-eyed glance. "It was good. Too good. There's no way it could've lasted."

She relaxed then, understanding and appreciating his attempt to lighten the mood. "Yeah, there's no way you could've kept up that stamina."

He shifted to face her. "I've never had complaints about my stamina."

She shifted to face him. "Have you ever had marathon sex for two days in a row?"

He pinched his chin between his thumb and index finger. "Not really."

"So, in normal circumstances, your stamina is fine . . . for a man your age."

"Hey!" He grabbed her legs and ripped back the blanket. Before she could process his intention, he'd wrapped strong fingers around her ankles and began tormenting the bottom of her feet.

She howled with laughter. "Mike! I'm ticklish."

"I remember."

Though strong, she was no match for his strength and he was merciless. Her lungs burned as she laughed too hard to fully take in air. Finally, he released her feet, only to move to her sides. She wiggled, arching her back and lifting her hips in an effort to displace him, but froze when she found his face inches from hers.

His breath feathered across her cheek. Submitting to the tingling in her fingertips, she reached up and slid her hand through his tousled hair, swept her fingers across his brow. His gorgeous eyes—a blue so beautiful they would forever be her baseline for the hue—searched hers, growing more molten by the second. Reading her assent, his head descended at an achingly slow pace until—finally—their lips touched.

God, he could kiss. It was a skill he'd mastered. He knew how deep to take it, how wet to make it, how slow to go. In a blur of movement, he shifted their positions, so he was sitting on the sofa and she straddled him. They sighed in unison when their bodies connected, like two interlocking pieces. Coming home.

He moaned and deepened their embrace. The force of his desire was palpable and it would've frightened her, except her own longing was just as intense, just as needy. His lips left hers and trailed down her neck. He sucked at her rapidly beating pulse, the scruff of his stubble an exquisite bite against her skin.

"I thought I'd imagined it," he murmured.

"Imagined what?" she panted.

"How good you tasted."

He captured her mouth again and she lost herself in his kiss. His tongue swept into her mouth, breaking down any barriers, insistent on not allowing her to hold anything back, while his fingers massaged her bare skin beneath her shirt. She melted, grinding the heat of her core against the hardness of his erection.

His hands gripped her hips, meeting her halfway.

She would never get tired of this feeling. Of receiving pleasure from this man and giving it in return. What would it be like to have access to these sensations anytime she wanted? To have him inside of her anytime she wanted?

Uh-oh.

She recognized the route these thoughts were traveling; knew they culminated at a dead end.

Shades of their weekend all over again. She'd just cautioned herself about being too close to him. A few minutes longer, they'd be as close as two people could physically be.

She severed the kiss, her lips tender and achingly swollen. He palmed her face and pressed his forehead against hers, the sound of their heavy breathing harsh in the silence between them.

"We can't do this," she whispered.

"Why not?"

"I'm carrying your baby. You have a girlfriend. I still plan to leave. Take your pick."

"Indi—"

She pushed him off her, aware that his reluctant acquiescence made it easy, and stood. "Thank you for the tea and crackers. I'm going to go back to bed."

He remained seated on the sofa, his hands clasped between his thighs, his head bowed. She'd almost reached the hallway when his solemn voice stopped her.

"If I'd woken up in time and asked, would you have stayed?"

If your own mother didn't love you enough to keep you, why should we?

Her heart fractured, but she told him the truth.

"No."

Chapter Twelve

INDI SAT ON the granite countertops, his navy blue bed sheet wrapped loosely around her naked body. Soft music emanated from wireless speakers and she arched her back, swaying sensuously to the beat.

They'd fallen asleep after a morning of energetic sex and had awakened ravenous . . . this time for food.

"So I've got milk, bottled water, coffee, cereal, bagels, and cream cheese," he said, reading from the list on his phone. "Anything else?"

"That should be good for now. We can always order again."

"Good point." He completed the list and submitted his order. "I love grocery delivery services."

"They have those in most major cities, right? I'll have to call the next time I don't feel like going out to shop."

"It'll be about an hour." He let his gaze travel from the rounded smoothness of her shoulders, along the line of her *slim thighs, down to her polished peach toenails. "What will we do to pass the time?"*

Her bright eyes sparkled. "Let's play a game."

He braced his arms on either side of her thighs, leaned in, and captured a kiss. "What, like Monopoly?"

It wasn't what he'd had in mind but—

"Never have I ever."

He frowned, nibbled on her ear. "Played Monopoly?"

She laughed, her shoulder ascending to dislodge his caress. "No, the game. Never have I ever."

His head jerked back. "Really?"

"Yeah. Why not?"

"I don't know, maybe because I haven't played it since college?"

She smiled softly. "In college, you haven't lived enough for it to be truly worth playing."

She was so fucking sexy. He couldn't get enough. He dipped his head again, nuzzling the satiny glide of her jaw, inhaling her warm vanilla scent. "Refresh my memory. It's been a while."

She rested her arms on his shoulders and delved her fingers into the hair at his nape. "I say 'never have I ever' and I name an action. If you've done it, you take a drink."

Grimacing, he closed his eyes and leaned into her touch. "Screw that. After last night the tequila is still flowing through my veins."

"It doesn't have to be alcohol. What about water?"

"Water? I thought it was a drinking game."

"It's actually an ice breaker."

He trailed a finger along the edge of the sheet and

crooked his finger in the cloth above the valley between her breasts. "I don't think we've had any problems getting to know each other better."

She pushed his hand away. "Do you want to play or not?"

He sighed and straightened. "Fine. You start."

"Okay. Never have I ever masturbated in front of my partner."

His heart stuttered. "You're starting there? No easing into the game?"

She bit her lip, her eyes lowering. "I didn't take you for an 'easing into it' kind of guy."

Warmth engulfed him. He clenched and released his hands. "I usually am, but you've turned me into a total horndog. I'll have to make it up to you. Start over."

"Huh?"

His lips quirked. "The game. Say it again."

She smiled, placed her foot against his stomach, and pushed him back. "Never have I ever masturbated in front of my partner."

Neither moved.

She tilted her head, dark brown waves trailing over her shoulder. "You haven't?"

He shook his head, his gaze never straying from hers.

"A first for both of us," she murmured, letting the sheet drop.

Mike watched it tumble down her chest, catch on her pebbled nipples, and pool around her waist.

He shivered. "You take my breath away."

She tossed her hair back, touched trembling fingers to her neck and slid them down to rest against the tops of her breasts. She took her bottom lip between her teeth and leaned forward. "You ready for this?"

Oh, hell yeah. His heart thumped against his rib cage, a rhythmic call to arms. He reached for her, but that cock-blocking foot intervened again.

She nodded to his pants. "Show me."

Impossibly, the pace of his heart intensified. Could a man die of pleasure?

He released the button on his pants, slowly drew down the zipper. He stole a glance at her, saw her tongue dart out, watched her eyes follow the metal teeth's reveal. . .

He slipped his hand inside and pulled his dick free. He rubbed his hand along its hardened length using the precum already beading on the tip to lubricate his stroking.

"That's it," she said, her voice low and husky. "Now, come here."

Not even the strongest gravitational pull could've kept him away. She pushed her fingers into his mouth and his tongue slid along the slim digits, getting them wet. She pulled them out and replaced them with a quick flick of her tongue, before leaning away from him.

Without breaking eye contact, she took her wet fingers and rubbed them on her nipples until the brown nubs glistened. Her lashes fluttered, her eyes rolled backward, and a moan slipped from between her lips.

His knees threatened to give way. "Babe, you're killing me," he groaned.

"Good. Don't stop."

He rocked his hips forward, his cock heavy in his hand, as she let her thighs fall open. His breath came in pants.

"Can you help me again?" She held out her fingers.

Abso-fucking-lutely. He sucked them. Hard.

She trailed her fingers down her belly and through the dark brown curls, to the node of pleasure nestled within the folds. Tweaking her clit, she allowed her head to fall to the side while she rubbed herself in a circular motion. She raised her left hand to squeeze her breast, rolling her nipple between her thumb and forefinger.

His senses were on overload. The musky sweetness of her desire, the siren sound of her moans, the pulsing hardness in his hands. And the sights? His gaze rested nowhere, bounced everywhere. The jiggle of breasts, her parted lips, the nimble kneading of her fingers, the shadow of her lashes against her upper cheeks.

They flew open, revealed her striking eyes glazed with passion. She slid two fingers inside.

Fuck.

Their eyes met. Melded. He couldn't look away. This was sexier than anything he'd ever seen, anything he'd ever experienced. Her eyes held the answers to every question he'd never known to ask. It could take a lifetime to sort through them all.

And she was leaving tomorrow.

Her shoulders seized. "Mike. I'm coming!"

In a show of sinfully erotic choreography, her back arched, her torso undulated, and her body spasmed. Moans issued from her in a stream of verbal pleasure so intense, it made him light-headed. He grabbed a condom from his back pocket, tore the wrapper with his teeth, and covered himself before she'd caught her breath.

"Never have I ever seen anything as hot as that," he said, hooking her knees over his elbows and surging into her tight passage. *"We'll try for slow. Next time."*

MIKE COULDN'T SHAKE the residual sensuality from his dream the night before. Technically, it'd been a memory of the sexy game he and Indi had played their weekend together. He smiled to himself. He'd never think of the drinking game in the same light again.

Play. That was an accurate way to describe their interaction. Sure she drove him crazy with her need to oppose him—for no discernible reason he could see!—but she also brought out a lighthearted side of him. He winced. Had he actually made boxes of tea sing and dance the other night? Yeah, he had. For her.

Even when they'd stood listening to the Youth Alliance choir, in an empty lot out in the suburbs, he'd been content, far happier than at all the society galas in San Francisco. He looked forward to being in her company more than anyone else's . . . even Skylar's.

The other woman was fantastic. Chic, refined, intelligent. They enjoyed the same things and had much in common. Skylar was a calming presence; she kept him grounded.

Indi made him soar.

When the elevator doors opened on Computronix's executive floor, Anya's pursed lips and foot-tapping form was the first thing Mike saw. It wasn't unusual for the brand manager to pop by his office for a quick consult.

But waiting for him before he'd even cleared the threshold ...

His stomach churned with apprehension, and for good reason. He wasn't a stranger to Anya's displeased reception. During the early days of Adam's preparation for the HPC presentation—when the genius's response to Anya's promotional strategy had often reduced her to clenching her teeth so tightly sparks shot from her molars—Mike had assumed the mantle of her human complaint box, a service she'd utilized early and often.

"When did you plant it on me?"

She stopped short, her set jaw and alert gaze fading into rapid blinking and a furrowed brow. "Excuse me?"

"The tracking device." At her continued blank stare he elaborated, "How did you know I was on my way up?"

"Oh." The metal stud beneath her lower lip jiggled. "I told Norm to call me the second you drove onto campus."

Note to self: Remind the gate's security guard that Anya wasn't the one who authorized his biannual bonuses.

"Adam's not here and the HPC is selling well. Why are you reinstituting our walk-and-talks?" He nodded to the receptionist and headed down the corridor to his office suite.

Anya hurried to keep up with his long stride. "I understand that most of your life is private and none of my business. But *you* have to understand that Adam's presentation and romantic declaration to Chelsea, the HPC, and their fairy-tale wedding has put Computronix—and by association, both of you—in the national spotlight. You're celebrities whether you want to be or not."

Adam and Chelsea's love story had generated a lot of interest. It was impossible to determine if that exposure translated into sales for the HPC, although the device was so revolutionary it didn't need it. Still, he'd encouraged Adam to lean into the publicity.

"What does that have to do with me?"

"Adam is the face of this company and his relationship with Chelsea has captured the public's curiosity. You—your lives—have become part of Computronix's brand and the care and feeding of the company's brand is my concern."

These were the times he missed Adam's directness. "And?"

"Did you not understand what I said?" she asked, her tone shrill and abrasive.

He shot her a censoring look. While he was never one to throw his title around, he ran this company and worked hard to be worthy of the respect that came with the title.

She swallowed. "I'm sorry. It's been a busy morning."

Mike frowned. "It's only eight-thirty."

"Even though Computronix has never put out a statement, it's common knowledge that you and Skylar Thompson have been seeing each other—"

Skylar? Is that what this is about? Had she mentioned him in passing to the press while in New York? Had some old picture of the two of them resurfaced?

"—so you can understand why the press, being the vultures they are, would scent fresh blood in the air, especially given the parallels with Adam's relationship with Birgitta."

What did the nasty scandal involving Adam and his ex-fiancée—a model who'd cheated on him and broken off their engagement after Adam had informed her of his Asperger's diagnosis—have to do with him and his relationship with Skylar?

"Anya, I have no idea what you're talking about and I don't have time to play twenty questions. If you require my response to or action on anything, you have about one minute to give me a concise rundown. I have a conference call with a company in China starting soon."

The color deserted her already pale visage. "Then you haven't seen this?"

With one hand, she flipped open the cover of her tablet and ran the nimble fingers of her other hand over its surface. She angled the device so he could see the screen.

Everything in him iced on the spot.

The hideous headline—*"Has Finance's Famous* It *Girl Been Replaced?"*—isn't what captured his attention. It was the picture below it. On the left side, a photograph of him and Skylar on a step and repeat at a gallery opening two months ago. In formal attire, her arm nestled in the crook of his elbow, they looked polished, successful, cohesive. On the right, him and Indi watching the teenagers from the Youth Alliance during their serenade. Except whoever had taken the picture had captured them watching each other instead of the performance. Even if they hadn't been holding hands, there was no mistaking the longing and awareness that sizzled between them. He wasn't observing two strangers bonding over a good concert. He was staring at a man and woman who shared a palpable connection.

A point that would be apparent to anyone who saw the picture.

Son of a bitch!

He took the tablet and skimmed the article. The video of the kids singing had been uploaded to YouTube, reaching over three million views in the past few days. Some intrepid reporter had seen the video and recognized him, noticed the trucks in the background, and decided there was a story to investigate. Although Griffin had kept his promise with a terse "No comment"—the reporter had put two and two together, disclosed his belief about the donation, and stirred speculation about the "new" woman in his life.

He pulled out his cell phone. He needed to give Indi a heads-up, let her know photographers might be camped out in front of his building. They'd only identified him, but it wouldn't take them long to name Indi. Especially once this week's issue of *People* magazine landed on the shelves. The last thing either of them needed was a picture of her entering or leaving his home.

He jotted off a quick text, telling her to stay indoors, that he'd explain it all after his meeting. He and Indi might need to relocate. Of course, if the paparazzi cared enough to camp out at his condo, his house in Palo Alto wouldn't be safe, either. Maybe they could stay at Adam's place in the mountains for a few days? Until this all blew over.

"The media office has already received requests for interviews and they've forwarded them to me. How do you plan to respond?"

"I don't."

"We have to. We've started a precedent with Adam and Chelsea."

"I'm not Adam."

"I'm aware of that, but the implication is that you're cheating on Skylar and—"

Fuck!

He dialed Skylar's number. It was almost noon in New York. It went straight to voice mail. Was her phone off or was she refusing to take his call?

He dialed again . . . and left a message. "Skylar, when you get this message, give me a call. It's urgent."

"Sir." Evan hurried to his side. "The conference call has already started. You really need to get to your office."

"But we need a plan," Anya said. "Choosing not to respond is an option, but not a good one."

His chest felt like a sponge squeezed to within an inch of its life. Anya's panic, Evan's urgency, Skylar's possible telephonic rebuff, chaos supplanting the calm and order he preferred in his business and his life. None of this would be happening if Indi hadn't charged into his life with the finesse of a tornado.

He exhaled sharply, his nanosecond of self-pity over. "Anya, you're right, we need to react to the inquiries, but I can't right now. Go back to your office and come up with several sample responses to appease any interested parties then begin drafting protocol on how we should handle this issue in the future. I'll find you when I'm done with my meeting."

Without waiting for her to reply, he strode to his office, Evan falling into step beside him. "Send Skylar flowers. The same kind we sent on Valentine's Day. I don't know her address in New York. You can call her office to get it."

Like putting a bandage on a gaping wound, but it'd have to do until he could talk to her and not her voice mail.

When he'd completed his conference call over an hour later, there'd still been no response from Skylar.

Sully rapped once, then entered his office. "Dude, you're fucked!"

Mike didn't know why the attorney even bothered to knock. He never waited for permission. "You're not helping."

"Have your plans changed?" Sully shoved his hands into the pockets of his slacks. Although it was barely midmorning, he'd already shed the jacket and tie. "Because that picture does not look like two people planning to give a child up for adoption. It looks like a couple eager to make another one."

He clenched his fingers into a fist. "It was a misconstrued moment in time."

"Uh-huh. I hate to break this to you, but unless both you and India were simultaneously looking at other people who happened to be just outside the frame, there's no mistaking the heat rays bouncing between the two of you." Sully lifted one shoulder. "It put *me* in the mood."

Damn.

"Have you talked to Skylar?"

Mike didn't answer. He buzzed Evan. "Did you order the flowers?"

"Yes" came his assistant's brisk voice. "They promised they'd deliver them by midafternoon."

Sully rubbed his jaw. "You don't really believe a bouquet will solve this problem?"

Mike slammed his palm flat on the desk, embracing the pain radiating up his arm. "No! Current situation to the contrary, I'm not an idiot. But I have to do something."

"You could fly to New York, talk to her in person."

Better than a bouquet, except—"I'm responsible for Indi while she's out on bail."

Viv Sutton had called yesterday, informing him she'd filed her notice of appearance with the court and would reach out to the district attorney's office to set up a meeting before the arraignment.

"Take her with you."

Oh, that was sure to get Skylar's forgiveness. Show up with the other woman in the picture, the same woman who happened to be pregnant with his child, the same child he planned to raise.

Sully must've read the look on his face because he waved a hand, "Bad idea. Never mind. Forget I was here," he said, leaving the office.

"If only I could," Mike muttered.

Everything was on the line. He'd known it might come to this, but that would have been because of the choices *he'd* made. He hated that someone else's actions were forcing his hand. This picture wouldn't just affect his relationship with Skylar, it could very well affect his deal with TTL.

What did it say about him, about their relationship, that he was more concerned about the latter?

Maybe nothing about him, but everything about Indi and the feelings she aroused in him.

Two nights ago, the late hour had forced him from his desk. But instead of making the turn that led to his house in Palo Alto, he'd kept going, heading back to San Francisco.

And to Indi.

She'd asked him why and he'd told her the truth. He'd been drawn back to her and their child, unable to stay away. Walking into the condo had been a homecoming. Everything in him eased, reinforced with a sense of peace.

Whether that was tied to Indi or Nugget or the both of them, he'd yet to determine. He thought he'd have more time. It looked like his time was running out.

Evan buzzed him. "Your mother's on line one."

And the hits kept on coming.

"Who's the woman in the picture?" Barbara's normally loving tone was coated in disapproval and reserve, the censorious voice of his rare youthful indiscretions.

He winced. "You saw it?"

"Your sister sent me a link to an article."

Mike gritted his teeth. He was going to kill Morgan.

"I thought you were dating Skylar Thompson. I've tried to not push or get involved in your affairs, but your father seems to believe your relationship is serious."

Nothing would make his father happier. "With that

type of woman by your side, the sky's the limit," Robert had said, when he'd called after a picture of Mike and Skylar had appeared in the San Francisco society pages.

"It's not what it looks like," he told his mother.

"It looks like you're seeing two different women. Which is your business. You're not married. But I hope you're being honest and upfront with both of them about your intentions." A pause. "And using protection."

Good God! Is this what it'd come to, taking advice about his sex life from his mother?

"I don't think your father's seen it. Yet."

One more thing he'd have to deal with. If Robert thought Skylar personified the wind beneath his wings, what would he say about Indi?

"So you're still coming this weekend?"

"I'll be there."

"Good. Should I add a plus one for you?" His mother's voice was the essence of innocence.

He wasn't fooled.

Mike rolled his eyes skyward. "What happened to not getting involved in my affairs? Don't you have enough on your plate?"

Between Indi and the baby, Skylar and TTL, and dealing with his father and his sister, he had more than enough to keep *him* busy.

"Fine. I'm off to make sure Katherine Givens doesn't skimp on the decorations for the reception after the ceremony. I'll see you tomorrow."

And he was off to inform Indi about the imminent family gathering.

Chapter Thirteen

THE SMALL COASTAL Northern California town of Barton Park was an idyllic place to grow up and Mike usually enjoyed his trips back to visit his family.

But this time there'd be no early morning family surfing trips to the beach, no drive to the state park to hike the waterfall paths with Morgan, no stroll to the local winery to watch his mom taste the seasonal flights.

He'd be showing up for his father's celebration . . . with Indi in tow.

Oh, she'd argue he could leave her behind and she'd proven she could take care of herself in the unfamiliar city, as long as she refrained from breaking and entering into anyone else's home. But he'd be away for three days. What if Indi was gone when he got back? And while he knew she understood the consequences of leaving the jurisdiction while still on bail, her impetuousness could override her judiciousness, her recent brush with the criminal justice system his chief case in point.

But that picture . . .

Maybe he should head to Barton Point without her. Despite what he'd told Sully and his mother, the picture was *exactly* what it looked like. He'd stupidly believed he could relegate Indi and their weekend together to an inconsequential footnote in his life. Yet that picture—taken by an objective third party—proved that neither of them was as impervious to the other as they'd professed.

Which complicated his life in fiendish ways.

He would raise his child, either with Indi's consent or the court's involvement, but if Skylar had seen that picture—and it was time to face the facts: she had— would knowing the depth of the attraction between him and the baby's mother affect her reaction to Nugget and her decision to marry him? And what chance did the deal with TTL have without Skylar by his side?

Shrugging his shoulders to try to alleviate the sudden tightness that had taken hold like a trespassing squatter, he entered his condo . . . and was immediately welcomed by the tantalizing smell of home-cooked food.

Indi.

A quick scan of the kitchen and living area failed to yield the woman who'd invaded his life, his home, and his thoughts. A pop of color materialized in his peripheral vision. Indi stood on the balcony that spanned the back of his condo, wearing bright blue leggings and a hot pink tank top with straps that crisscrossed her upper back.

She'd pulled her braids into a ponytail on the crown of her head.

His heartbeat shifting into high gear, he sat his phone and keys on the counter and watched as Indi settled on her belly and then, in a fluid, lithe gesture, rose up until it looked like she was doing a push-up. In between one breath and the next, she lifted her hips and bent her body to an inverted V. Several seconds later, she lifted one foot in the air. Gracefully, she brought the leg down and surged forward into a low lunge between her hands. Stretching that leg back, she lowered her body into the push-up position and the entire routine began again.

He poured bourbon into a glass and leaned his hip against the wall. The orange glare of the setting sun speckled through the downtown skyline and alighted on her limber form. She was stunning. He'd known his share of beautiful women, but something about this one captivated him—had from the first moment he'd seen her. It wasn't just her looks: her enticing warm vanilla scent, the husky timbre of her voice, the dewy suppleness of her skin. She was ambrosia to all his senses. He reached down and adjusted himself. Did getting turned on by a yoga session make him a pervert?

India straightened and brought both arms over her head, swaying slightly from side to side. Pressing her hands together, she lowered them in front of her. Her chest expanded, then deflated, and her posture relaxed. She turned and jumped slightly when their gazes met. His breath clung to his lungs like an anxious toddler and they stared at each other for a long moment before she looked away.

He exhaled.

"When did you get home?" she asked, meeting him in the kitchen after entering through the sliding door.

He refused to admit he'd been standing there gawking at her.

"I just walked in," he said, handing her a bottle of water.

"Thanks." She twisted off the top and took a lengthy swig.

It gave him another opportunity to watch her—unobserved—an activity that was fast becoming his go-to diversion. Initially, he'd believed her to be this waif of a woman. He'd eventually discovered that, though she was slender, she was strong. Even now, with her arms bare, he could see the definition in her biceps, the leanness of her hips, the power in her thighs.

He brushed his knuckles down her side. She shivered, but didn't move away from his touch.

"You're barely showing."

It was true. If he hadn't enjoyed an intimate and days-long seminar on the shape of her body, he'd be fooled into thinking the gentle swell in her lower abdomen was natural and not evidence of the existence of their baby.

"If it weren't for the nausea, I could pretend I'd just indulged in apple pie topped with Jamoca almond fudge ice cream"—she gestured airily to her chest—"the day after my new boob job."

Oh yeah, he'd definitely noticed those. They'd felt amazing crushed against him. What had once fit nicely in his hand now looked to overflow his palm.

"Didn't you do some of those poses during our weekend together?"

He realized what he'd given away a second too late.

Way to sound like a stalker. You told her you'd just walked in.

Her eyes widened, but she nodded and answered his question. "I've been practicing yoga for a while. It makes me feel powerful and at peace in my body."

Relieved she didn't call him out, he asked, "Is it dangerous for the baby?"

"No. I read the pamphlet Dr. Kimball gave me. As long as I stay away from Bikram yoga—"

He paused, the tumbler halfway to his lips. "Bikram?"

"Doing yoga for an hour and a half in a room that's over one hundred degrees."

"Why in the hell would anyone do that?"

She laughed. "I'm not a regular practitioner, but I have tried it a few times."

"But not while pregnant?" It sounded more dangerous than beneficial.

She perched on one of the wooden bar stools that matched his cabinets. "Just regular yoga. As long as I listen to my body and don't engage in any overly strenuous poses, doing this is actually good for me and the baby."

He nodded. Then said, "I got a call from my mother."

She stiffened and her lashes swept down to create

dusky shadows beneath her eyes. "Did you tell her about the baby?"

"No, but she knows about us."

"There is no 'us,'" she said, playing with the water bottle's plastic top.

He clenched his jaw at her continued insistence of their non-status. "She doesn't know who you are, but she knows that we may have been . . . involved."

Her fine brows crammed toward one another. "That makes absolutely no sense."

He picked up his phone and pulled up the photo Anya had texted to him.

Her hand flew to her mouth. "Is that from—"

"The Youth Alliance, yes. Congratulations, we're in the society pages."

"Do they know who I am?"

"No, not yet. But with the *People* magazine spread coming out, it won't take long." And because he couldn't help himself, he added, "Which is why I told you to stay in the house."

"I didn't leave," she protested.

"But you went out on the balcony. Easy pickings for anyone with a telephoto lens."

"If you'd explained the reasoning behind your demand, instead of shooting off a terse text, I probably would've stayed inside." She bent her head to study the picture then lifted wide, light brown eyes. "And your mother saw this?"

"Uh-huh. My sister showed it to her."

She bit her lip, leaving a tantalizing trail of moisture behind. "What did you tell them?"

"Nothing."

She shoved a hand on her hip. "Don't you think it'll be a little hard to hide the fact that you're suddenly raising a child?"

Excitement stole the moisture from his mouth. "Does that mean you've made a decision?"

She winced. "I'm just saying . . ."

His sprouting enthusiasm shriveled and died on the vine. "I didn't tell my mother anything because I'd prefer to do it when I see her tomorrow."

"Is she coming to San Francisco?"

"No, I'm going to visit them. The town where I was born is throwing a gala in my father's honor."

"Impressive. What did your father do?"

"He's owned a very successful commercial real-estate business for the past thirty-five years. He was also the mayor for sixteen years."

"So you're like the town's first son?"

He'd never thought of it in that way, but there had been major perks growing up in Barton Point as the son of Robert Black.

A few disadvantages, too.

"Sounds like fun." She finished the water and tossed the bottle in the recycling bin. "You should have a good time."

"We both will."

"Excuse me?"

"You're going with me."

"Oh no." She jumped down off the stool and walked out of the kitchen.

He followed her. "Oh yes."

"How do you plan to explain me, the baby, the picture, and your girlfriend?"

It sounded like the title of a raunchy comedy from the seventies.

"This weekend is about my father. The last thing I want is to answer questions about our convoluted situation."

Or hear his father's unwanted opinions about the mistakes he was making in his life.

"But showing up with me," she said, facing him, her voice low, her hand flat on her stomach, "after your mother and sister have seen the picture—"

"I'll figure out something to tell them." He tilted her chin up, allowing his fingers to caress the fine bones of her jaw. "I've been clear about the fact that I want to keep our baby. If you come with me, I can refer back to this visit when they ask me about the mother. So you won't be a stranger."

The seconds stretched between them until he almost choked on his anticipation. He knew she was angry about the insult implicit in his invitation, but he wouldn't change his mind.

Just when he thought he'd have to pull another reason from his ass, she finally nodded. "Okay."

"Good." Damn, her mouth. He swept his thumb along her bottom lip, then dropped his arm, his hand flexing at his side. "I called Viv this afternoon and confirmed you could leave the city without violating the conditions of your bail."

He saw when she understood the implication of his words.

She tilted her head to the side and crossed her arms over her plumper breasts. "You cocky bastard! You were *that* sure of your ability to get me to agree?"

"You were always going to go; I never planned to leave you here. But your cooperation will make it a more pleasant experience."

"YOU'VE BEEN QUIET for the past two hours and we still have another hour left. Do you plan to sulk the entire way?"

She rested her chin on the palm of her hand and stared out the car's window at the passing scenery. "I'm not sulking."

She was.

Other than Chelsea, Indi did her best to keep all of her involvements superficial. She'd learned the wisdom of relating casually at an early age. Yet the day after he'd sprung this little getaway on her, she was heading up the coast to spend the weekend with the family of her unborn child's father.

She'd successfully ignored him for the first part of the trip, but it appeared that approach would no longer be tolerated. Ah, well . . . She called upon all the lessons learned from traveling with strangers.

Be friendly. Avoid drama. Remain positive. Engage in neutral discussions.

"Your sister goes to Stanford, right?"

"For the time being."

She turned away from the window, frowning. "What does that mean?"

"My mother said Morgan was thinking about taking a semester off."

"Oh." She returned her gaze to the craggy coastline. "Taking some time off can be a good thing, especially if she's not mentally prepared for the next stage or she's working so hard that she's starting to lose focus."

He huffed a laugh. "Why am I not surprised by your reaction?"

So much for nice, neutral traveling conversation.

"My reaction is totally reasonable. Your sister isn't a child; she's a grown woman. She knows what's best for her spirit, even if that offends your notions of propriety."

"First off, she's not a grown woman. She's only nineteen."

Her lips twitched at his testy tone. "Last time I checked, that was considered an adult."

"She's always been a little reckless, a little headstrong."

"Reckless? She attends Stanford, hardly the place for irresponsible juveniles."

"Maybe *reckless* isn't the right word. Impetuous, emotional."

"I would think her being emotional is something you would want to nurture."

He'd meant *different*. It appeared Morgan Black wasn't happy to toe the family line the way her older brother did.

"I do. But you can't make big decisions based on feelings. In the real world, actions have consequences. What if she decides not to return? What will she do?" His hands tightened on the wheel. "If wanting to make sure my sister makes a prudent decision means I'm a bad person, then I'll accept that label."

"It doesn't make you a bad person. A tad controlling, maybe . . . but you've got to let her make her own decisions. It's her life, not yours."

"And I'm supposed to take advice from a charged felon?"

"You don't know how to play fair, do you?"

"I'm just stating the facts."

Control freak, thy name is Mike. She rolled her eyes. "I hate to break it to you, but you don't know what's best for everyone."

"Actually, I don't claim to know what's best for everyone, just the people in my life. It's my job to protect them."

There was such certainty in his voice, she knew he believed what he said.

She shivered. "Good thing I'm not in your life."

"You may not be, but our baby is."

Speaking of Nugget . . .

"What did you decide to tell your family about me and the baby?"

"I'm still working on it, but I may not tell them anything on this trip. It would be too much to drop on them and we're only here for the weekend." He glanced over at her. "Is that going to be a problem?"

"This trip wasn't my idea."

"I was referring to your morning sickness, though your nausea can't tell time for shit."

It was true. She never knew what would bring on the nausea, but it happened every day at different times. The good news was once she gave into it, she was generally okay. There were bouts of tiredness throughout the day, but the actual vomiting took pity on her and stayed away.

"I think I can hide it for two days." She cleared her throat. "What about me?"

"I'll tell them you're Chelsea's sister and you came to town before they got back from their honeymoon and I didn't want to leave you alone."

"And they'd buy that?"

"Why wouldn't they? I know you find this hard to believe, but I'm a good guy. Plus, you're not my usual—" He winced.

Type. Indi knew how to complete that sentence. She looked down at her hands in her lap. She was well aware of that fact.

Having decided silence wasn't a bad idea after all, she didn't initiate another conversation until they passed a quaint wooden sign bearing the town's name.

Mike rolled down his window and rested a bent arm on the door. "Welcome to historic Barton Point."

Indi felt like she'd ridden onto the pages of a Hans Christian Andersen fairy tale. Mike's hometown was quaint and charming with leafy tree-lined streets, cobblestone sidewalks, and rustic Tudor-style cottages. As they drove through the area Mike called the Shopping District, the bright sun, wispy clouds, and cool breezes

added to the picture of people appearing to enjoy themselves. A travelogue come to life. But—

"It's not very diverse," she observed.

Women carrying shopping bags, children riding bikes,
an older couple walking their dog, a group of teenagers
sitting around a stone fountain, a young family pushing a
stroller. She hadn't spied a brown face in the crowd.

Mike looked over at her quickly then gazed out of the
windshield and his window. "I never noticed."

"You wouldn't."

"Why not?"

"You're a rich, gorgeous white man. The world is your
playground."

"You think I'm gorgeous?"

She gave him her best "seriously?" look. "There's probably nowhere you ever go where you worry you won't be
welcomed. Or that you could be in danger."

"And you do?"

"Of course. I travel. A lot. As a woman and a person of
color, it's always a concern."

He nodded but didn't say more.

"Still, it must've been nice for you growing up here."

"It was."

"Let me guess." She took in his traveling attire: dark
washed denim that molded to his thighs as he shifted
gears and a blue-and-white patterned button-down peeking from the V-neck collar of the wheat-colored cashmere
sweater that stretched across his broad shoulders. "President of the Honor Society, captain of the football team,
and homecoming king."

His features tightened. "Wrong. I played baseball."

"I bet you were the most popular kid in your class."

"And you were probably arguing on the debate team or protesting with the Sierra Club."

Her smile died. "I never had time for extracurricular activities." She turned to study the view from the passenger side window.

It was hard enough focusing on her schoolwork when her stomach growled in hunger and exhaustion stole her concentration.

Fifteen minutes later, on the northern outskirts of town, Mike turned the car between two stone pillars and followed the long driveway as it curved upward and ended at a large house on the hilltop, surrounded by tall trees on three sides.

"We're here."

He exited the vehicle and the sound of waves crashing against the shore burst in and assaulted her ears, before he closed his door and headed to the back of the car.

She leaned forward and pressed her hands against the exquisite leather dashboard as sensation careened in her belly.

I wish you could see this, Nugget. It's incredible.

Large metal-framed windows appeared carved into the stacked-stone facade of a storybook castle condensed into a home. Two turrets, topped by clay-tiled roofs, bracketed a massive one-story structure that achieved the notable feat of being as approachable as it was impressive. Colorful flora dotted the professionally groomed landscape.

This was a home filled with happiness. Where the children were wanted for more than the income they brought in. Where the mother and father loved—not just tolerated—each other. In those few moments, Indi imagined all the birthday parties and sleepovers, all the holidays and vacations.

All the love.

All the family.

The front door opened and a petite older woman, her dark hair pulled into a sleek chignon, stepped outside. Spying them, her cheeks lifted in happiness and she hurried down the steps. Mike met her halfway, setting their luggage down and walking into her waiting embrace.

Even in the absence of their voices, Indi knew the other woman had to be his mother. His coloring and size probably came from his father, but his core features—his eyes, nose, and mouth—were all her.

The older woman's gaze finally left her beloved son and trailed over his shoulder to the car. Mike jerked around and his posture stiffened, like he was surprised to find her still in the vehicle. He motioned for his mother to give him a moment, then he jogged back over and opened Indi's door.

Uncertainty held her immobile and the masculine planes of his face softened. "It'll be okay," he said. "I've got you."

She inhaled and nodded slightly before taking his proffered hand and stepping out of the car. *You've traveled all over the world. You've done some amazing things. You can talk to this woman.*

At least she looked good, glad she'd decided on the flowy, paisley-print maxi dress that complimented her skin tone and camouflaged her midsection—which had suddenly popped out this week. Okay, not popped out, but there *was* a slight roundness where before she'd been flat. She called on all of her experiences rolling into unfamiliar towns, meeting new people, and putting them at ease.

"Hello, Mrs. Black. I'm India Shaw."

"India. What a beautiful name." Mrs. Black's smile was so welcoming, Indi couldn't help but return it. "You're Michael's friend from the picture, right?"

Crap. A direct hit.

But she didn't let her smile falter.

"I'd like to think we're friends." She tilted her head. "Are we, Michael?"

She saw his slight wince, recalled a moment from their weekend when he'd placed small, wet kisses on her bare thigh while she'd trailed her fingers through his blond strands.

"What are you thinking about, Michael Black?"

He'd playfully shrunk away from her touch. "Don't call me Michael. Only one person addresses me that way, and the last woman I want to think about right now is my mother. In fact . . ." He'd swiftly pinned her so she was flat on her back, his broad shoulders blocking any light. "I need to do something drastic to recapture the mood."

His fingers and tongue worked in tandem to ensure thoughts of anything else ceased to exist.

The memory receding, she glanced at Mike, startled

to find his darkened blue gaze raking over her body. His nostrils flared and the tip of his tongue darted out to wet his lip. Her nipples pebbled and heat pooled at the apex of her thighs.

Was he reliving the same moment?

His mother's head swiveled back and forth between them, like a spectator at a tennis match, and Mike finally remembered they weren't alone.

He cleared his throat.

"Yes, that was Indi and she's my friend," he told his mother, though his gaze lingered on Indi. "She's actually Chelsea's sister. She's waiting for Chelsea and Adam to return from their honeymoon and since she doesn't know anyone in the city, I invited her up here with me."

His mother nodded and patted his chest. "My Michael, always a shining knight."

Mike shot her a triumphant smile.

"And, India, please call me Barbara. You're in for a treat this weekend. The town is honoring my husband and I was on my way to the venue to check the place settings." She turned to Mike. "Katherine said they sent over the wrong ones and the correct ones won't be here in time. Plus, with everything going on with your sister— Ah, please forgive me. I'm sure you'd like to come in and freshen up after your trip."

Mike grabbed their bags and motioned for Indi to precede him. They followed his mother into the house . . .

Where the twin odors of garlic and lemon almost knocked her off her feet.

Barbara placed a hand on Indi's arm. "Are you okay, dear? You don't look well."

Mike narrowed his eyes and sat their bags just inside the front door.

"No, I . . . sometimes the long car drives . . ." She took another deep breath and her stomach revolted. "Is that garlic I smell?" She hoped the bright note she tried to inject into her tone was successful.

Barbara smiled brightly. "Oh yes. Esme is making garlic chicken and basil, one of Michael's favorite dishes."

Shit.

"—redid the west wing of the house," Barbara was telling Mike, "and that's where you'll be." She tilted her head to the side. "Should I have Esme prepare a second room?"

"Yes, Mom. I told you, Indi and I are just friends."

"Of course. But I also know young people usually mean something else by 'friends.'"

"I'm not *that* young. Tell Esme to make up another room."

"That's not necessary," Indi said, trying to breathe through her mouth as Nugget began salsa dancing in her womb. "I can make my own bed."

"Nonsense. It'll only take her a few minutes. Esme . . ." Barbara called, leaving the room.

Indi could feel the sickness gathering steam. She shifted from one foot to another and took several deep breaths, but tears pricked her eyes at the futileness. She'd so wanted to make a good impression. But as nausea roiled in her gut, she knew she'd have to jettison her concern over how she would be perceived. Head bowed, she tugged on Mike's arm. He placed a hand on the small of her back and she braced herself against him.

"The bathroom?" she managed through clenched teeth.

Before he could answer the front door opened and a young woman, sporting black leggings, a white tee, and a jean jacket, walked in. She took one look at them and screamed.

"Mike!"

She launched herself into his arms and Indi stumbled back several steps to avoid becoming a casualty.

Mike hugged the young woman, resting his chin on the top of her head. "Hey, Morgan."

She hit his shoulder. "Don't start."

"I didn't say anything." He laughed, easily fending off her blows.

"You didn't have to. Your tone told me a lecture was coming."

Through the burn of acid settling in her chest, Indi nodded, familiar with that look and tone of voice.

The motion must've caught the young woman's attention because she finally addressed Indi. "I'm Morgan, Mike's sister. I know," she said, placing a hand on her hip and tossing back her sleek fall of dark brown hair, "the family resemblance is ah-mazing." Her black eyes, tilted at the corners, sparkled.

"Practically twins," Indi deadpanned. A mistake, as another rush of garlic-tainted air invaded her lungs.

Morgan tapped Mike on the chest. "Get ready. He-Who-Must-Not-Be-Crossed is behind me."

"That's not funny, young lady," Barbara said, joining them once again.

"Yeah, it is."

Indi had no time to wonder at the reference as the acid in her chest decided to continue its journey upward. She grabbed Mike. "I need a bathroom. Now."

He opened his mouth—

"Morgan, we're not done with this conversation!"

A tall blond man stood in the doorway, backlit by the sun. Wearing a meticulously tailored suit, he cut a polished and commanding figure. Mike's father?

Indi actually inhaled.

Of course, that was the worst thing she could've done. The breeze from the open front door mixed with the air in the foyer, stranding Indi in the swirling center of a garlic-fragranced vortex.

There was no way she was keeping this down. Unfortunately, she still didn't know the location of the nearest bathroom . . .

Exiting the way she'd entered, she brushed past the newcomer and out the front door, ignoring Barbara's frantic call, Morgan's surprised laugh, and Mike's deeply felt "Fuck!"

Reaching the metal railing, she doubled over and threw up in the house's beautiful landscaping.

Chapter Fourteen

MIKE PULLED THE bedroom door closed behind him and walked slowly down the hallway.

When he'd left home for college, patterned paper had hung on the walls and thick carpet covered the floors. His mother's renovations hadn't been relegated to only the bedrooms in the west wing; she'd rejuvenated the entire section with pale gray paint and white oak hardwood floors.

He'd finally gotten a devastated Indi to settle down. She'd apologized profusely after the incident, had even offered to replace the ruined plants with "new, clean flowers." Not that she knew anything about gardening, she'd informed him—weakly fighting off his efforts to tuck her into bed—but she'd worked at a plant nursery one summer after high school. It had taken over an hour and a promise to go to the Barton Point Farm & Garden Store later, but she'd finally slipped off to sleep.

He'd lingered there for several minutes, watching her sleep, her arm curled around her belly protectively. She claimed she'd be unable to raise Nugget, but her actions showed a woman who'd already grown to love the life she carried within.

"Hey." Morgan leaned against the wall, her fingers flying over her phone.

"Hey."

"Dad's waiting for you in the study."

As he got closer to her he saw the scripted *C*—the Computronix's logo—carved into the back of the device. He shoved his hands into his pockets. "What are you doing?"

"Don't worry," she said, her fingers never ceasing on the screen. "I'm not posting the video of your girlfriend upchucking in our bushes." She finally looked up. "Although I could have. It was priceless. Especially the look on Dad's face."

Mike could easily imagine his father's clenched jaw and curled lip, though he'd missed seeing it, having run after Indi to make sure she was okay.

He'd gotten there in time to gather her braids away from the mess.

"And I thought the drama this weekend would come from you and Dad voicing your concerns in stereo about me studying abroad."

"You want to study abroad?"

"Didn't Mom tell you?"

He shook his head. "She said you wanted to take time off from college."

"That's what Dad's calling it because I'm breaking away from his plan." She pounded a fist against her thigh and pushed away from the wall. "He acts like I intend to bum around Europe with a backpack, picking up guys and smoking weed. I'll still be pursuing my education and getting credit that will go toward my degree."

His father's viewpoint wasn't surprising. Robert Black had specific aspirations for his children and their own feelings were rarely part of the conversation.

But maybe his father had a point this time. Morgan had never mentioned studying abroad before.

The first couple of years attending a university could be overwhelming. Adjusting to the academic differences between high school and college, making new friends, and negotiating living with a roommate, learning general life skills like laundry, preparing a budget, shopping for food—these were experiences that could paralyze even the most intense student. Was Morgan running away from the stress of her new situation instead of buckling down and overcoming the challenges she might be facing? He would be doing his sister a disservice if he played into her capitulation.

He tousled Morgan's hair. He knew how much she hated it, but its thick, razor-straight texture reminded him of when she was a little girl and she'd first come to live with them. She'd stare up at him, awe brightening her eyes. *"Jjog-eulo,"* she'd say—which they learned was Korean for *up*—and hold out her chubby arms. He'd pick her up, cuddle her close, and promise her that nothing bad would ever happen to her again.

Plus, big brother, little sister. Annoying her was an integral part of their familial bond. He couldn't help himself.

"Why do you want to study abroad?"

"I—" She licked her lips and her gaze veered away from his. She exhaled. "It'll look great on my transcript. And in today's competitive market, international skills and knowledge will help me stand out to potential employers."

A pat, impressive answer but Morgan's hesitation—her overall aura of shiftiness—set off his bullshit meter.

"Stanford is consistently ranked as one of the top five best universities in the world. There's no expertise you can acquire from studying abroad that you can't get, and in superior quality, from here."

She straightened, her shoulders falling back into a strong, defiant posture. "But if I study abroad, I'll have access to classes and subjects that wouldn't be available to me at Stanford."

"That's what the internet is for. Whatever interest you have, you can find an online webinar to suit your needs and fit around your class schedule."

"What about the educational and personally enriching benefits of immersing myself into a new culture?"

"There are language and culture houses on campus. If you're interested in a particular country, I'm sure you can find other students from that region."

Morgan scrunched up her face. "There's more to learning than what you find in books."

"Say slackers who think hitchhiking across the country or weaving yarn bracelets should count the same as attending lectures and passing exams. They have their benefits but parlaying them into college credit isn't one of them." He flicked a finger against her chin. "I'm sorry but you haven't given me a valid reason to support your leaving Stanford."

"It's only for a year!" she said, throwing her hands in the air. "You know, Mike, you sound just like Dad. If no one has had the balls to tell you this to your face, I will: You don't know what's best for everyone!" She flounced away in those awful wedge sneakers.

Someone *had* recently told him something similar and he could confirm she was pretty ballsy.

Sighing, he pinched the bridge of his nose, squeezing his eyes shut. One uncomfortable conversation down, one more to go.

There were many occasions when he'd sat in the study, listening while his father voiced lecture after lecture as if on a mission to download his morality into his son's mind. Mike never remembered the details, only the gist—use your fists as defense, never offense; treat women the way you'd want someone to treat your sister; greatness is for those who never settled for good enough—but the night of the accident was the sole standout. Though it had happened sixteen years ago, he remembered everything, his torn and muddied clothes, the stinging scrape on his elbow, his mother's sobbing in the background, the shocked disappointment on his father's face. That evening, the oak paneling and cherry bookshelves seemed to be closing in on him, punishment for the fatal consequences of his lapse in judgment.

He swallowed, knocked on the door, and waited until he heard the familiar, "Come in."

His eyes widened as he looked around. The dark paneling had been removed in favor of light-colored walls, and the beautiful hardwood floors from the hallway were on display.

Robert read the incredulity on his face and grumbled, "Your mother couldn't stop after the west wing. She renovated it earlier this year. Claimed it wasn't a gentleman's club."

Robert was a formidable man, but Barbara was more than his match. That parity was what Mike had been looking for in a wife, what he'd hoped to model his own marriage after.

"Been following the performance of the HPC." Robert tapped his knuckles on the desk. "Very impressive. The stock has risen steadily since the presentation."

Did his father believe he wasn't aware of that information? Mike settled into a beige armless, tufted chair. "Yes, it has."

"The added publicity of Adam proposing to his wife was a boon."

He crossed his right ankle on his left knee. "I can assure you Adam didn't do it for promotional purposes. He doesn't think that way."

"Maybe not, but it helped. I'm sure his wife appreciated it as brilliant strategy. She's in PR, right? With Beecher & Stowe?"

Mike wasn't surprised his father knew about Computronix's major players. The other man often extolled the benefits of doing research and obtaining as much information as possible.

"The harder you work, the more preparation you do, the luckier you'll be."

"She just made partner."

Robert nodded. "Adam picked well. With his Asperger's, it's good for him to choose a woman who's communicative and sociable. You'd do well to pick in a similar vein."

Here we go.

He remained silent, knowing his response wasn't required.

"You've been dating Skylar Thompson for a while."

"I have."

"She's a beautiful woman, very accomplished."

He tilted his head back and met his father's stare. "Yes, she is."

"Exactly the type of woman a successful businessman should have by his side."

"That's your opinion."

"Is it one you share?"

He did. And until very recently, he'd been the businessman in that scenario. However, the scenario was shifting, as was his image of the person who should be by his side.

"I've been spending a lot of time with Skylar discussing a business proposition between Computronix and ThomTexteL."

"What kind of proposition?"

"One I can't discuss with anyone outside of a few key people in the company."

Robert frowned. "But I'm your father!"

The Father Maneuver. "I know who you are."

His father straightened in his chair. He hated having his goals stymied. "Who is this woman you've brought to our home?"

Add graying hair and eighteenth-century clothing and Robert would be right at home in a Jane Austen novel.

"I'm sure you already know this because Mom filled you in. Her name is India Shaw and she's Chelsea's sister."

"I wasn't aware Chelsea Bennett had any siblings."

"Why would you be aware of anything regarding Chelsea's background?"

"She married the CEO of Computronix and as a shareholder—"

The shareholder card.

"—I have a right to know about anything that would affect my investment."

Researching Chelsea's professional life? Maybe, although it still felt intrusive. But digging into her personal life, her upbringing . . .

Had his father always been this arrogant and controlling? He'd valued Robert's opinions, appreciated that his father helped to instill most of his core beliefs. Because of his father, he'd learned honor, ambition, and confidence and believed the older man epitomized those traits.

But as he sat across from Robert, his judgmental attitude on display, Mike realized the negative aspects of those traits and began to wonder if Adam and Jonathan didn't have a valid point about the weight he placed on emulating his father's choices.

With Morgan's accusation of his resemblance to Robert ringing in his ears, he leaned forward and rested his elbow on his bent knee, his father in his crosshairs. "Adam and I own the company—you're a small shareholder. Your interests gives you zero right to investigate the people who work at Computronix, or anyone on the periphery. That's *our* job. If you're concerned about the way we're running the business, you do have the right to sell your shares. I'd be happy to take them off your hands at full market value."

It was the voice he used to establish his position in meetings with older executives new to dealing with Computronix. The ones who assumed he'd fall for anything they offered because they'd been around longer than he and Adam.

Those men were quickly disabused of that notion.

He had to give his father credit: he couldn't hold his son's gaze but he didn't back down. "Was my report wrong?"

"No," he allowed after a brief interval. "Indi's not her biological sister. She's her foster sister."

"Foster sister. So she has no family?"

He stiffened, aware Indi would find Robert's questions and tone of voice insulting. "She has Chelsea. And now Adam."

"No biological family?"

"As the father of an adopted child, I'm surprised you'd make the distinction."

"Yes, well." Robert cleared his throat. "What does she do?"

"She's not here for a job interview. What does it matter?"

"If you're thinking about dating her—"

"We're not dating"—technically true, though he'd consider their current situation a great deal more intimate—"but if we were, it'd be my business."

"Why then would you bring her to our home, especially for this event?"

"I didn't want to leave her by herself in the city. She knows only Chelsea, Adam, and me."

His father narrowed his eyes. "There's something you're not telling me."

Now it was his turn to glance away as he shrugged.

"I'm the head of this family and this is my house," Robert insisted. "How can I protect you all if I'm missing pertinent pieces of information?"

He recognized the irony of his father telling him the same thing he'd told Indi. He stood. "Then we'll leave."

Robert waved his hand. "No need for the dramatics. Sit down."

He stayed, but remained standing, bracing his arms on the back of the chair he'd just vacated, his tolerance at an all-time low.

"I saw the picture. There's something between you." Robert held up his hand when Mike would've interrupted. "I've got eyes. She's a beautiful woman, but she's not the one for you. Send her back to San Francisco. Trust me, son. I only have your best interests at heart."

A part of Mike understood that now. If he ever believed Nugget was making a decision that would bring him harm, he'd do everything in his power to steer him in the right direction. He basked in the feeling of kinship with his father. "I know."

"And we didn't survive the disastrous fallout from the accident only to have you throw all of your accomplishments away by following your johnson instead of your brain."

Irritation over his father's newest tactic warred with amusement over his choice of words. The irritation won by a landslide.

It had been a while since his father had felt the need to mention the accident.

"Is this where you blame me again for sneaking out?"

Robert was calm. "I never blamed you. I simply said it was a school night. You should've been home."

He clenched the back of the chair so tightly his knuckles whitened. "Greg didn't die because I snuck out of the house. He and the guys were already wasted when I got to the park."

"Which is exactly why you should've said something when they decided to climb the cliffs."

"I did!" He pushed away from the chair, the force of his reaction causing it to tip precariously on its side, before righting itself. "I told them not to go."

Robert stared at the chair before fixing his gaze on

his son. "How hard did you try? They were drunk—you weren't. You should've been the responsible one that night. How many times had I told you to do what's right, not what's easy?"

Apparently, his conscience blamed him as much as his father did.

"At least you don't need to concern yourself with the consequences of my decisions anymore."

"Don't I?" He could tell from Robert's look and tone that he was referring to Indi.

"No. I've been doing a damn good job for years, starting with going into business with Adam."

Instead of with you.

He didn't say it, but they both knew that's what he'd meant.

Robert's lips tightened until his mouth resembled a crease between his nose and his chin.

An uneasy silence settled between them. Mike cleared his throat and raked a hand through his hair. Robert toyed with the cap of his Brooks Brothers fountain pen, the one he'd often used during his time as mayor. It sat mounted on an acrylic block in a place of honor on his desk.

Finally—

"I've scheduled us for a round of golf in the morning at the country club."

Mike sighed. "I haven't held a club since the last time I was here."

"I promised several of the town council members and our county board supervisor that you'd play a round while you were here. You know the whole town is proud of you and your accomplishments."

He knew. Barton Point was small, with a population of just over five thousand. He'd known most of these people his entire life.

"What about Indi? It's rude to invite her here and then abandon her."

"She'll be fine. Your mother will take care of her, especially now that she's sick," Robert muttered, shaking his head. His desk phone rang and he glanced at the caller ID before picking it up. "I have to take this. Think about what I said."

His own phone rang as he closed the door behind him.

"Sully. Give me a second."

He crossed the great room, slid open the glass panel, and stepped out onto the balcony. He was welcomed by the slightly hypnotic sounds of chirping nocturnal creatures intermixed with the waves softly lapping against the shore. He inhaled deeply, the bracing tang of the salty air a hit of rejuvenation. How many people could claim part of the Pacific Ocean as their backyard? Nestled among the trees, the vastness of the water before him, he could be master and commander of the world.

"What's going on?"

"I found an attorney for you. Kenneth DeRosen. He comes highly recommended. Specializes in fathers' rights."

"Fathers' rights?" He braced a hand on the stainless-steel railing. Had Sully lost his fucking mind? Mike wasn't interested in associating with bitter men who

ranted about "feminazis" out to castrate their manhood.
"Not those men who call themselves victims and advo-
cate kidnapping their children or burning down court-
houses?"

"No. DeRosen has carved out a very successful and
well-respected practice representing men in divorce,
child custody, and child support cases. He was booked
solid for the next five months, but I managed to get you
an appointment in a couple of weeks."

Even though Indi appeared open to the idea of letting
him raise Nugget, Mike knew he'd still need an attorney
to draw up the paperwork and ensure everything was
handled properly. A referral was still necessary, though
his reasons for one may have changed.

But a fathers' rights attorney? It felt like throwing the
first punch before the argument even began.

"You don't have to hire him," Sully said, correctly in-
terpreting his silence. "This is just a consult. He'll answer
your questions, explain the procedure. If you don't like
him, we'll find someone else."

His friend had a point. Mike needed to do his research, determine his options, figure out the best strategy to win. It's what he always did, the bedrock of his
success.

Sully continued. "I gave his office my cell number, so
they'll text me initially with your confirmation. I told
him a little about your situation and, although each case
is unique, he seemed to imply that courts wanted to keep
families intact unless one of the parents is unfit."

"Thanks. I appreciate your looking into this, especially with the possibility of an HPC infringement case looming."

"Do you want to keep the appointment?"

In the end, it was his responsibility to protect his family. Indi hadn't agreed to give the baby to him. Hell, despite her fervent claims, she could change her mind and decide to raise Nugget herself. A better alternative than adoption, in his opinion, but where would that leave him? Would his son or daughter's remembrances of *their* childhood feature him as a faceless lecturer, trying to impart as much information as possible in the spare time they had together?

His fingers tightened around the bar. He wouldn't be a visitor in his child's life.

"Yes."

Chapter Fifteen

THE HEAVY DARKNESS of exhaustion receded inch by inch and the reality of her surroundings began encroaching on Indi's peace. Crashing waves, the caw of birds, salt in the air—

Oh no. No, no, no.

She reached for the dream prayer once again. Please be a dream. Please be a crazy, whacked-out dream brought on by indigestion and not a living, breathing nightmare where she'd actually vomited in the family's expensive landscaping.

She cracked open an eye. She was lying on her left side, her head resting on her bent elbow. Gauzy, sheer curtains were pulled back to reveal a stunning view. On the far horizon, vibrant reds and purples bled into oranges and yellows, disclosing the late hour. She should get up and properly apologize to Mike's family, but she wasn't ready to show her disgraced face.

Not yet.

She covered said face with both hands. What must they think of her? A strange woman shows up unexpectedly with their son, barely speaks, and then bowls over his father and anyone else in her way to puke in their artistically designed garden.

Well, she couldn't hide out in this room all weekend. She wasn't a coward. If she'd remained afraid of the metaphorical bogeymen on the other side of the door, she'd still be stuck in the Midwest, free from all of her travels and experiences.

But first, she should change. Freshen up.

She untwisted the folds of her dress and swung her legs around—her bare feet touching the cool wood floors—and sat up, taking a moment to let the world adjust. She reached for the charm around her neck and feeling warm skin, looked down.

Cold tentacles claimed space in her belly. She wasn't wearing her necklace. Her fingers skipped frantically along the cobalt blue duvet, her gaze searching until she noticed it pooled on the nightstand. She slipped the silver chain over her head and inhaled its minty fragrance.

Serenity.

Feeling slightly better, she stood, arched her back, and looked around. Earlier, the nausea twisting her stomach had claimed her total focus. Now, she was able to appreciate the slate-gray walls, recessed lighting, and the black leather king-sized platform bed. But no luggage. Her shoes were lined up neatly in the corner, but her weekend travel bag with her changes of clothes and, more importantly, her toothbrush was nowhere to be seen.

Maybe it was still in the foyer where Mike had first set it down.

She traversed from hardwood to area rug back to hardwood to get to the door. She opened it. Sniffed gingerly.

A faint trace of garlic, but not as overwhelming as before.

The long hallway opened into an enormous great room, a shiny kitchen situated on its far end. A linear gas fireplace bifurcated a structural wall, stacked with the same stone that covered the front of the house, the focal point for several seating arrangements. A low glass-topped coffee table, supported by sculptural wooden legs, sat on a dark area rug and a sleek ceiling fan kept the space airy and cool. Despite the modern contemporary ambience of the home, colorful accents and framed family photographs littering every available surface proclaimed it an inviting space.

Movable glass walls showcased the impressive view of the cliffs, water, and beyond. Through the one open panel, she could hear the deep timbre of Mike's voice and a high-pitched tone she recognized as belonging to his sister, Morgan, although she couldn't make out their words. She wanted to venture out and join them, but her mouth felt like a porta potty before a marathon. She needed to rinse and then chug some water first, temporary measures until she could find her toothbrush.

"Glasses, glasses, glasses," she muttered to herself.

The kitchen was huge, separated from the great room by an L-shaped counter, lit overhead by two chandeliers. The counter could easily seat eight people, four on each side. White cabinets, some backlit and glass fronted, encircled stainless steel appliances.

"Can I get you anything?"

Indi jumped at Barbara's composed tone. Turning, she found the older woman standing in the doorway.

Mortification tingled across her nape and settled in her cheekbones. "Um, I was looking for a glass for some water. I was thirsty."

Barbara walked over to the refrigerator and pulled out a bottle of water. She handed it to Indi.

"Thank you."

Barbara's bright blue gaze swept over her in an experienced, comprehensive manner. "Would you like a cup of herbal tea? Orange spice, ginger with chamomile, or raspberry?"

"The ginger with chamomile would be wonderful."

Barbara filled a navy blue teakettle with water and placed it on one of eight gas burners. "How about some toast?"

Her stomach echoed in hunger. "I'd kill for some toast . . . not literally," she amended. She peered down at her interlocking fingers. "You're being so nice considering what I did. I—I can't apologize enough for—"

Barbara shrugged. "You couldn't help it. Pregnancy hormones."

Shock hit Indi like the Ice Bucket Challenge. She stumbled backward until the counter dug into her hip.

Barbara laughed, the sound throaty, bawdy, and slightly at odds with her proper lady facade. "Oh please. I've been around the block and I made an educated guess. I might've been wrong but, considering your reaction, I guess I'm not."

So much for hiding it for two days. She hadn't lasted ten minutes.

Barbara raised her hands, palms facing outward. "I'm sorry. It's none of my business. It's my maternal instinct. You'll learn about it soon enough," she finished with a self-deprecating eye roll.

Indi ran her fingers through her long braids. It *was* Barbara's business. She was Nugget's grandmother and, if Mike had his way, she'd probably be involved in Nugget's life. They'd decided not to tell his family she was pregnant and, while that cat was out of the bag and on its way to Mexico, the main factor—that Mike was the father—was not. Until she apprised him of this new development, she needed to keep that secret under wraps.

"It's okay. It's all been . . . unexpected."

Barbara took down two mugs and placed them on the Carrara marble countertop. "How far along are you?"

"About fifteen weeks."

"Have you told anyone yet?" Barbara's soft voice held a lulling, hypnotic quality.

Indi couldn't help but answer, though she fudged the truth. "No."

The other woman disappeared into the large pantry and reappeared a second later, holding a loaf of bread. "Not even your family?"

"Chelsea doesn't know."

"What about your mother?"

Shame thickened Indi's throat. She dropped her chin to her chest, let her braids swing forward to cover her cheeks. "My mother isn't a part of my life."

Barbara paused. "I don't understand. Did she pass away?"

Indi almost laughed. It said a lot about this woman that the only way she could imagine a mother not being a part of their child's life was if they were dead.

"No. Or I guess it's more accurate to say I don't know. If she's passed away. I don't know where my mother is. She dropped me off at an emergency room when I was four years old. I spent the rest of my childhood in foster care."

The lines of Barbara's face eased in compassion. "I'm so sorry, honey."

The kettle whistled and on her way to the stove, Barbara reached out and squeezed Indi's forearm. That one gesture was almost her undoing. While Barbara switched off the burner and pulled a tea towel from a drawer, Indi inhaled and exhaled in an effort to retain her composure.

"Thank you, but I'm fine. I got through it intact." Unable to bear the other woman's sympathetic gaze, Indi looked away. "Others aren't so lucky."

"That's true." Barbara placed tea bags in both mugs and added the boiling water. "You said your mother dropped you off. *You*, not you *and* your sister."

"Chelsea?"

Barbara nodded.

The questions were intrusive and if asked by anyone else, Indi would've wondered—aloud—if the interrogator had a fulfilling life since they spent so much time pondering hers. But she had the feeling Mike's mother wasn't asking to stockpile ammunition for gossip but because she actually cared. And that made it easy for Indi to respond.

"Chelsea isn't my biological sister. We shared a foster home for about eight months and we never lost touch. She's the closest thing to family I have."

"Not anymore."

Indi's head reared back and she gaped at Barbara—who pointed at Indi's belly. "Your baby. You, your baby, and its father, if he's in the picture. You're creating a new family."

Indi caressed her stomach. She hadn't thought about it in that way before. She'd been so busy thinking about all the things Nugget would prevent her from doing, all the negative things that would happen if she raised the baby, she'd never considered she was creating the one thing she'd never had.

Since turnabout was fair play . . . "Did you find Morgan through the foster care system?"

"No. Sit down. You look like you'll fall over any second." Barbara waited until Indi had taken a seat on one of the white quilted leather bar stools before she returned her attention to their drinks, steeping the tea bags then throwing them away. "Sugar or honey?"

"A little sugar, please."

Barbara added it to the cup and placed it, and a small

plate of toast, in front of Indi, patting her shoulder and settling on the bar stool next to her.

"When Robert was mayor, we participated in a cultural exchange with our sister city in South Korea. While there, we visited one of the orphanages. There was this little girl I was drawn to and by the end of the visit, I couldn't bear to leave without her." Barbara blew on her tea, took a cautious sip. "Of course, it wasn't that simple. There was a lot of red tape involved. But it was worth it. In the end, we got Morgan."

The look of love on Barbara's face blinded Indi and in that instant she envied the younger girl, who'd possessed something so special, people from halfway around the world hadn't been able to resist it.

"Mike mentioned his father had been mayor."

"Many years ago. Barton Point was founded in 1899 and Robert's family was one of the first to settle here. The Blacks have always believed in public service and giving back to the community, Robert more so than others. Hence the party this weekend."

Indi took a bite of toast and followed it with a sip of tea. Moments later, satisfied when her stomach didn't evict its contents, she said, "If I'd known it was such an important family event, I wouldn't have intruded."

As if she'd had a choice.

"We're happy you can join us."

"I'm not sure your husband or your landscaping would agree."

Barbara laughed. The sound warmed Indi, and an answering grin lifted the corner of her lips.

"Robert will be fine. He needs to be challenged and shaken up every once in a while. It's good for him. Michael does, too. Sometimes he seems too much like his father." Barbara lifted her cup but took no action to drink from it, her gaze going inward then flickering, as if she remembered she'd spoken aloud. "I love my husband immensely, but it doesn't mean I'm blind to his faults."

Interesting.

"I haven't known Mike long, but he strikes me as a very honorable guy. I do know he takes his responsibilities very seriously."

"That he does. He used to be so carefree . . ."

Indi's curiosity was piqued. She tried to imagine a carefree, happy-go-lucky Mike . . . and failed. Intense. Yes. Principled. Of course. Passionate. Definitely. But carefree? Not even during their weekend together, when he spent most of the time completely naked or, at the very least, shirtless.

"I can't imagine Mike without the weight of the world on his shoulders."

"He was quite different as a boy." The memories were like the sun breaking through the clouds. "Always smiling. He'd grab my face between his hands and blow raspberries on my cheeks. Called them bubble kisses. He had this lightness about him."

Her expression became overcast.

Indi leaned forward. "What happened?"

"Life," Barbara said, waving her hand in a breezy manner.

But Indi knew it was anything but.

"Thank you for this," she said, gesturing to the light meal in front of her. The tea calmed her stomach and the toast closed the gnawing hole created by throwing up the little sustenance she'd managed to keep down. "It really helped."

"I'll also make a note to throw out any leftovers from dinner. What was it, the garlic?"

Just hearing the name of the food made her stomach roll. She nodded.

Barbara smiled. "When I was pregnant with Michael I was sick the same way. And not just the first trimester. The entire pregnancy. I had to go into the hospital twice to prevent dehydration. Just be thankful you'll be spared that experience."

Would she? Or did Mike's crazy mutated genes mean Nugget would make her sick for the next six months?

"And don't worry, the food at the gala will be suitably bland. You shouldn't have any problem at all."

Indi choked down the last piece of toast. "Uh, I wasn't planning on going."

"Nonsense. You must attend with us."

"But I have nothing to wear."

"Which means we'll have to go shopping tomorrow." Barbara picked up her mug. "I'm glad you're feeling better. I'll see you in the morning."

"Mrs. Bl—Barbara?"

The other woman turned around.

"I can't seem to find my luggage. If it isn't too much trouble, do you have a spare toothbrush I can use?"

Chapter Sixteen

FOR ONLY THE second time in the past sixteen years, Mike was keenly aware that he wasn't inclined to take his father's advice.

When he was growing up, he thought his father was one of the wisest men he knew. Mike had always believed there'd be no greater life than having what Dad had, and following his counsel seemed like a great way to get there.

And yet . . .

"You honestly believe that you're bound to the same choices your father made?" Adam asked.

Jonathan nodded. "You do have a tendency to treat your father's life and words as gospel."

"There's nothing wrong with following in my father's footsteps. He's a great man."

"What worked for your father may not work for you. Men become great when they forge their own path," Adam argued.

A conversation from a year ago.

Is that what he'd been doing? Substituting his father's judgment for his own? He was extremely confident about his work choices, but in his personal life . . .

Maybe he *should* send Indi back to San Francisco. She didn't need to be here. She couldn't leave, the bail requirements and pending criminal charges a virtual tether. If he was honest with himself, he'd admit that he'd insisted she come on this trip because he was drawn to her, had enjoyed this past week in her company.

Reason enough to rethink his position on his father's advice.

He walked out of the ensuite bathroom after brushing his teeth and washing his face, using a hand towel to wipe the remaining water from his jaw and chest. He froze when the bedroom door opened and Indi walked in holding a toothbrush.

She gasped, her widened eyes scorching a trail from his bare torso to the top of his jeans. His breath hitched in his chest in response to the heat in her eyes.

She opened her mouth then glanced behind her and shut the door. "Are we sharing a room now?"

Anticipation set his heart pounding and he smiled. "Do you want to?"

She crossed her arms, emphasizing those pregnancy-plumped breasts. "Why are you in my room?"

"I'm not. This is my room."

Wrinkles rippled across her unblemished forehead. "This is the room I woke up in." She pointed to the corner. "My shoes are over there."

He'd never tire of looking at her, her face animated with every emotion she experienced. His palms itched to stroke her creamy skin.

"You may not remember, but your room wasn't ready. After the whole throwing-up-in-our-front-yard incident, I carried you in here."

"Right." She bit her lip, her light brown gaze sliding from his. "I'm sorry."

"Stop it. You have nothing to apologize for. Esme made up your room while you were resting. I moved your bags over there. Guess I forgot about the shoes," he said, attempting to make her smile.

It worked, briefly.

Indi trailed her fingers along the dark wood edge of the dresser, rearranged a vignette of vases. "Your mother knows."

"Knows what?"

She glanced at him from beneath her lashes. "That I'm pregnant."

The air whooshed from his lungs. "You told her?"

"Of course not!" She shifted a container of twisted bamboo. "She guessed. Said she'd been sick the same way with you."

"I can't believe she hasn't come after me." He rubbed the back of his neck. "Or told my father."

Indi shook her head, her braids spilling over her shoulders. "She doesn't know you're the father, just that I'm pregnant."

"Huh." He expected to feel relief, but disappointment? "What did she say?"

A soft smile graced those kissable lips as she straightened the pile of artistically arranged books. "She was really sweet about it. I told her a little about my upbringing and she said with this baby I'm creating my own family."

Indi had just met his mother, yet she'd shared a part of herself few others knew. His mother and the mother of his unborn child. Two amazing women.

She placed both hands on her belly. "I'd never thought of it that way before."

For a moment he allowed himself to unravel the tangled, complicated conflict of this situation and imagine he and Indi were just a couple who planned to raise their child together. He smiled at the unexpected sense of peace that shrouded him.

"She also invited me to the gala."

He halted in the act of putting on a shirt, his head surfacing through the collar of his crewneck tee. "Of course you're going to the gala."

She shifted, jamming a hand on her hip. "You never said anything."

Shirt finally on, he smoothed down the fabric and glanced up in time to notice her staring at his covered chest as she made a sound of protest in her throat.

He raised both brows. *Like what you saw?* "I didn't think it was necessary. Why else would I bring you?"

She flushed and tightened her jaw. *No!* "To keep an eye on me. I'm prepared to stay here while you share this with your family."

"You're carrying the next generation of Blacks." He

surrendered to the urge, penetrating her personal space and placing a hand on her stomach. "You *are* family."

This close, her aroma carried more notes of mint that its usual vanilla. But it still fit. Somehow scents seemed one-dimensional until mixed with her essence and turned into an alluring fragrance.

"The baby is. I'm not," she whispered.

He reached forward, laced his fingers through hers. "Don't do that."

Her moist lips parted and her lashes fluttered. "Do what?"

Her voice was breathy. Unbelievably erotic. Blood rushed to his aching cock.

"Put distance between us." He skimmed his fingers up her bare arms, the rise of her flesh a testament to his effect. Palming her cheek, he stared into her eyes. "It won't work."

When their lips met, she moaned, her hands fisting in the fabric at his waist. The softness of her breasts pushed against his chest, the heat between her thighs pulsed against his straining cock. And still it wasn't enough. Angling his head, he devoured her, his tongue sweeping into the hot recesses of her mouth, staking a claim, giving and receiving pleasure. He wanted all of her. More than that, he wanted her to crave him, until all her thoughts of leaving died on the vine before they could be nurtured.

She'd tried. Had walked away when he'd been in no condition to stop her. The existence of Nugget brought them together again, entwining their lives forever. And God help him, he didn't possess the strength to let her go a second time, even when reliable counsel cautioned that he must.

They broke apart, his body seconds away from ceding to desire's assurance that air was less important than her kiss. He inhaled, taking in a lungful, and then leaned his forehead against hers. God, he loved her bottom lip. He brushed his thumb over it and, as he'd known she would, she scorched its pad with the tip of her tongue.

It was always like this between them. Hot. Explosive. Complete.

How could the woman who was wrong for him make him feel so right?

His pulse thrashed loudly, as if to smother the burgeoning thought. She'd said they weren't family, but they could be.

They could raise Nugget together.

The thought was enough to jerk him out of her embrace. He took a step back, shoved appeasing hands through his hair.

She shook her head, her pupils dilated. "You've got to stop doing that. It's not fair to me or Skylar."

Indi was right. He'd never kidded himself that his relationship with Skylar was a love match. Hell, she'd confessed as much before she left. He thought they'd make a good team and their companies would both benefit from his idea.

But Indi and Nugget were game changers. And he was being drawn toward them and the life they could build together. Was that even possible, especially when Indi was dead set against it? Surely a trip around the world wasn't worth abdicating participation in her own child's life? They didn't have to get married, but they could both be involved in raising him.

Indi sighed, the sound weighty and weary. She gathered her braids, lifted them, and placed them over one shoulder. "It's important to you to handle your responsibilities and I know keeping Nugget is part of that. But I'm not. This isn't a two-for-one offer. If I give the baby to you, I'm still leaving."

Irritation boiled his blood. Despite his earlier warning, she was trying to push him away.

Maybe you should let her.

Clearly, her proximity was having an unforeseen effect on his objectives. He'd seesawed from requesting that Indi let him raise Nugget instead of putting him up for adoption to entertaining thoughts of the three of them. Together. As a family.

Was he losing his mind? Maybe it was his integrity. Just a few days ago, he'd intended to propose to Skylar. But now, between his burgeoning feelings for Indi and Skylar's refusal to return his calls or texts, that scenario seemed to be fading faster than footprints in the sand at high tide.

They both needed some distance. It was probably best to go along with her attempts to disengage.

For now.

"How are you feeling?"

"Much better, thank God. Your mother made me tea and toast."

She looked better—the simple act of not throwing up

was a huge improvement—but the smudges under her eyes and the imperceptible droop to her relieved smile was a testament to her long day.

"What would you like to do tomorrow?"

Fuck golf. What would he rather do, spend the day with his father at the country club or hang with the irresistible woman carrying his child?

Guess he meant distance in the metaphorical sense.

"I don't have anything to wear to the celebration."

He rubbed his hands together. "We'll go shopping."

"Your mother said she'd take me."

Try again, honey. "Do you mind if I tag along?"

"If you want to."

"I do." He fingered a braid. "You're always doing something different with your hair. It was long and loose at the engagement party, curly at the wedding, and now braids."

She shrugged. "Hair is just another way to express myself. Like an accessory. I don't feel the need to keep it one way."

All the styles flattered her. And he liked the variety.

"I didn't mean to barge in," she said, moving away from him, her braids sliding across his palm. "Where's my room?"

Determination rippled in his chest. He didn't want her to go, ached for more time in her company. "We can hang out a little. Wanna watch some TV?"

She snorted. "No thanks. If I recall correctly, our ideas about quality TV differ greatly."

He exhibited a little mock outrage. "There's nothing wrong with *The Capture.*"

"Unless you're the rare person who fails to find animals hunting and killing their prey entertaining."

"I only watched that one episode with you. And to be fair, I'd started it while you were taking a bath. At least it's better than the medical show where the doctor finds time to perform cutting-edge surgeries in between sex with the chief of staff and fighting off the zombie apocalypse."

She pointed at him. "That show has won awards."

"Probably because the judges lost valuable brain cells every time they screened it." Blood flowing, he grabbed the remote and pointed it toward the forty-eight-inch flat screen HDTV mounted on the wall. This was his Indi: passionate, opinionated, engaged. He couldn't handle her indifference. "I know something we'll both enjoy."

A minute later, the introduction to *Battle of the Cake* appeared on the screen.

"Yes!" Indi climbed on the bed and settled back against the mound of pillows his mother insisted on displaying, though he relegated most of them to the floor before he went to sleep. She groaned. "My kingdom for a slice of cake."

"You don't have a kingdom and you can barely keep any food down."

He received a throw pillow in the face for telling the truth.

During their weekend, when they'd taken a breather, they'd played a fun game to determine who'd control the remote. He'd liked his chances—he was known for his willpower—but she'd executed this move with her finger and he'd been spent. Literally. His punishment for failing to outlast her? *A Clockwork Orange*-type viewing of a show where four expert bakers battled to see who could build the best cake creation based on a theme.

Cake, for god's sake!

Ten minutes in, he'd been hooked. He didn't care about the baking, but he'd been enthralled by the strategy involved in deciding what to make in the time allowed, the structural engineering of building cakes that towered over four feet, and the competitive nature of chefs who were at the top of their game.

But the best part? Watching Indi watch the show.

Her comments were more entertaining than the competition itself.

"That cake is too big. You won't be able to carry it to the structure!"

"There's not enough time for fondant—switch to buttercream!"

"Do these people even watch the show before they come on? You can't use artificial flavor extract, the judges will notice it!"

Starting the episode, he tossed the remote on the mattress and followed it, basking in her shrieks of laughter as she tumbled sideways. When she righted herself, he headed toward his favorite viewing spot: her lap. Before he laid his head down, he hesitated. "Is it okay?"

"To lay your head here? I think so. The doctor didn't caution against it."

Maybe she didn't, but he wasn't willing to take the chance.

"Google it," she said, pausing the image on the TV.

Locating his bag, he reached into the side pocket and pulled out his customized HPC. He hooked it behind his ear and powered it on.

"They're so cool," Indi breathed, her awe of the device that had catapulted his company to the top of the tech industry apparent.

He smiled. "Have you used one?"

"The last time I stayed with Chelsea. The day before the wedding it was glued to her ear."

Before he knew what he was doing, he told her, "We're working on a new version."

"Really? That seems fast. The HPC just came out."

"It's been a year. We've got to keep growing. Now, you can't share what I'm about to tell you with anyone."

"Ooh, does this call for a super-secret, double-dare pinkie swear?"

He flattened his lips. Was this a good idea? He hadn't even told his father, but he was about to share classified Computronix information with a woman who acted like they were getting ready to share secrets at a slumber party.

"Indi."

"Okay, okay. I promise I won't tell anyone what you're about to tell me."

"Thank you. We're beta testing a new device that will allow you to use the HPC with a screen or monitor. Even though the whole point of the HPC was to make full computing completely portable, a lot of people still want to focus on something concrete instead of the air."

She listened intently and nodded her head. "I can see that."

"So we've created this cube that will not only stream the HPC's data digitally, but will also deliver media over the internet without involving a cable company."

"That would be great for cord nevers, like me."

"Exactly!"

"Does this have anything to do with your relationship with Skylar? ThomTexteL owns cable companies, right?"

He should learn never to underestimate her intelligence. He wanted to answer her question, but he didn't want to reintroduce Skylar into their time together. Not after he'd gotten her to stay. He settled for a brief, business-like response. "We're looking into acquiring the exclusive rights to their cable channels."

"So you could screen them through the cube? That would be huge for Computronix. I can't believe a tech company hasn't thought of providing their own exclusive digital content yet."

"We have. Like with the HPC, we want to be the first to get it to market."

She bit her lip. "That makes it a very important deal."

He didn't trust the soft, contemplative tone of her voice.

"Enough of that. Back to our search." Within seconds he'd typed in the request. "At fifteen weeks, the baby is small and very well protected within your uterus. Slight pressure is okay, as long as it's comfortable for the mother."

When she didn't respond, he tapped her arm. "Hey."

"Right. Baby small and well protected. Sounds like we're good to go." She patted her lap.

Relieved, he powered down the device. "It said Nugget is the size of a lemon. Should we change his name?"

She laughed. "No, you goof."

"You're the one referring to our unborn child as a lump of metal and I'm a goof?" He tossed the HPC on the dresser and crawled back up the bed. "Tell me if it gets uncomfortable."

"I will."

He pressed play on the remote and the show continued. A brief kiss to her belly then he shifted and gingerly placed his head on her upper thigh. That episode ended and another one began.

Contentment.

That feeling, and her fingers combing through his hair, were the last sensations he remembered as he drifted off to sleep.

Chapter Seventeen

It was, quite possibly, the perfect way to wake up.

There wasn't a panicked reanimation or a startled jolt to consciousness. Instead, awareness came to Indi slowly and peacefully and with it, the realization that the comforting presence which had invaded her dreams and wrapped her in a cocoon of protection came from the warm, solid body pressed against her back.

Indi had fallen asleep somewhere between episodes three and four of *Battle of the Cake*. When she'd awakened in the middle of the night, needing the bathroom, she'd been nestled against Mike's broad chest. She'd debated heading to her room, but she still didn't know where it was located. In the end, she'd slid back into the bed, turning her back to him. A moment later, a strong arm had pulled her close to him and she'd been unable to resist the heat of his body.

Mike's breathing was even, his chest rising and falling steadily. With one of his muscled arms still curved around her waist and his hand flat against her lower belly, she felt safe and protected in a manner she'd never before experienced but one she'd always craved.

She feared of moving an inch, believing any action would shatter the gossamer-thin tranquility of the moment. And she needed to remain in his embrace for as long as possible, soaking it all in, imprinting it in her memory, before she dragged herself away and began rebuilding her armor, one layer at a time. So as the sky gradually lightened and a new morning dawned bright and hopeful, she lay there and marveled at the feel of his soft cotton shirt against her cheek and neck, at the exquisitely rough sensation of his jean-clad thigh pressed between the bare skin of her legs.

She couldn't allow herself to get more involved in his life. She shouldn't be sharing late night confidences with Barbara or agreeing to spend any more time than was necessary in his company. It was starting to feel real—like they were an actual couple—and she could never allow that. It's the reason she'd left him after their weekend together. It would be so easy to pretend that they could be a family and raise Nugget together. But with continued proximity, how long would it take before he realized she wasn't the right woman for him? Before he realized he'd made a terrible mistake?

The distressing thought overrode her caution and she shifted against the mattress. Mike's arm flexed against her.

Crap. So much for stealing away.

"Good morning," he said, his voice a husky caress against the side of her neck.

She shivered. "Good morning."

"Did you sleep well?"

"I think so. I don't remember sleeping badly. You?"

"I slept like a log. Do you know what time it is?"

She squinted at the small digital alarm clock on the nightstand closest to her. "Six thirty-four."

"Damn," he half said, half yawned. He managed to stretch without removing the arm that bound her to him, and the feel of his body elongating with grace and power reminded her of a large feline. Kind of like his previous car's namesake. "My father will be expecting me to go with him when he leaves in an hour."

Thank God. Problem solved. Crisis averted. "Maybe you should go. After all, you're here because the town is honoring him. I'm sure he'd enjoy spending time with you."

"I think you misunderstand my relationship with my father," he retorted, his breath tickling the hairs at her nape. "Don't worry, I'll tell him to go on without me and then you and I can head to the Shopping District, grab some breakfast."

Her brain chanted, *That wasn't the plan! That wasn't the plan!*

Her mouth said, "Okay."

Traitor.

"But first . . ." His arm tightened and he pulled her back against his hard body.

She gasped as heat flooded her, attempting to burn through her resistance. "Mike?"

"Hmmm?" He nuzzled the skin beneath her jaw.

"We said we weren't going to do this."

"Do what?" He nipped the spot where her shoulder met her neck and the nerve endings that stimulated her erogenous zones roared to life.

Nobody affected her the way he could.

Nobody.

Her lashes fluttered and she tilted her head back, allowing him easier access. "This."

His hand eased its way up her torso until it closed around her breast. Even as she cursed the fabric that prevented skin-on-skin contact, she arched into him, her nipple pebbling against his palm. His tongue swirled against her skin and she moaned, her pulse pounding loudly in her ears.

"Am I hurting you?" he whispered.

"No," she breathed.

"Good. Because I'd never do anything to hurt you, Indi."

To prove his point, he stroked her silhouette like a patron admiring a rare piece of art. His fingers skimmed along her side, dipping in at her waist and flaring out at her hips. He continued until the fabric ran out and when he reached the hem of her dress, he slid his fingers beneath and branded her bare skin with his touch.

How had she gone so long without this contact?

Grasping the crook of her knee, he lifted her leg and placed it over his thigh, opening her throbbing core to his caress. His thumb smoothed over the cotton of her panties and when he found her clit, he flicked the digit back and forth across the sensitive nub.

She felt herself getting wet, knew the evidence of her arousal must have made itself known because he groaned. "Fuck that's sexy."

No, *he* was sexy.

She needed to touch him. She reached behind her, grasped the hard ridge of his hip and tried to pull him closer. He cooperated by grinding his cock against her ass while his thumb still worked her clit. It felt so good. But she wanted more.

Finally, he slipped his fingers beneath the waistband of her panties and touched her. Her body remembered his touch, remembered this feeling and it opened for him, welcoming him home. She was still wet from his teasing and he coated his fingers in the moisture of her arousal. It allowed him to stroke slowly and leisurely through her folds, teasing her clit, running his fingers around the rim of her pussy, without dipping inside.

She writhed against him, panting, her body on fire. A sweet tension built in her lower belly. It was so close, the pleasure she sought, her body one large quivering mass of sexual need.

"That's it, baby. Come for me. Show me how good it feels."

The tension snapped and waves of pleasure encircled her, catching her up in a whirlwind of pure bliss, leaving her slightly sated, but aching—it was a sexual amuse-bouche.

Still, it wasn't enough. It would never be enough until he was deep inside of her. She'd reached for the fastening to his pants, her fingers fumbling with the closure, when he grabbed her hand.

"We can't," he said, his voice harsh, his breathing heavy.

Son of a bitch!

The scent of their arousal hung heavy in the air and she was acutely aware of her exposed position. She snatched her hand away, lowered her leg, and tried to move away from him, but he held her close.

"This isn't about you. Skylar . . ."

How many times would it take for her to remember she wasn't his type? He'd told her as much in the car. In fact, if it weren't for the baby, she wouldn't even be here.

She was such an idiot.

She tried to push him away but he wouldn't budge. "Let me go."

"Indi—"

"Let me go."

"Indi—"

"Mike, you're hurting me!"

He immediately released her and she scooted to the far edge of the bed. The cool air felt good against her flushed skin.

He hadn't hurt her, not physically in the way he'd thought, but in a way that was more painful.

"Go with your father. Or not. But I can't see you for a while."

"I can explain—"

"Either you leave or I will."

When the door closed behind him, she grabbed a pillow and sagged against the headboard. Pressing her face against the soft cushion, she yelled into it, allowing it to absorb all of her hurt, anger, shame, and frustration.

She'd wanted distance. She'd gotten distance.

"WHAT'S THE DEAL with you and my brother?"

So much for a pleasant morning of retail therapy, Indi thought.

The Barton Point Plaza was the epitome of elegant yet casual shopping, with a bilevel open-air mall anchored by a restaurant that reminded her of a ski chalet. With the bright sun and cool breeze, she would've loved strolling along the flower-lined walkways getting to know Barbara, but issues with the gala had cropped up, requiring the older woman's attention and Mike had decided to accompany Robert to the country club anyway, a fact for which Indi was immensely grateful. After what had happened between them this morning, she couldn't have borne spending several hours in his company pretending she hadn't been eviscerated by the aftermath of their foreplay.

That had left her in Morgan's custody.

Neither of them appeared to be happy about the situation.

Indi squinted, glad her eyes were hidden behind sunglasses. "Excuse me?"

"You've told my parents some bull story about hanging with Mike while Adam and Chelsea are on their honeymoon—"

"That's not bull," she interrupted.

"Whatevs. I heard Dad and Mike talking about it. He's not happy."

Who? Their father or Mike?

Morgan stopped walking and placed her hands on her hips. "You can lie to our parents about why you're together, but I know there's something else going on."

Great. Mike's little sister fancied herself a modern-day Nancy Drew.

"Morgan—"

"I saw him."

"Saw him what?"

"I saw him coming out of his room."

"Morgan!" An older woman in black pants and a coral cardigan—her pinched expression somehow managing to smile—called from across the courtyard. "Looking forward to the gala tomorrow."

In the brief time since they'd parked the car and traversed the lot to the plaza, numerous people had greeted the young woman, declaring their surprise at seeing her home and asking after her family.

Morgan waved. "I'll tell Mom I saw you, Mrs. Eames."

The woman walked on and Indi pondered Morgan's statement. Did she know something or was she fishing for information?

"It's his room. Where else would he be?"

Morgan raised a delicate brow. "It wasn't where *he* was. It's where *you* were. I saw you coming out of the same room a little later."

Be cool, Indi.

She'd failed in her efforts to keep the pregnancy a secret. And while her condition didn't need to remain private, their relationship—the prior one, there was nothing between them now—should.

"My room wasn't ready and I was tired. It was strictly platonic."

Cool as a baked potato straight out of the oven.

"Yeah, I've heard being pregnant is exhausting. The hormones. Or maybe it's all the effort expended setting traps and digging for gold?" The younger woman crossed her arms and cocked her head to the side, a smirk marring her beautiful features.

Did Morgan find this amusing? Or did the little shit imagine this was a scene from one of those god-awful reality shows? It made her think of the women she met in Charleston. Who thought they could utter any insulting or demeaning affront as long as it was followed by a syrupy sweet "Bless her heart."

A red haze clouded her vision.

"It's true," she said, her tone acerbic. "Before the pregnancy, I'd never have been rude enough to ask how it feels to be adopted, considering the Blacks aren't your real parents. Or, what's going on with Stanford? Are you dropping out because you can't hack it? But it's like you said, I'm experiencing these exhausting pregnancy hormones. What's *your* excuse?"

Agony bloomed on Morgan's features and guilt curdled Indi's satisfaction. She tilted her chin upward and gazed at the bright sky. "I'm sure I can find my way back to the house. Why don't you go hang out with your friends or something?"

She spun on her heel and headed away from Morgan. She'd actually started to feel better after the incident yesterday, due in large part to her conversation with Barbara and her night with Mike. But her *morning* with Mike and this encounter with his sister was just the push she needed to reestablish her guard and remember her place. Which was alone. She wasn't a part of this or any other family, despite Mike and Barbara's nice words.

If it were up to her, she'd go back to the house, pack her things, and make her way back to San Francisco on the next train. But she wasn't sure she wanted to call Mike's bluff regarding the bail. Plus, if she left, Morgan might disclose their argument as the reason why and despite her attitude, Indi didn't want to cause trouble between her and her brother.

She passed a small boutique where the window showcased various sheaths in classic muted tones. She'd never consider these dresses; they looked confining, unimaginative, uninspired. But she wanted to blend in, not stand out, and this seemed like the clothes people would wear at the gala.

"May I help you?" The saleswoman smiled.

Indi slipped off her shades and tightened her fingers on the strap of her shoulder bag. "I need a dress for a gala tomorrow night."

"The Chamber of Commerce event for Robert Black? Cutting it close," the brunette observed. She strode over to a rack and waved her hand, like a spokesmodel on *The Price Is Right*. "These are our most popular styles."

Indi smiled in thanks and flipped through the hangers with little enthusiasm. Black, off black, jet black. Light beige, honey beige, golden beige. Were they the only colors? Navy too racy? She closed her eyes, wiggled her fingers, and let her hand drop on fabric. *Tell her what she won, Bob!* Was it the honey beige or the off black?

Did it matter?

"That's not the dress you're going to wear, is it?"

Indi stiffened at Morgan's voice. She opened her eyes to find the young woman skimming through the garments, her nose wrinkled.

"Why?" She may not be proud of how she responded to Morgan, but that didn't mean she was ready to forgive her.

"Mike is an extremely eligible bachelor and everyone will be interested in the woman on his arm. You'll have to wow them and in this"—Morgan flicked a hanger containing the golden beige dress—"you'll totally blend."

"That's the plan. And I told you, there's nothing between your brother and me."

"Maybe, maybe not." Morgan hesitated and her bravado deflated, like a fallen soufflé, her shoulders sagging. "Either way, I was rude earlier, way out of line. I'm sorry."

Indi softened, believing the remorse to be sincere. "No problem. And I apologize for my comments."

Morgan waved a hand in a manner reminiscent of her

mother. "I deserved it. I was acting like a brat. It's nothing you've done. I . . . I'm having some issues with my father right now and I just wanted to get him off my back. I figured if I could offer Mike up to him, I'd get a break. It was a bitch move."

Don't get involved. It's none of your business.

Yet Morgan's pain was difficult to ignore. She was Mike's sister and Nugget's aunt. If there was something she could do to help the younger woman, she should.

She squeezed Morgan's shoulder. "You want to talk about it?"

Morgan nodded. "But not here. There's a coffee bar a few doors down."

Ten minutes later, they sat on a cobblestone half wall in one of the small courtyards bordering the plaza. Indi took small sips of her mint and honey iced tea—grateful when her belly graciously accepted the offering—and waited for Morgan to initiate the conversation.

Morgan played with the lid of her insulated coffee cup. "Chelsea is your foster sister, right?"

Indi's eyes widened. She'd thought this had to do with Morgan. She was tired of talking about her childhood, had discussed it more in the past week than in the past ten years. She rubbed a hand across her belly and stared at the people walking past the alcove. "Yes."

"Were you ever adopted out of the system?"

Her stomach churned. "No."

"Do you know your parents?"

She glared at Morgan but all she saw was openness and sincerity. She hadn't imagined the other girl's anguish, so she inhaled and called upon a little more patience. "My mother left me when I was really young. I never knew my father."

"You don't remember her?"

"Not really. I have flashes of memory, but she could walk in here and sit next to us and I'm not sure I'd know her."

Not that she hadn't looked.

"I have the opportunity to study abroad for my junior year and I want to go to Seoul, South Korea. It's where I'm from." Morgan sighed and placed her cup on the wall. "My father has a different opinion."

"He doesn't want you to study abroad?"

"Oh no, he'd be happy for me to study abroad. He'd just prefer I went to Europe. When I told him I wanted to see where I was from, he said I was from Barton Point."

Tears added luster to her midnight dark orbs.

"Do you know before college I only saw a handful of people who looked like me?" Morgan dropped her chin to her chest and shook her head. "I was called all kinds of names and I hated how I looked. At night, I would pray to God that I'd wake up in the morning and look like my mother."

Indi's heart broke for the little girl who'd had tons of love, but who'd still grown up feeling like a part of herself was missing.

"I have this memory," Indi whispered, Morgan's pain a mirror image of her own, "of a brown-skinned woman with light brown eyes, in a plaid coat. When I was little I used to look at every black woman who fit that description and wonder if she was my mother. I did that for *years*."

Morgan shifted to face Indi, her body humming with energy. "Then you understand that urgency to know where you come from. I love my family. I'm not trying to hurt them. But I need to learn about my heritage and this will give me the opportunity to do so while I'm getting college credit. I thought Dad would praise my resourcefulness."

Indi pulled Morgan in for a hug. She did understand. It was something she'd wondered her entire life. Fortunately for Morgan, her journey to find her origin story may have a happier ending. There was no reason for Indi to look into her past. She'd been left behind, like garbage.

Isn't that what you're doing with Nugget?

"Is everything okay, Morgan?"

They looked up to see an attractive older couple watching them anxiously.

Morgan wiped her eyes and dredged up a smile. "We're fine, Mrs. Polson. This is India Shaw, a friend of the family."

Mrs. Polson nodded. "We'll see you tomorrow at Robert's party."

"Been looking forward to it," the man—Mr Polson?—said.

"I'll tell my mother I saw you," Morgan parroted.

"Please do. Take care. Good to meet you, Miss Shaw." Mrs. Polson clutched her husband's bicep and the pair continued walking.

Morgan pulled the elastic band from her hair, raked

her fingers through the thick strands, and reset her ponytail high on the crown of head. "That's the problem with being from a notable family in a small town. You're always on display."

Indi saw it from another point of view. "But it's nice to have so many people watching out for you. She didn't know me and thought you looked upset. Something may have been going on, and her intervention might have stopped it."

Morgan fumbled with the scalloped edge of her white T-shirt, a large gold-foil heart emblazoned across the chest. "I guess."

"You're surrounded by people who love you and care about your welfare. As someone who had too little of that, I urge you not to take it for granted."

"I don't. But sometimes love isn't enough."

It wasn't? That was news to Indi; she'd always believed it was. If she'd been lovable enough, her mother would've kept her, her foster parents would've been kinder. She might've found a place to belong.

In her experience, love was the most important thing when you never had enough of it.

"Come on," Morgan said, jumping off the wall. "Let's go shopping. I know a boutique that is perfect for you. Plus, if we're here any longer, Mrs. Polson will probably have the BPPD drive by just to make sure I'm okay."

Indi laughed. "What do you mean by 'perfect for me'?"

"Look at you."

Indi stared down at her ankle boots, jeans, and Aztec-print poncho. "Yeah?"

"You have this genuine boho chic vibe. Exotic, ethereal, but strong. You'd overpower a beige silk sheath. We need to find a dress that's worthy of you." She bumped Indi's shoulder with her own. "One that will make Mike's eyes bulge out of his head."

"There's nothing between your brother and me!"

That's it, baby. Come for me. Show me how good it feels.

"You keep telling yourself that."

Chapter Eighteen

WHEN SKYLAR'S PICTURE flashed across Mike's cell phone screen during golf on Saturday morning, relief lightened the ever-present cache of tension hugging his shoulders. He hadn't stopped reaching out to her since the picture of him and Indi went viral, but she hadn't answered his texts or returned his calls. There was the possibility her distance could be explained by a hectic work schedule, but he knew that wasn't the reason.

She'd been hurt by what she'd seen and he couldn't blame her. That's why they needed to talk.

But it didn't mean he looked forward to doing what had to be done.

He waved off Robert and the other members of their foursome and—ignoring his father's pinched expression—answered the phone.

"Who is she?" Skylar's voice was cool and direct.

He shouldn't have expected anything less.

He wouldn't insult her intelligence—or his—by pretending not to know to whom she was referring. He strode away from the midmorning crowd converging on the clubhouse's patio and headed to a private gazebo bordered by a small pond. It was a breathtaking location, seen in photos of hundreds of weddings the club had hosted over the years.

Ironic.

"She's Chelsea's sister. Her name is India Shaw."

"Did you meet her at the wedding?"

"No. I met her for the first time at their engagement party."

"But you've slept together?"

He stroked his brow, wishing it was that easy to smooth over this situation. He owed Skylar this discussion, but he didn't intend to get into salacious details.

"You and I weren't together when it happened."

"But we're together now." For the first time, a note of ire spiced her tone.

He shoved a hand into his pocket. "We don't need to do this over the phone. We can talk when you get back."

"We need to settle this. I have another week of meetings here in New York and this picture and the questions it invokes are an unwelcome distraction. Are you still involved with her?"

"Not in the way you're probably envisioning, but yes."

"I don't need to imagine anything. I saw the picture."

Had he done this before, broken off a relationship? He must have and yet he couldn't remember it being this difficult, though he knew he was doing the right thing.

He dropped onto the bench, removed his sunglasses, and inserted the stem into the collar of his shirt.

"This isn't going to work out, is it?" Skylar quietly asked.

"No." If there were a silver lining, it would be that he hadn't proposed to her. Breaking an engagement would've been worse.

"That's a shame. I think we would've made a hell of a team."

He agreed and that was the problem. They'd both approached their relationship as another business opportunity. They'd taken turns canceling their dates if more pressing work matters came up. And when they did get together, they'd been strategic in choosing the right venues, to maximize the benefits to their respective companies.

Nothing about Indi's arrival into his life had been convenient and yet he'd made time for her. Being with her emphasized the enjoyment, the happiness, and the fun that had been missing with Skylar.

"You don't need me to tell you this: you're a fantastic woman. You're smart, beautiful, successful. The perfect catch, just not for me."

"You're right, I don't need you to tell me." A slight pause. "But it's nice to hear."

His gaze darted over the golf course, noting the contrasting light and dark green lines mowed into the fairway from the tee to the putting green. Now the question he needed to ask, but, considering what he'd just done . . .

Ah, hell.

However, before the universe could brand him a grade-A son of a bitch, she said, "I'll talk to Dad about the OTTo deal."

"Are you going to support the deal or advise against it?"

He was prepared for either outcome. If Skylar and her father decided not to proceed with the deal Mike had offered, he'd simply explore other options. The non-compete clause in the contract Franklin Thompson had signed when they'd toured the Industrial Design Lab applied only to TTL approaching another tech company. It had no effect on Computronix's ability to seek out an alternate cable media conglomerate.

"Would it change the status of our relationship?" she asked.

What the fuck? He'd considered the notion she'd reject the idea of them working together, but to use the deal to force him to remain in the relationship? "No."

"That's what I figured." She sighed. "Your offer is a good one and I'm excited about the prospect of being first in this new arena. He may be reluctant because of the change in our situation, but I'll advise him to accept it."

Something she said bothered him, but the billow of gratitude filling his chest engulfed that small displeasure. He exhaled. "Thank you."

"Give me a few weeks to complete our work here and put together the team who'll be working on the project. We'll be in touch."

His company would assemble its own group whose job it would be to work with their TTL counterpart on the logistics of the project and bring it to fruition. From start to finish, it could be a couple of years before Computronix and TTL were ready to announce the joint venture. Hopefully, enough time would have passed that when he and Skylar needed to interact, they could do so without tension.

"Good-bye, Mike."

"Skylar, wait," he called out, identifying the comment that chafed like clothing against a newly acquired sunburn. "You said you 'figured.' Figured what? That I wouldn't change my mind? Knowing how important this deal was to me, why did you make that assumption?"

"Because in all the time we dated, you never looked at me the way you're looking at her in that picture."

When the call ended, he placed his cell on the bench beside him and released a huge breath. It was done. For the first time since Indi had reappeared in his life, the weight of juggling multiple expectations had been lifted from him. He was no longer torn between what he wanted and his responsibilities. He was free to pursue Indi with no barriers or pretense between them.

It was the reason he'd pulled away from her this morning. Wrapped around her body as she'd moaned in pleasure from his kisses and caresses, he'd been a heartbeat away from sliding his throbbing cock into her warm, wet heat and satisfying the gnawing hunger that had been building since their weekend together all those months ago. But in the end, he couldn't go through with it. He hadn't wanted to taint the possibility of their future together with accusations of infidelity. Both women deserved more than that.

He grabbed his phone. And now . . .

"Go ahead and draft the TTL contracts," Mike said several moments later when he'd connected with Sully.

The calendar may proclaim it a Saturday morning, but Mike knew he'd find the attorney in his office, hard at work.

"The deal's going through?"

"Probably. I want to be ready in case it does."

Sully whistled. "I'd assumed flowers were played out. Nice to know going old-school can yield dividends."

Mike frowned. "What are you talking about?"

"The bouquet you ordered for Skylar."

He realized he'd need to be prepared to answer queries about their breakup. Something simple and discreet that would leave no doubt about the status of their association but wouldn't feed the cheap gossips.

"Skylar and I ended our relationship."

That worked. And when delivered with his the-matter-is-closed tone, it should be enough to stunt any further questions.

"She broke up with you?"

Except, he was talking to Sully. A man who'd fight a junkyard dog for a bone he wanted . . . and win. The downside of working with men he respected and liked enough to consider friends. Although Adam would never have asked. Not because he didn't care, but because he'd have assumed Mike would talk further about it if he wanted to.

"It was a mutual decision."

"I'd call 'bullshit' but if the deal's alive it must be true.

Scorned women aren't known for being generous toward those who've spurned them. What does this mean for you and India?"

"It means I'm going for it."

"Good. Meeting with Kenneth DeRosen is a good start."

This had nothing to do with issues of custody regarding the baby. The unresolved nature of his relationship with Skylar had been bothering him, not because of concerns about the deal, but because he knew he couldn't move forward with Indi until things with Skylar were settled. Now that they were and he'd admitted to himself what he wanted, there was nothing standing in the way.

"Not just the baby, Sully. All of it. The baby, Indi, *and* me. I'm going for it all."

"Dude, you're the steadiest guy I know but in the span of a week and a half you've been . . . unpredictable."

"Is that a bad thing?"

Not that Sully's opinion would change what he felt, but it'd be nice to know his friend supported his decision.

"Are you sure? Is there a chance you're confusing your feelings for her with what you feel for the baby?"

It was a good question. He thought back to their weekend together, to how she'd evoked feelings in him he hadn't experienced before, how charged he'd been to see where it could lead.

And the absolute rage he'd felt when he'd awakened to find her gone.

No, his feelings for Indi had been engaged long before he'd known about the baby.

"I appreciate your having my back, but I'm not confused about anything."

"Then congratulations. I'm happy for you. I'll get started on the contracts."

Mike disconnected the call.

What to do now?

He knew what he wanted. But Indi seemed set on believing their involvement was a short-term proposition. Even if she agreed to give him Nugget, she still seemed to think she'd be leaving him after she had the baby. He knew he had an effect on her, that his feelings weren't one-sided. He also knew she could connect to another person; after all, there was her deep love for Chelsea.

He just needed Indi to see that Chelsea wasn't the only person to whom she could entrust her heart.

"HI THERE, MIKE," a voice called out. "You waiting to get a manicure or a pedicure?"

He straightened from his spot reclining on the wooden bench outside the local day spa and smiled at one of his mother's friends when she and her dog stopped to chat. "Neither, Mrs. Stone."

"Barbara got her nails done on Thursday, so you can't be waiting for her. I heard Morgan was in town. She's probably getting something outrageous done for your father's gala. You know how the kids are these days."

He bent down to pet her cocker spaniel and nodded noncommittally, seeing no reason to disabuse her of her incorrect notion.

"The new *People* magazine came out yesterday. Your partner and his new wife were on the cover. They even had pictures inside of the ceremony." Mrs. Stone winked at him. "You looked very handsome."

His new smile was forced, though he doubted the other woman could tell the difference. "Thank you."

He'd forgotten about the release of the issue with Adam and Chelsea on the cover. He hadn't heard anything from Anya. He wondered if anyone had put two and two together and verified the woman in the picture with him from the Youth Alliance event was Chelsea's sister.

"I'm looking forward to tomorrow night. My daughter's in town and she'll be attending with me." Mrs. Stone wiggled her fingers in farewell. "Maybe I'll tell her to save you a dance?"

He waved as she continued down the street. He pulled his phone out to check the time, then shifted on the bench. It shouldn't be much longer now.

As soon as he'd finished his call with Sully, he'd begged off lunch and drinks at the country club. He'd intended to spend the rest of the day with Indi and that required some special planning on his part.

He wasn't above bribery. If letting her experience the perks of being with someone in his position and seeing that he was willing and more than able to provide for a family is what it took to convince her they could raise Nugget together, as a family, then that's what he'd do. Fuck stoicism. He'd plan and scheme like a general taking a pivotal hill in battle if it got him what he wanted in the end.

And what he wanted was Indi and their baby. More than he'd ever wanted anything in his life.

The door next to him opened and Indi stepped from the building, her face shining, her eyes bright. When she caught sight of him, uncertainty eclipsed her features and she faltered for a fraction of an instant, before heading over to him.

He stood. "Did you have a good time?"

"The massage was fantastic." She looked away and fingered a braid, before swinging her gaze back to him. "Thank you."

Delicate bubbles of satisfaction rose in his chest. "I'm glad you enjoyed it. When I mentioned your nausea they suggested an aromatherapy session."

"I was worried at first—aromatherapy can involve some concentrated, intense scents—but the technician said they had a delicate blend that worked well for a lot of their pregnant clients." She held up a little black satchel adorned with the spa's logo. "They gave me a sample to take home."

If it managed to mitigate her queasiness, he'd ask his mother to pick up a larger order for Indi and ship it to him.

"When Morgan dropped me off after shopping and lunch, I didn't expect anyone to pick me up. I could've made my way back to the house."

"I didn't mind waiting." *Come on, Mike. Be real.* "Actually, I wanted to."

She studied him, her manner slightly cautious. "It's a beautiful spa. And really popular. When did you have time to make the reservation?"

"This morning after golf."

"And they managed to fit me in on such short notice?"

He nodded. An appointment opened up . . . after he'd dropped his name.

She bit her lower lip. "Why?"

He almost groaned. That lush bottom lip would be his undoing. "Why what?"

"The massage, your waiting for me. They're sweet gestures, but . . . I mean, after this morning, why are you doing this?"

He knew she wasn't ready to hear the lengths he'd go to in order to make them a family, but there was one thing he could tell her that was long overdue.

"To apologize." He reached for her hand, his fingers sliding against her palm. "For forcing you to come and deal with my family when you could've stayed back in San Francisco and for putting you in an awkward position by acting on my interest in you while still being with Skylar. I'm sorry."

She inhaled sharply and stared down at their joined hands. "I accept your apology." She smiled. "As funny as it sounds, I'm glad I came. Your mother is a sweetheart and I even enjoyed spending time with Morgan."

"How was shopping with her?"

"Well, the beginning wasn't a walk in the park, although we *were* in a courtyard of sorts . . ."

He laughed, glad that she was talking to him again. "But it turned out well?"

"Yeah. We had a long talk."

"I hope it helped."

Between her desire to leave school and her outburst at him during their conversation last night, it was hard to ignore that his little sister had acquired a bit of an edge.

"She's growing up and trying to find her place in the world. It's hard to know how far you can go when you don't know where you're starting from," Indi said, in a voice that hinted the words were more than a slogan on a framed wall hanging.

That didn't make any sense to him. They were Morgan's family. She came from right there in Barton Point. She'd had a privileged upbringing, just as he had. She could go far. It was expected that she go far.

But the last thing he wanted to do this afternoon was to get into a discussion about adoption. Even if they were only discussing Morgan, he didn't want Indi to equate his sister's situation with Nugget's. Instead he wanted to focus on him and Indi as a couple, and soon, with Nugget's birth, a family.

"Would you like to go for a walk before dinner?"

"What about your family? Shouldn't you spend time with them?"

"My mother will be finishing her checklist for the gala tomorrow night and my father . . ." He shrugged. He didn't really care what his father would be doing.

He continued to hold her hand as they strolled along parts of the downtown area. When they passed certain places, his subconscious would call up memories from his childhood and hanging out with his friends. He'd never anticipated moving back to Barton Point, but there were areas around the Computronix campus that possessed a similar small-town vibe. Maybe they should consider making Palo Alto their permanent home base. Provide Nugget an upbringing similar to his own.

"What do you think about Augustus?"

"I don't know him."

"Not the person, whoever he may be. As a name."

Her head jerked back. "For who?"

"For Nugget. He'd never forgive us if we didn't come up with something else to call him."

Her fingers tightened around his. "I'm not raising him, so it doesn't matter what I think."

"But if you were . . . what kind of names would you like?"

She tried to pull her hand away. "This is stupid."

He wouldn't let her. "Come on. I'm curious."

She exhaled forcibly and was silent so long he thought she wouldn't answer him. Then she said, "John. David. Thomas."

"Really? They're so boring."

"Exactly. Those are the names you always find on pencils and magnets and cups. When I was little, I'd see kids with those little license plates engraved with their names. Mary. Beth. Sue." She shook her head. "They never had unusual names like India."

"I had the opposite experience. I didn't think there was anything cool or memorable about Mike." He lowered his voice. "Don't tell anyone, but secretly, I yearned for a name like Jagger or Axl."

"Who would I tell?" she asked, laughter spilling from her, as she leaned into him, her upper body shaking with her mirth. He reveled in her amusement, in his power to bring her a different kind of enjoyment.

"What about Michael Jr.? Or MJ?" she asked, when she'd finally caught her breath.

He grimaced. "Uh, no."

"Why not?"

"Because I'd want him to carve out his own identity. I never want him to feel that he has to follow in my footsteps."

He was realizing the unconscious burden of carrying that expectation. He wouldn't do that to his son.

They passed a baby store and he stopped. The last time he'd pushed her to celebrate the pregnancy, he'd gotten her to consider letting him raise Nugget instead of putting him up for adoption. The stakes were higher now. "Wanna go in?"

"No."

"I won't buy anything. Let's just look."

She jerked her hand from his and took several steps away from him. "What are you doing?"

"I thought we'd look in the store."

Her eyes widened. "You're unbelievable!"

He knew she didn't mean that in the good way.

"It's not a big deal." He shifted to allow a few women to pass around them and enter the establishment. "We can keep walking."

Her voice got louder. "The pictures, discussing baby names, and now you're trying to get me into that store?"

A few people stared in open curiosity. He grabbed her arm. "We can't discuss this here."

At the end of the block they rounded the corner to a side street where there were fewer pedestrians.

She turned on him. "Your arrogance is astonishing! Stop pushing me to do what you want me to do. I told you I'm not raising this baby."

"You might change your mind."

"I won't. You don't understand."

"You're right, I don't. Why don't you want to raise him? You already told me that you love him and it can't be the money; I said I'd pay child support. You wouldn't have to work another day in your life."

"It's not about your money!"

"Then what is it about? Help me to understand."

She crossed her arms over her chest, tightened her lips, and shook her head.

"Are you going to let me raise him?"

Her bark of laughter was devoid of real amusement. She tilted her head skyward. "You want to raise him, but you don't even realize what it'll mean."

"What are you talking about?"

A tiny cynical smile marred the perfection of her mouth. "Do you understand he won't be like you?"

He narrowed his eyes. "Explain."

"He'll be biracial. Half black, half white."

"I know that," he said, insulted by her insinuation.

"But do you *understand* what that means? He may have some of your features, but superficially, he may not look like you. Are you ready for that? For the stares you'll get, the assumption that he isn't yours or that you adopted him? Will you be ready to answer his questions about why he looks different and how that makes him feel?"

He hadn't considered those issues and he should've. But they didn't change what he wanted.

"What about Skylar? How do you think she'll feel raising another woman's child? She'll get those same stares, those same questions? Have you thought about that?"

"Skylar's reaction isn't important any—"

"The hell it isn't! An entire genre was founded on the premise of the evil stepmother. I don't want my child to be the recipient of her negative attitude, whatever its source."

"I get what you're trying to tell me, but won't this be a concern for any adoptive family?

They all will have to deal with those stares, answer those questions. Have *you* thought of *that*? Unless you plan to limit Nugget's chances of being adopted by specifying he can only be placed with an interracial couple?"

Her posture sagged, like the anger that had held her upright suddenly abandoned her. "I—"

He cupped her shoulders. "I'd never let anyone say or do anything to hurt our child. Skylar's reaction," he didn't miss Indi's flinch when he said the other woman's name, "isn't important because I'm not involved with her anymore. We ended things."

She stiffened. "What?" Not waiting for his response, she brought her arms up to break his hold. "No! That's not what I wanted. Please tell me it didn't have anything to do with me."

He couldn't lie to her.

"I can't. It had everything to do with you."

Chapter Nineteen

THE IDEA THAT Mike had broken off his relationship with Skylar—because of her!—had sent Indi into a tailspin. Her heart pounded frantically in her chest and she'd shifted into airplane safety mode, her gaze ricocheting around the area, searching for the nearest exit. Mike must've taken one look at her face and seen her intent to flee because he'd ushered her to the car before the thought to run in the opposite direction had taken root in her mind.

He'd driven a few miles out of town to a gorgeous, modern bed-and-breakfast perched on a cliff's edge.

"This place serves the best dinner in town. I made reservations for us, but now . . . Let's get a room where you can relax and calm down and we can talk about this away from the intrusive and opinionated eyes and ears of my family."

Which is how she found herself standing in the center

of a large bedroom decorated in a warm but neutral palette, the only concession to color being the brilliant blues of the ocean and sky and the vivid greens of the trees and lawn seen through the glass sliders.

But Indi wasn't in the proper frame of mind to appreciate the beauty of her surroundings.

"Just last night you were telling me how important this arrangement with her company would be to Computronix and now you're telling me you broke off your relationship and risked the deal? Because of me?"

"I'm not worried about the deal."

"How can you say that?"

"OTTo will still become a reality, whether it's with TTL or some other cable company."

She rubbed her fist against the tightness in her chest. His answer should've mollified her. Instead, her irritation grew. Because her feelings had nothing to do with the deal. He was hurtling every obstacle between them until he'd finally be close enough to see he'd wasted his time. He'd realize there was nothing lovable about her. And to hear him say the words—

"I'm tired of talking about Skylar and Computronix," Mike said. "I want to talk about us."

She glared at him. "There is no *us*. We're having a baby, that's all."

"It's more than that, and you know it."

"You're delusional. Don't be stupid. Call Skylar. Ask for her forgiveness."

"No."

Desperation clawed at her insides. She strode over to

the door and slammed her hand against it, the reclaimed material rough against her palm.

"I'm going to leave," she threatened, her back to him. "I'll walk out of this room and never look back."

His voice, when it came, was the embodiment of calm. "If you do, I'll just follow you."

She let her arm drop to her side as she turned and propped herself against the door. "Why won't you just give up?"

He crossed the room and stood close enough to invade her personal space and make her aware of him. "It's not in my nature."

Damn him. He was stripping away her defenses, one layer at a time. She'd give anything to believe in his pursuit, to consider what would happen if she gave in to him and let him close, let him in. But she didn't need to assume. She knew. She couldn't surrender to his demand. The risk was too high.

She stared up at him, played her ace. "What if I let you raise Nugget?"

He didn't know she was already leaning in that direction. That her discussion with Morgan had cultivated the idea that it might be better for Nugget to be reared by one of his parents than by strangers, especially considering the issues he might face.

Mike slowly shook his head.

"Why not?" She had to try one more time. She pushed against his chest; the solid muscle failed to yield. "What more do you want from me?"

He braced his left arm on the door and leaned in until

he was all she could see and hear, his scent permeating the very air she breathed.

"I want to finish what we started this morning," he said, tracing a finger down her cheek and along her jawline. "And this time I don't want to stop until I'm so deep inside of you, I can't tell where I end and you begin."

Warmth suffused her entire body. Dear God. How was she supposed to respond to that?

He kissed her, his lips brushing against hers in the softest of caresses. Back and forth at first, and then, taking little nips, like she was a delicacy to savor and relish. She wanted to resist him, to meet his intoxicating tenderness with reserve, but her defiance evaporated into a puddle of longing at her feet. From the moment they'd first touched, her body had trumpeted what her brain had tried to ignore: she was in danger of losing her heart—her very soul—to this man.

His tongue swept confidently inside, sure of its welcome and right to be there, while his right hand slid beneath her top and settled on her waist, squeezing the bare skin and sending bolts of pleasure careening to her nerve endings.

He broke the kiss and she murmured a protest, not wanting to sacrifice the delicious sensations flooding her. She opened her eyes in time to catch his struggle for control. His chest rose and fell harshly and a slight flush bloomed upon his cheekbones. He clenched and released his hands.

"Are you okay?" she asked, smoothing her hands across his broad shoulders clad in a navy blue and white striped polo shirt.

"It's been a while since we've done this. I'm determined to take my time."

He drew her away from the wall and toward the enormous four-poster bed situated in the middle of the room. He spun her around until her knees touched the mattress and she fell back onto the plush bed. Squatting down in front of her, he proceeded to slip off her boot.

She tightened her leg. "I can do it."

He glanced up at her, his eyes the clear sparkling blue of an aquamarine gemstone. "I know. You can do anything you put your mind to. But I want to do it for you."

When he put it like that, all reasonable and romantic, how could she refuse?

He removed her other boot. "Stand up."

She did. He unfastened the button on her jeans and lowered the zipper. The promise in that sound caused her breath to catch in the back of her throat. Hooking his hands in the waistband, he pulled the denim over her hips and down her legs. He helped her step out of them and when she would've reclined on the bed, he gripped her hips tightly.

"Not yet."

At the sight of this powerful man on his knees before her, she was inundated with a swell of feminine power. He lavished hot kisses on her belly and when his tongue flicked and teased her navel, she grabbed the back of his head and pressed him closer, her body trembling in anticipation of that tongue stroking her just a little lower. She slid her fingers through his hair, mussing it to acti-

vate his curls. She gripped those thick strands tightly as
his tongue rasped along the waistband of her panties.

Then those, too, were discarded and tossed over his
shoulder and she was naked from the waist down. There
was something sinfully erotic about her position—

"Spread your legs for me."

—but she felt no embarrassment. During their time
together he'd seen, teased, and kissed every part of her
body and vice versa.

She went a step further, lifting a foot and placing it on
the bed rail.

He groaned and his expression tightened. "Aww, babe,
what are you trying to do to me?"

"I'm only giving you what you want."

Licking his lips, he spread her folds until her very core
was laid bare before him. His thumb disappeared into
his mouth for a brief second and then it was back, rubbing against her clit, pressing inward and upward with
a skillful ease that powered her desire. She watched him,
transfixed by the intensity on his face as he stared at her
pussy. Finally, he looked up and the glittering fever in his
gaze flayed her.

"I'm going to devour this sweet pussy and make you
come so hard you can't breathe."

And he did.

Time and space receded until she existed in a vortex
of pleasure. In a distant part of her mind—the one that
existed purely for her survival, telling her when to inhale,
exhale, and swallow—she hoped no one occupied the

room next to them. She couldn't have kept quiet if her life depended on it.

"Hmmm, I love the sounds you make," he said, groaning and clutching her tighter. "I could come from that alone."

He adored her with his tongue as if he were being graded on his technique and nothing less than an A plus would do. He varied his approach, alternating between a stiff, probing tongue that burrowed into her clit with sweet pressure and a slow, rhythmic tongue that lapped her folds and clit jointly with one wide and languid lick. One. The other. Both. It all drove her wild. And when he slid two fingers inside of her and said, "You taste so fucking good, I can't get enough," his hot breath ruffling her sensitive nub, she almost came. Possibility became reality when he curled those fingers upward and massaged the magic spot along the front inner wall of her pussy.

The orgasm that ripped through her was so vivid, it *did* steal her breath. She bucked, writhed, and trembled while he held on tightly around her waist, licking, sucking, and finger fucking her until the storm passed. Her legs gave out and she collapsed back on the duvet like a limp noodle.

He rose to his full height and, his eyes never leaving hers, slowly brushed the back of his hand across his wet, glistening mouth.

Sweet Jesus.

He swung her legs around until she was lying fully on the bed. "Don't go anywhere."

Air was taking its sweet ass time filtering back into her lungs. "Where would I go?"

She couldn't move now if the Dalai Lama himself demanded it.

"Taking your presence for granted is a mistake I don't plan to repeat."

Oh, she had a response for that, but then he was stripping off his shirt and it was so damn distracting. Forming words was impossible when faced with the smooth expanse of his broad chest and the sleek muscles in his biceps and forearms. His abs were hard and flat but not ripped like some action figure come to life or a 'roided-out gym rat.

He was perfect. She could gaze at him forever.

"I'll trade you."

Why was he still all the way over there? She forced herself to focus on his words. "What?"

The corner of his mouth ticked up. "Between us we could clothe another person. Your shirt for my pants."

She'd been wrong. She could move. She just needed the right motivation.

She grabbed the hem of her shirt, intending to rip it off when he shook his head.

"We have forever together. There's no need to rush. Take your time."

She wanted to correct him—who said anything about forever?—when she noticed the gleam in his eye, the supreme confidence in his stance. He was feeling really good about himself. And he should be. He'd delivered on his promise. But she couldn't let him think a mind-blowing, earth-shattering orgasm would always render her more compliant. It would, but he didn't need to know that.

Take her time? Ask and ye shall receive.

She lowered her eyes and let her lashes drop as she rose up on her knees. She rested her hand at the base of her throat, let her fingers play in the divot between her neck and collarbone before walking them over to one shoulder and then skimming them across to the other.

"Indi?" he whispered.

She lifted her gaze to meet his. Saw the shock, heat, and hunger stamped across his features. She slid her tongue out to dampen her bottom lip, before clenching it beneath her teeth.

He swallowed. And his cock rammed against the front of his pants.

He unbuttoned them and pushed them off his hips, but she shook *her* head when he reached for her.

Now this part would be tricky. She knew *what* to do, but she'd never tried it. Still, the look on his face—like he was on a low carb diet and she was a hot buttered dinner roll—was enough to motivate her to continue.

She crossed her arms, grabbed the hem of her shirt, and stretched it down and away from her body. Undulating her torso counter-clockwise, she lifted the garment over her head in one fluid movement and let it fall off the bed.

Score!

She shook her head, letting the fall of her braids hide her exhilarated smile.

Almost done . . .

She reached behind her and undid her bra, tossing it in a wide arc to land on the floor across the room. His eyes followed the garment, but snapped back to her form, as if he couldn't wait to see what she did next.

Hiding her smile, she bent forward and shimmied her shoulders, letting her breasts jiggle. She palmed them, holding one in each hand and then compressing them together, so they met in the middle of her chest, squeezing her throbbing nipples between her index and middle fingers. She arched her back and tilted her head to the side, letting him take it all in, before falling back onto her elbows, her legs crossed, her body completely naked.

The air in the room was so charged she could feel sparks of electricity dancing upon her skin.

Mike cleared his throat. Twice. "What the fuck was that?"

"Bartender in a Burlesque club. Vegas."

She blinked and he was out of his pants. He growled and pounced on the bed, yanking her ankle so she fell flat on her back as he hovered on all fours above her.

"Look at me." He gritted his teeth, determined to get the words out despite the effort it cost him. "No more running away from me. I'm in this for the long haul and we'll figure it out. Together."

He leaned forward and braced himself on his elbows, so he didn't burden her with his weight. When he slid into her, the intimate fullness of their joining made her dizzy.

He froze and his brows slammed together. "Is this okay? You on your back?"

She was more than okay. She was tremendous, fantastic, exceptional. Nothing had ever felt this good. How had she ever thought she'd be able to put it behind her and move on?

She nodded and tightened her inner muscles around him. He mumbled something inaudible and began to slowly stroke inside her, the ridges of his engorged cock grazing against her sensitized flesh with each joining and departure.

She slid her fingers through the hair at his nape, down the sides of his neck, across his shoulders. She wanted to touch him everywhere. She couldn't be close enough, wanted to take all of him, to consume him and be consumed by him.

"I've missed this pussy. It's mine . . ."

Ooh, dirty talk. Yes . . .

"Ahh, this pussy missed you . . . fingers and vibrator not cutting it . . ."

" . . . vibrator not doing it right. You'll have to show me . . ."

She raked her nails into his defined pecs, dragged them down his abs and around to his firm ass, squeezing the flesh and trying to bring him closer, but it was physically impossible.

Her head thrashed back and forth on the pillow, the pleasure almost too intense to handle. He captured her mouth with a kiss, stilling her while quickening his pace. It didn't take long to revive the tingles that pulsed in her lower belly. They'd lain dormant after the first time, but they'd never gone completely away. They roused and sparked to life and she strained for them, eager to experience the fireworks again, only this time he'd be there with her. So close . . .

"Mike, baby, don't stop . . ."

She lifted her hips, met him thrust for thrust.

"That's it. You're so fucking beautiful when you come. Come for me . . ."

His words tipped the scales and sent her soaring as light exploded behind her eyelids and her body shuddered and quaked in the stunning aftermath of her climax. He sped up his pace, his movements losing all semblance of coordination and control as his body slammed into hers and he roared her name, following her into the chasm.

When she'd finally taken in enough air to speak, Indi said, "She didn't know what the hell she was talking about."

He lifted himself off her and she smiled at the dazed, clouded look on his face. He peered down at her. "Who?"

"The fabulous and fertile celebrity mom from that pregnancy book. My sex dreams couldn't hold a candle to you."

INDI LAY ON Mike's chest, his arm thrown casually around her shoulder, her fingers trailing across his smooth skin. His heart beat soundly beneath her hand. They'd cracked opened the glass doors a little while ago, and the faint sounds of the crashing surf struggled up to serenade them. She hadn't wanted to disturb the peace they'd managed to find, but something was nagging at her and she needed an answer.

"When I talked to your mother last night, she mentioned you used to be different when you were younger. More carefree and easygoing. At first I thought she must be joking, but she wasn't. She didn't say what happened, just hinted something had."

He exhaled and Indi's head rose and fell with the movement. "When I was sixteen, I disobeyed my parents and snuck out on a school night to hang with some friends. I knew I wasn't supposed to—my gut was telling me it was wrong and I could hear my father's voice in my head—but I was so tired of his goddamn lectures."

He lifted his head and braced his folded arm behind it. "They'd been drinking before I even got there. I figured I'd stick around and make sure everyone got home safely, only . . . one of the boys wanted to climb the cliffs. I told him no, but he didn't listen, and the other guys kept egging him on, so I got annoyed. I started to leave, but then I heard this yell. I turned and I saw Greg— He'd lost his balance. That moment where he teetered on the edge— I tried to run back up and—I don't know, grab him and pull him back—but it was too late. He fell and broke his neck."

Though there had been some starts and stops, he'd delivered the entire tale in a flat monotone.

She gasped. That's *not* what she'd been expecting.

"No! Oh, Mike. Baby, I'm so sorry." She threw her

arms around him as a slight tremor coursed through his body.

"It was my fault. I knew we shouldn't have been there. If only I'd tried harder to convince them not to climb the cliffs."

He squeezed her close even as he threw an arm over his eyes. She pressed soft kisses across his chest and up the side of his neck, wanting to impart any comfort she could.

"Did you get in trouble?"

"No. We all told the police what happened. The other kids got citations for drinking in public. A boy died and I got nothing. I should've listened to my dad."

She wasn't going to sit there and witness his self-flagellation.

She grasped his chin in her hand and turned his head to face her. "You were a kid. You did what kids do. You snuck out to be with your friends. You didn't drink. You definitely didn't push him. Those were his choices."

"But I was the sober one. If I'd only tried harder to talk them out of climbing the cliffs—"

"I want you to think about what happened and how much blame you're carrying around today. Then I want you to pretend Nugget had been in your situation."

He hissed and his body actually jerked beneath her hands.

"Would you want him to suffer the way you are? The correlation between what happened and your responsibility for it isn't accurate. Let the guilt go. It's not contributing to anything. It's only eating you up inside."

He pulled in a deep shaky breath and closed his eyes. She hoped he was considering what she'd said. The idea that he'd shouldered such guilt at a young age saddened her.

She kissed his chest. "You're a good man, Mike," she whispered.

His lashes flew up. "I'm not looking for compliments."

"I don't think you hear this one often enough. And I'm talking about you, not your company or your accomplishments. There are a lot of people in this town who respect your father and I'm sure he's done some amazing things. But you are an amazing person. You struck out on your own when it would've been easier to accept the life your father was willing to hand you. You helped your best friend find love, even when doing so could have negatively affected your company, you're almost single-handedly supporting a youth housing shelter for the next five years, and despite the rude way I handled our initial parting, you posted my bail when I called and accepted my word about Nugget without a paternity test. You're even willing to raise him on your own. Nugget will be lucky to have you."

His muscles tightened beneath her cheek. "Does that mean what I think it means?"

No take-backsies. "Does it have to mean anything?"

He rose, his muscles flexing and releasing, and pulled her to a sitting position. His light blue gaze searched hers. "You're damn right it does."

"Okay, fine. Yes, I've changed my mind about the adoption. You can raise Nugget."

He didn't let her go. "And you'll give us a chance? I mean, if I'm as amazing as you say I am . . ."

She tried to pull away but the stubborn man wouldn't let her. She looked down at fingers that twisted the ecru colored duvet. "Doesn't all of this seem like it's happening too fast? It hasn't even been two full weeks."

His hand cupped her cheek and combed through her braids. "When two people connect, the length of their acquaintance is irrelevant."

She grabbed his wrist, brought the back of his hand to her lips. "I wasn't expecting this. Everything's happening so fast and I need some time. Can we keep it between us? For a little while longer?"

It would give her the opportunity to learn if she could trust her feelings, to work on giving up her independence, to see if she were ready to accept this family they'd created . . . and to try to overcome the agonizing fear that they wouldn't accept *her*.

HOURS LATER, IN the early morning light, Indi stared at the man lying next to her. When animated, he was the most exhilarating person she'd ever known. But when slumber softened the edges of his face, her heart hurt with the effort it took to contain her emotions. He wanted her and, God help her, she wanted him, too. She had no idea if their relationship, or their family, could work, but they had about five months before Nugget was born to see what would happen.

And she didn't intend to waste any second of it.

She tossed the blanket aside and trailed her hand down his naked body until her fingers grazed his dick nestled in a thatch of dark blond curls. She took it in her hand and smiled slightly as it began to grow and harden. She felt the graze of his knuckles against her cheek and her mouth watered. She started with his nipples, flicking her tongue against the rosettes until they pebbled. She kissed and licked her way down his torso, rubbing her chin against the bristled path that led straight to what she desired.

She took him in her mouth, his musky scent driving her insane. She fondled him with her right hand while her tongue worked the deep ridge at the base of his head. The moisture from her salivating lips slid down his shaft and helpfully lubricated her firm strokes. When she tasted the bloom of his precum, she moaned and opened her mouth as wide as she could to take him in further.

She felt his hands tangle in her braids and she smiled against him but she didn't stop what she was doing. She suctioned her cheeks, as she worked him in and out, her tongue sliding alongside the bottom half of his cock, the roof of her mouth massaging the top. His hips began to pump, and the notion that he was fucking her face was such a turn-on she slid a hand down to play among her drenched and swollen folds.

"If your goal is for me to come in your mouth, you're close to succeeding." A lethargic passion weighted his voice.

She withdrew from his cock with a soft *pop.* "Next time. I promise."

He studied her from beneath heavy-lidded eyes. "It seems we're assembling a substantial fucking to-do list. It may take a long time to work our way through it."

She straddled him and bent forward to press a wet, hot, openmouthed kiss to his lips, her ass in the air. She straightened . . . and slid down on his shaft.

They sighed in unison.

Bracing her hands on his chest, she arched her back and rotated her hips, grinding her clit against his pelvis. He groaned and dug his fingers into her hips as she shivered at the remembered pleasure gathering low in her belly.

"You can do it, Mike. You're the most determined man I know."

Chapter Twenty

HIS BODY HUMMED like a tuning fork out of pitch, seeking the source of its recalibration.

Where was she?

Mike leaned against the back of a chair and once again checked the time on his phone. With the visual confirmation that only ten minutes had elapsed since his last inspection instead of the hour he'd feared, he slid the device back into the inner pocket of his tuxedo jacket and tipped his head back to glare mutinously up at the ceiling. Early evening sunlight poured in through the great room's glass walls, projecting shadow lines across every surface it touched. Living on the West Coast and circulating in the social sphere he did, he'd come to terms with being dressed in formal attire when the sun was out but he'd never get used to the oddness. It made him feel like a moneyed lethargic lothario goofing off while everyone around him worked.

"This is ridiculous!" Robert paced the perimeter of the room, the line of his jaw harder than the stone on the fireplace. "The gala started thirty minutes ago. Why am I still home?"

Mike eyed the other man. He'd bet one of his two limited bottles of Jefferson's Presidential Select bourbon his father didn't feel uneasiness in his suit. Robert Black wore his classic tuxedo as if he'd been born wearing a bow tie and satin peak lapels.

He sighed. "Because the ladies are still getting dressed."

"How is that possible? Your mother has known about this event for months. If she needed hours to get ready, she could've built them into her schedule so we could be on time."

He sympathized with his father's impatience, but his restlessness was pushing Mike to the edge.

"You're acting as if this were an aberration. From what I remember, you two always do this dance: you're ready before she is, she takes her time, and when she finally appears, you kiss her cheek and tell her she was worth the wait."

When he was younger he'd thought the tender display gross. Like most kids, he really wanted to believe his entrance into the world came via stork and not because his parents—*gasp!*—did *it*. As he'd gotten older, he'd appreciated the outward displays of love and affection his parents shared. Had wanted that for himself.

He just hadn't anticipated the package in which it would arrive.

His father waved a negating hand. "I can't even claim

her lateness is exacerbated by extra company. She and your sister dragged India off when you both returned home after lunch . . . five hours ago! In five hours I can play a round of golf and still have time left over for a meal." Robert pivoted crisply and narrowed his eyes. "Which reminds me, unless the two of you came in late after your mother and I retired and then snuck out early before we awakened, it appears you stayed out all night. Together."

Mike's cock hardened as memories slammed through him. Of Indi on top of him, her thighs squeezing his hips. Of her breasts teasing and enticing him to reach up and take a dark nipple between his lips. Of her torso moving between his hands as he turned her over and slid from her front entrance to the rear . . .

He returned Robert's gaze, aware that no doubts or misgivings clouded his eyes. "And if we did?"

Robert inhaled deeply through his nose and exhaled through his mouth. "We talked about this. You're a handsome, wealthy, successful man at the dawn of your career. Between you and Adam, Computronix has the ability to become the biggest technology company in the world. But you need to listen to me; I've never steered you wrong before. The right woman by your side can boost your standing in ways you'd never imagine. Skylar Thompson is the right woman—"

"For someone else!" The words claimed their independence from him in righteous fury, mocking his own previous inability to do so. He was not going to allow his father to copilot his life anymore. He completed his assertion in a calmer, but no less resolute tone. "Skylar is a wonderful woman, but she's not for me."

Surprisingly, Robert chose not to argue the point further. He glanced at his watch, muttered a low curse, and strode to the door. "I'm not waiting another second. You bring them along when they finish primping."

"Of course." Mike waited until his father crossed the great room and reached for the doorknob. "I only hope you've considered how much you'll enjoy the evening with a pissed-off Barbara Black by your side."

A low blow, sure, but his father had squandered his generous mood.

Robert's spine straightened, as if some unseen hand squeezed his shoulder blades together. "Fine," he said. "I'll be in the study."

"No need to do that. We're ready," Barbara said, her voice a feminine hacksaw, cutting through the tension in the room.

Finally!

Mike sprung from his perch and turned to see his mother glide into the room in a floor-length navy blue dress with capped lace sleeves and draped folds that gathered at her waist.

"You look lovely, Mom."

"Thank you, dear."

His father tugged on his cuffs, twisting the onyx and platinum links. "Barbara, it shouldn't take five hours to get ready for an event."

"Stop pacing, Robert," she said, arching a look in his father's direction while she accepted Mike's kiss on her cheek. "It takes as long as it takes. Besides, you're the guest of honor. We don't need to be there as people arrive. The family should make an entrance."

Robert started toward her. "There's making an entrance and there's being late."

She patted her dark hair, riotous curls swept behind an ear. "It's called being *fashionably* late. Isn't the end result worth a little extra time?"

Robert's face softened. "You'll always be worth it."

Mike's smile—formed from his father's obvious adoration of his mother—crumbled as he noted the room's last two entrants. He spared a glance for Morgan long enough to note how grown-up and poised she looked in a light purple strapless dress with a full gauzy skirt that ended above her knee.

But as much as he loved his sister, she'd be a footnote in the ode he'd compose about Indi.

She also wore a strapless dress, though hers was cream, and it molded to her plump breasts, offering a teasing sample of the pleasing entity covered by the fabric. An interesting sunburst design adorned the bodice in rippling shades of blue that not only added a dramatic element to the dress, but also hid the slight bump that had finally appeared announcing Nugget's presence. Her braids had been pulled off her face and secured at the crown of her head, the long ends falling gracefully down her back.

He swallowed.

She was, without any hesitation, without any equivocation, the most beautiful woman he'd ever seen.

"Look at his face," Morgan said, laughing. "I guess that means we picked the right dress."

Hell yeah, they did.

Foregoing conscious intent, he crossed to her, only to halt when she tipped her head to the side, a groove creasing her subtly makeup-enhanced brow and her fingers gripping the cream-colored box masquerading as her purse.

I wasn't expecting this. Everything's happening so fast and I need some time. Can we keep it between us? For a little while longer?

Then she should've worn a different dress.

Fuck.

His hunger for her rampaged inside his chest like a leashed predator scenting his prey. He wanted nothing more in that moment than to reach for her, slide an arm around her waist, slip his other hand under the fall of her hair, grip the back of her neck and take her lips in a kiss that left no doubt in the mind of any of the room's occupants, including her, that she belonged to him. That she carried his child. That they *would* be a family.

But . . . he'd promised her.

He cleared his throat. What was up with his sudden esophageal issues? "You both look beautiful," he said. "Shall we go?"

TWO HOURS LATER, the Barton Point Country Club's ballroom was packed with people Mike had known his entire childhood. The hardwood floors gleamed and white linen-topped tables were spread along the periphery. Another large table was elevated and placed at the front of the room. Crystal chandeliers created a soft glow. If their lateness had been noticed, it hadn't been commented upon. Throngs came forward to talk to his parents, marvel over Mike and Morgan, and seek an introduction to Indi. Several people thought she looked familiar, but no one had been able to tie it to the *People* magazine spread.

Dinner was served and at the end of the meal the mayor toasted his father, thanking him for his many years of service and his countless contributions to the town. Robert's speech was a master class in public speaking: he thanked the town for the honor, declared his undying loyalty to Barton Point, and professed his love to his family. Respect and admiration shone on the faces surrounding them and Mike was struck by the facility with which his father switched between his public persona and his private. None of these people would recognize in the good-natured, jovial man before them the glacial-gazed patriarch who tolerated nothing less than total submission from his children.

Afterward, Mike pulled Indi onto the dance floor as the string quartet cycled through the venerable playlist reserved for the country club crowd. Once again, he marveled at the dichotomous experience of having her in his arms—the tension her nearness eased being replaced with a taut desire her proximity stoked. This is what he'd wanted from the moment he'd seen her in the dress. In her matching heels they were almost able to dance cheek to cheek. Almost, but not quite.

He pressed his cheek against her temple and inhaled. She smelled amazing, her usual warm vanilla scent kicked up a notch. Mixed with something . . . exotic? Floral?

He nibbled the tip of her ear.

"Stop it," she hissed.

She butted his head to dislodge him and the sapphire and diamond studs she wore—his mother's, he recognized—brushed his chin.

He flexed the hand that caressed her hip and leaned back so he could look into her face, aware that the motion brought the lower half of their bodies into intimate contact. She gasped and swept her tongue out to lick her bottom lip. The corner of his mouth lifted in a salute of her response to him.

"I can't help it. You smell incredible."

"It's a new scented oil I bought. But that doesn't matter. If you keep nibbling my ear, pressing me close, and nuzzling my neck, people will suspect there's something between us."

He hated to burst her delusional bubble, but she hadn't realized her mere entrance with the family, at *his* side, declared to all who'd attended that there was something very definitely between them. He'd dated his share of women, and a lot of it had been reported in the San Francisco society pages, but he'd never brought them home to meet his family, let alone invited them to a family function. For all of his intentions to propose to Skylar, he hadn't told her about the event.

No, Indi's presence at the gala was enough to convince half the attendees they were seriously involved. And his don't-even-think-about-it stare to any man who dared gawk at her longer than politeness decreed was enough to convince the other half.

"Don't you like it when I nibble your ear, press closer to you, and nuzzle your neck?" He executed every action immediately after listing it.

Her face softened and her lashes lowered. "Of course I like it."

Any blood that had managed to remain attached to his brain cells took the expressway south to his cock. If she insisted they had to keep their relationship a secret during this visit, then it was time for them to leave.

He growled into her ear. "We are hitting the road tomorrow morning as soon as we wake up. That'll get us home by eleven and me inside of you by eleven-oh-five."

Her answering smile was slow, knowing, and dick-stirringly sexy. "I hope—" Her eyes suddenly focused on something over his shoulder.

"Indi?"

She shook her head but when their bodies shifted in dance, her head swiveled on her neck to keep that something in her line of vision. Her lips tightened. "I'll be right back."

"Indi—"

She slid from his grasp before his fingers could tighten to keep her near.

Dammit.

Flashes of cream wove between the circulating couples

as he tried to follow her, but well-wishers impeded his progress and he lost her in the crowd.

He exhaled, raked his fingers through his hair.

"You must be so proud of your father."

He smiled and nodded his head to the umpteenth person who'd repeated that sentiment to him. "I am, Mr. Walker."

Neal Walker had been a Barton Point High School guidance counselor and the faculty adviser to the Future Business Leaders of America club.

"I met your friend. She's a lovely woman." Mr. Walker dipped his head slightly to the side. "A bit unusual, but I found her charming."

He resisted the urge to shout in triumph. There she was . . . talking to Morgan?

"I don't know if your father mentioned it, but my grandson, Ronnie—Ronald, was just accepted into Stanford."

"Congratulations." His sister's gestures were animated but Indi grabbed her wrists and lowered them, giving the appearance of trying to calm her down. His attention swung back to the man in front of him. "He couldn't attend a better school."

"He's really nervous about it, and since it's your alma mater, I wondered if you could maybe talk to him . . ."

Morgan kept trying to get around her, but Indi parried the move by stepping in front of her. Finally, Morgan placed a firm hand on Indi's arm, said something that caused Indi to stumble back a couple of steps, then strode with purpose across the room toward—

"Never mind. I know how busy you must be and I—" Shit.

"I'm sorry, Mr. Walker," he apologized, his upbringing kicking in, manners on autopilot. He took out a business card and handed it to the other man. "Have Ronnie give me a call. I'd be happy to talk with him."

Mr. Walker tapped the card against his closed fist. "You've always had this ability to achieve whatever you've put your mind to. I remember the beginning of your sophomore year when the principal doubted your ability to set up a small in-school supply store. You made him eat his words with a huge opening the week of Valentine's Day."

The memory surprised a laugh from Mike. "Sales were helped by the single long-stemmed red roses I stocked. I knew lots of guys were feeling the pressure to do something romantic for their girlfriends."

"You could've argued to keep the money or given in to the pressure to give it to the school. But establishing a small scholarship in the name of Gregory Hazlett after the accident, well . . . it was just a hint of the wonderful man you'd grow up to be." Sincere admiration warmed the other man's gaze. "We're so proud of you, Mike."

Mike braced himself for the spiked ball of guilt that materialized in his gut whenever Greg's name was mentioned. To his surprise, though he felt a measure of grief, the guilt he'd harbored for so long failed to appear.

Indi. She'd urged him to let it go. And he had.

Letting *her* go?

Not an option.

"Thank you, Mr. Walker. It was good to see you. And please, give my best to your wife. Would you excuse me for a moment?"

They shook hands and Mike stared at the spot he'd last seen Indi. She was gone. Instituting a methodical grid search, he let his gaze skim over the crowd until it finally alighted on the lithe figure he sought. He stopped her with a touch to her shoulder, the skin on skin contact sending currents of sensation up his arm. "What's going on?"

"You may want to get your mother and head to the vestibule." Indi shook her head and bit her lower lip. "I tried to tell her this wasn't the place to confront your father, but she's adamant."

Confront his father? About what, studying abroad? Here?

Following Indi's discreetly pointed finger, he saw Morgan approach his father, who sat holding court near the dais. She spoke into his bent ear. Robert straightened and frowned down at her, but he excused himself from his round table of admirers and followed his daughter. Indi was right; they were heading toward the small foyer connecting the large hall to one of the ballroom's side entrances.

"Hurry," he urged, lengthening his stride to cover the distance.

Indi's refusal stopped him. "This is a family matter. I don't think I should be there."

He grabbed her hand and stroked his thumb along her knuckles. "How many times do I have to tell you? You're family now. Come on."

They stepped into the middle of a heated conversation.

"We're not doing this here," Barbara said, her rapid blinking doing nothing to diminish the sheen of her eyes. Though her distress was unmistakable, he quickly discerned that the main disagreement was between his father and his sister.

"If you think I'm going to pay for you to run off halfway around the world, you'd better think again."

"I don't need you to pay for it. There are programs and scholarships available. I'll find a way to cover the tuition and fees myself."

"You'd like that, wouldn't you? To have everyone think I can't pay for my daughter's education—"

"This isn't about you," Morgan said. "It's about me and my heritage."

"Of course it's about us," his father said, dismissing her assertion. "Your mother and I have loved and raised you for eighteen of your nineteen years, and after a year and a half of college you decide to shit on all we've done for you?"

Morgan flinched. "That's not what I'm doing."

"That's what it sounds like to me."

"Because you're not listening." Morgan threw her hands up, her frustration evident. "I love you, too, but this isn't about my love. Look around you, at all of the people here. They all look like you. No one here looks like me. Have you ever been called a chink? Or had someone sniff your hair and say it smelled like rice?"

His mother gasped. "No!"

"Yes," Morgan whispered, the word insufficient to house the pain radiating in her eyes.

"Why didn't you ever tell me?"

"Because I was a little kid. I thought if I didn't say it out loud, maybe you wouldn't notice I was different." She looked down. "I didn't want to hand you a reason to give me back."

Coldness sucker punched Mike in his core. He'd never known his sister had faced these situations or experienced such loneliness. If he'd given it a second of thought, he would've. His best friend had Asperger's. From countless conversations with Adam, he was aware of the feelings being different brought. He should've initiated the conversation, asked how she was feeling. That's what a big brother was supposed to do.

"You're not buying this are you, Barbara? We live in an upscale town. These people have been our friends and neighbors for years." Robert shook his head at his daughter. "I can't believe you would lob such vile and ugly accusations."

Morgan expelled a sound reminiscent of a wounded animal and crossed her arms over her midsection, turning away from them.

Mike frowned. How many times had he been a player in a similar scene, where his father had shot down Mike's thoughts and opinions and asserted his own? It'd been hard to see in his own life but watching Morgan go through it made him want to—

"I can."

Mike's head spun toward Indi. She was staring his father down, her bearing strong, expression defiant.

"Excuse me?" Robert said.

"I can believe Morgan's accusations." She wrinkled her nose. "I've experienced similar situations."

Morgan's posture slowly unraveled and she stared at Indi, trembling fingers pressed against her lips.

"I'm sorry. India, is it?"

Mike bristled. His father goddamn well knew her name. His hands curled into fists at his side. "Dad . . ."

"This is a family matter," Robert said to her, ignoring him. Big surprise. "It's none of your business."

Indi shrugged. "Family doesn't mean a lot to me. Friendship does." She left Mike's side and moved to stand next to his sister. "And Morgan is my friend."

Morgan squeezed Indi's hand.

His father narrowed his eyes. "After three days?"

Her eyes veered to Mike briefly before refocusing on her target. "When two people connect, the length of their acquaintance is irrelevant."

His heart shifted in his chest, as if awakening from a deep slumber.

She continued. "Morgan wanting to study in Seoul isn't a rejection of you as much as it's a way to embrace a part of herself."

Mike watched Indi, floored. She was incredible. She'd seen someone in need and rushed to help her. Even now, in the face of his father's prick-ness, she provided comfort to Morgan. She had an immense capacity for love and a nurturing spirit. Despite her fears and concerns, he knew she'd be an excellent mother. He just needed her to believe it, too.

An ugly sneer distorted Robert's features. "I'm sure someone somewhere values your viewpoint and opinion. I do not."

Anger veiled Mike's vision. "That's enough."

"If I understand your background, your experience isn't similar to Morgan's. We chose our daughter. She grew up in a loving family. You were shuffled through the foster care system."

Indi's mouth tightened, but she forged on. "That's why I understand. Take my advice—"

"That's just it. I don't want to take advice from an unmarried pregnant woman who probably doesn't know who fathered her child."

Blood thundered in his ears. "Dad!"

"Robert!"

The outrage in those voices echoed throughout the small antechamber.

Indi smoothed a hand down her braids. "Mrs. Black, thank you for your hospitality this weekend."

"India—" Barbara said.

Placing a hand on her belly, Indi turned to go.

Mike stopped her, cupping her face in his hands, his thumbs wiping away the tears he couldn't see, but he knew had to be there.

"I'm so sorry, baby," he murmured, pressing his forehead against hers. He needed the contact to stop himself from giving in to the violence that rippled beneath his skin. "I'll handle this. I promise he'll never speak to you like that again."

She gripped his wrists. "No, Mike. Please, don't do this."

"Let her leave, son. It's for the best."

He twisted to face his father. "Shut up," he ordered, the words barely coherent as they were steeped in his rage.

Robert's head snapped back, his shoulders stiffening.

"You've been wrong about a lot of things," Mike said, stepping into the welcoming embrace of his anger, "but never as wrong as you are in this moment."

"What are you talking about?"

"Mike, you promised!"

"Indi won't be unmarried for long," he said triumphantly. "She knows the father of her child. It's me."

A familiar but unexpected voice intruded upon the shocked silence.

"Then you have some serious explaining to do," Franklin Thompson exclaimed, his pale skin reddening with anger.

Chapter Twenty-One

OH MY GOD! What had he done?

And who in the hell was this random dude?

Indi pressed her hands to her heated cheeks.

"Mr. Black, we're ready to—oh, you're all in here." Another woman poked her head into the room. "The President of the Chamber of Commerce is ready to proceed with the formal presentation of the plaque."

No one spoke or moved, their bodies suspended in the thick and gelatinous tension that filled the space.

Feeling the vibe the woman said, "I'll tell them you need another five minutes." She held up a finger and reached into the wall to pull out a hidden pocket door, which she closed, giving them some much-needed privacy.

Only after she left did everyone shake off their stasis.

"Is that true?" Barbara asked, her gaze swiveling from Indi to Mike. "You're the father?"

Morgan looked dazed. "Indi's pregnant and Mike's the father? Holy shit."

"Goddammit, son!" Robert's voice was the loudest of them all. "How could you do this?"

Mike's eyes narrowed and a muscle ticked in his jaw. "I'm going to give you a warning and you'd better heed this one. Watch the next words that come out of your mouth."

Quadrupled expressions of shock covered the other faces in the room. Even Robert had heard and understood the leashed menace in his son's tone. His mouth tightened but he didn't speak.

Indi stared at Mike, her pulse racing at the speed of light.

He was angry?

She'd agreed to let him raise Nugget, had given him access to her body and her heart. All she'd asked was that he keep their relationship secret, just for a little while.

But he'd barely waited twenty-four hours to substitute her judgment with his own.

Her stomach twisted and she placed a hand on her belly.

I know it's not you this time, Nugget. This is a different kind of upset.

She shook her head at the father of her child. "You promised not to tell anyone."

"I know you were worried." Mike settled a hand on her waist and she stiffened. "But you don't have to be. Now it's all out in the open and we can deal with it together. You won't have to go through this alone."

She jumped when she felt a hand on her back.

"Michael's right. You're not alone anymore. You're part of our family," Barbara said, tears glistening in her eyes. Mike's eyes. "You're carrying my grandchild."

"I'm going to be an aunt. This is wild." Morgan smiled. "And we're going to be sisters."

"See?" Mike asked softly, his palm against her cheek. "Everyone's fine with it."

"Hello? I'm not!" Thompson raged. "You're supposed to marry *my* daughter!" His nostrils flared and spittle gathered in the corners of his mouth.

His daughter? The older man practically vibrating with fury, his suit rumpled, hair disheveled, tie slightly askew was Skylar Thompson's father?

When Mike shifted his stance, using his body as if to shield her from the angry businessman, she tilted her head to the side and glared at him. She didn't need his protection. She'd been taking care of herself for the past twelve years, thank you very much!

But his attention was focused on Thompson. "What are you doing here?"

"I'm making sure you honor your agreement."

Mike raised a brow. "As far as I know, we don't have an agreement. The contracts are still being sorted out."

"Not the deal! I'm talking about that day two weeks ago when we stood in your lab and you assured me, man to man, that you weren't dating my daughter just to do business with me."

Indi pursed her lips. Guess Mike was zero for two in the promises department.

"I know how it looks, but—"

"I'm glad you know how it looks because it looks like shit. It's only been two weeks since that conversation—two weeks!—and now you're announcing you've gotten another woman pregnant and you're marrying her?"

"With all due respect, sir, this was between Skylar and me. We've already talked and we'd decided to end our relationship."

Thompson waved his explanation off. "That's the same nonsense she said, but I knew it wasn't the entire story. When your father called and explained what was happening, I flew back here as fast as—"

"My father did *what*?" Icicles hung from each word.

Realizing what he'd said, Thompson's mouth slammed shut. He swallowed and his gaze swung to Robert—

Who stood there with his arms crossed in smug defiance. "Yes, I called him."

Barbara frowned at her husband. "Why did you get involved? It was none of your business."

"Of course it's my business. He's my son. Franklin and I were both concerned our children were making a dreadful mistake."

Mike's hardened gaze speared his father to the spot. "I may be your son, but I'm not a boy. I'm a man who doesn't need you to question my decisions. You'd better hear me, Dad. This is *my* life. You've already lived yours and you do not get a do-over through me." He paused and clenched his jaw. "Or Morgan. If she wants to study abroad, for whatever reason, she can do so. She's an adult and she's more than capable of making her own decisions about her education. And if you won't pay for it, I will."

"I don't need you to do that, Mike. Like I said, I can get financial aid. But thank you. All I ever wanted was my family's support." Morgan's tentative smile pierced through Indi's withdrawal. She knew what Mike's words meant to Morgan.

Barbara took her daughter's hand. "You have it. And don't worry, we *will* pay for it. We can discuss it, all of it, later."

At least something good would come out of this situation. But Mike wasn't done.

"Did you tell Skylar you were coming here?" he asked Thompson. "I'm sure she'll have a lot to say about your interference in her personal and professional life."

Thompson looked around at them like he couldn't believe this wasn't unfolding as he'd planned. He straightened, pushing his chest forward and his shoulders back. "I may have little standing with regards to her personal life, but in business, that's another story. One day Skylar will take over TTL, but today's not that day. Either you marry my daughter as planned or the proposed deal is off."

Indi's mouth flew open. This wasn't happening. She knew what he said, but she wouldn't let this happen. Not because of her.

Mike shrugged. "Then the deal is off."

Thompson and Robert exploded.

"Are you insane?"

"What has gotten into you?"

Indi moved to stand in front of Mike. "We should talk about this."

"There's nothing to talk about." Mike's physical stature and commanding presence worked to impose his will on the room's other occupants. "If he thinks he can blackmail me into marrying his daughter, he has no idea who he's dealing with."

Morgan gasped. "He's giving it all up for Indi? Unbelievable. I never thought he was a romantic."

"Shhh," Barbara said.

"Son," Robert said, "don't do this. Think about your company."

"Computronix will be fine. I'm done taking your advice. Indi and I will be together. And if you plan on being a part of your grandchild's life, you'll need to accept it."

This was the tenacious, ruthless man who'd helped build one of the most successful tech companies in the world while still in his twenties. Unfortunately, those traits weren't relegated to his business persona. He was determined to get his own way, despite what anyone else said.

Despite what *she* said.

Indi brought her hands up to massage her temples.

"Indi and I will be together . . ."

" . . . being a part of your grandchild's life . . ."

What happened to giving her space? It was way too much, way too soon.

"I won't forget this, Black. You've made a huge fucking mistake."

Thompson stormed across the room and after a brief

skirmish with the pocket door, he slid it open, only to be greeted by a large group on the other side.

Waiters carrying trays of champagne, most of the invited guests, and several members of the orchestra, stood assembled behind the woman who'd interrupted them earlier. Some openly stared, others looked away and attempted to initiate their own conversations, but it was clear from the awkwardness that permeated the space, they'd all heard at least part of the confrontation.

Robert threw his hands in the air. "Great."

Thompson pushed his way through the crowd and several moments later, the door that led out of the ballroom slammed shut.

"Umm, yes, well, when you didn't return after five minutes, the committee thought it might be fun to bring the presentation to you." The woman smiled, though it looked more like a grimace, and held out a beautifully engraved plaque in the shape of a shield. "Congratulations?"

Chapter Twenty-Two

THE CAR RIDE back to the house was uncomfortable.

They'd driven to the gala separately; Barbara and Morgan had gone with Robert in his car, while Indi had enjoyed some alone time riding with Mike. However, after the evening's events, Robert had been shocked to find himself his car's sole occupant.

When they reached the house, Indi had attempted to excuse herself for the night, claiming exhaustion, but Mike had steered her past the hallway that led to the west wing and straight into the great room. Infuriating man. And if she'd somehow managed to make it past him, she never would've been able to ditch Barbara and Morgan. The two women hadn't left her side.

"Why didn't you tell us?" Barbara asked Mike. She shifted her attention to Indi as she pulled her down on the sofa. "Are you feeling okay? Do you want some tea?"

Maybe it was the way she'd grown up, without people

caring what she did or where she went, but Indi found the attention smothering. Especially when she knew it couldn't last.

"I'm fine." She straightened the two picture frames on the side table next to the sofa.

She wanted to leave. But how? Hotwire one of the cars? Probably not a good idea when she was already facing felony charges. She had money. If she could get downtown, she could catch a bus. How would she get downtown without Mike knowing? It was too far to walk. Call a cab? She'd have to get out of the house unseen. Barbara and Morgan would have questions. Robert! He wouldn't interrogate her. Hell, he'd probably offer to drive her all the way back to San Francisco if he thought it would keep her from his son. Speaking of . . .

She hazarded a glance at Mike and found him frowning at her from his perch next to the fireplace. She looked away. He couldn't know what she was planning, could he?

Robert thundered through the front door. "Am I the only one who realizes this is a problem?"

Mike flicked his gaze heavenward. "Yes. You're the only one."

"Are you even certain the baby is yours?"

Indi stiffened.

Mike pushed away from the fireplace. "You're my father and I love you, but if you say another insulting thing—"

"Michael, no." Barbara stood. "Robert Black, your behavior this evening has been appalling."

"You all don't seriously expect me to remain quiet while my only son ruins his future?"

"We're about to have our first grandchild," Barbara said. "How about focusing on that?"

Apparently Robert was having a difficult time letting go. "What are you going to do now?"

"The deal will go through. Despite what Thompson believes, Skylar and I already discussed it. And if she somehow changes her mind, we'll find another cable conglomerate to approach. One of my reasons for choosing TTL was the convenience factor, but they aren't irreplaceable."

"And your relationship with Skylar Thompson?"

"For the last time, there is no relationship. I'm marrying Indi."

Oh really? Since when? Did it ever occur to him to ask her before announcing it to the entire town?

In two weeks she'd gone from having only one other person concerned about her welfare to having her future passionately debated by one of Barton Point's finest families.

How in the hell had that happened?

"We are not getting married," she said to the room at large.

"Of course you're getting married," Barbara said. "You're having a baby together."

"They don't have to get married," Morgan argued. "That's so 1980s. It's the twenty-first century. They can coparent." She looked at Indi. "It'll be easy if they live near each other. Do you live in San Francisco or Palo Alto?"

Indi was dazed. Did they hear what she'd said? It was

like she had no opinion of her own, or if she did, as if that opinion didn't matter.

"I don't live in either place," she told Morgan.

Barbara patted her knee. "Exactly where *do* you live, dear?"

"I move around."

"But you *are* going to settle down in San Francisco?" Barbara nodded her head as she asked the question, insinuating a positive response was the only proper response.

The thought made the hair rise on her arms. "I'm not settling down anywhere."

She could feel Mike's stare boring into her, but she refused to look at him. This was all his fault.

"But you have to." Barbara's expression was horrified. "You can't haul my grandchild around the country like a vagrant. Children need stability."

"That isn't my intention." She paused, aware that all eyes were on her. "I'm not raising the baby. I planned on giving him up for adoption."

Barbara's hand flew to her chest. "You can't do that!" She shot a look at Mike.

Morgan looked at her, confused. "You've been in the system. Why would you do that to your own child?"

"It's not always like that," Indi said. "Look at your experience. You were given to people who love you."

Mike's voice cut through the debate. "She's not putting the baby up for adoption! I've asked her to let me raise Nugget."

Morgan frowned. "What's a nugget?"

Mike rolled his eyes. "It's what she calls the baby."

"Another brilliant choice, son." Robert rocked back on his heels, his smug tone grating on her nerves. "You've given up an incredible woman and an important deal, and she doesn't even plan on keeping the baby."

"Shut up, Dad."

"I understand why you're frightened, but you don't have to be. You have us now. You won't have to do it on your own," Barbara said, her features soft with compassion.

Indi stroked the end of her braids, her stomach churning. "I'm not worried about doing it on my own. I've been on my own for years."

"Then what *are* you worried about?" Mike rubbed the back of his neck. "Whatever it is, I'll take care of it."

Morgan added her fifty cents. "Forget that. What about Nugget? What are you going to do when he wants to know his mother? To see where he comes from?"

"I—I don't—know. Yet. I just decided to let Mike raise him. We haven't talked much beyond that."

"Well shouldn't you figure it out? Unless you're willing to curse *him* to a life of looking at every black woman with light brown eyes and wondering if she's his mother?" Morgan's tone was accusatory.

"Morgan!"

Indi stood. She needed to go. Now. These people barely knew her, but everyone had an opinion about what decisions she should make and how she should live her life. She could call a cab. Did Barton Point have Uber? Who did she know—Jill! She'd had a wonderful time shopping with Chelsea's assistant after her visit with Dr. Kimball. If she called her, would Jill drive three hours to pick her up?

The doorbell rang.

Robert scowled. "Who in the hell would show up un-invited at this time of night?"

He left to answer the door and she heard a familiar voice. "Is India Shaw here?"

Relief rushed through her, stealing her knees' ability to hold her upright. She'd braced herself against the arm of the sofa and was halfway to toeing off the heels she'd worn all evening when Chelsea appeared in the doorway.

Indi couldn't recall seeing a more welcoming sight, save the night the guard had escorted her from the jail cell. She didn't know how she'd gotten here, or where she'd come from, but Chelsea still looked fresh and rested. Her long dark curls were pulled into a sleek ponytail at the base of her neck and the jeans, tank top, and cashmere duster she wore screamed traveler chic. Her sister's brown eyes took in the scene with one thorough, experienced glance before she hurried over and pulled Indi into a tight hug.

"Are you okay?" Chelsea whispered in her ear.

Indi was vaguely aware of the commotion in the background as Adam greeted the family.

She sighed and clutched at Chelsea's back, covering her eyes with a free hand, in case she was unable to curb the tears currently filling them. "I will be. How did you know I was here?"

"We got Mike's email about the charges."

"Email?" Mike had sent them an email? When? "But how? I thought you were at a tech-free resort."

"We will never do that again," Adam said. "If the lodgings do not provide decent Wi-Fi, we are not going."

Chelsea shot an amusingly resigned look at her husband. Her new brother-in-law was a handsome devil, tall and athletic with shaggy dark hair and eyes the blue of the darkest sapphire. But even with his resemblance to a dark sex god, he didn't make her blood sing like the blond archangel standing next to him.

"We were," Chelsea said. "But somebody'd had enough. We'd decided to leave a few days early and spend the rest of our honeymoon at the house in San Mateo. As soon as we left the resort, Adam powered up his phone and saw the message from Mike. We talked to Sully and got here as soon as we could."

"I need to get out of here. Now."

Chelsea sobered. "Okay. Where are your things?"

"In the bedroom."

No one tried to stop her as she left the great room and took the hallway down to the west wing. In the bedroom she'd been assigned, but had never slept in, she slipped on comfortable flats and pulled out her overnight bag. When she passed the dresser, Barbara's sapphire and diamond studs winked at her from her earlobes in her reflection in the mirror. She carefully took them off and left them in the small crystal bowl in the wardrobe.

It had been so simple in the beginning: go to San Francisco, tell Mike he was the father, give the baby up for adoption, continue with her life. How had she ended up here?

Because you deviated from the plan. You started to believe you were entitled to more.

And you were wrong.

Since there was no such thing as a clean getaway, Mike intercepted her before she could leave the room. "Where are you going?"

She added her toiletries to the bag. "I'm leaving with Chelsea and Adam."

He leaned a shoulder against the doorjamb and stared into her eyes. "I never thought I'd see the day when the adventurous India Shaw would let fear get the best of her."

She'd worked hard for that adventure. The first sixteen years of her life, decisions had been made on her behalf by people who didn't give a damn about her, only the paycheck her presence generated. She'd escaped that system as soon as she'd been able, and for the past twelve years, she'd taken care of herself and made her own decisions. And now, because of one little mistake, she'd lost her freedom to an unwanted pregnancy and the baby's father was trying to steal her autonomy.

She'd be damned if she let that happen. Once she gave birth to Nugget, her independence would be all she had left.

She flipped her braids over one shoulder. "I'm not afraid of anything."

"Then why are you running away from me?" He arched a challenging brow. "Again?"

"Did it ever occur to you that I'm just not that into you?"

Real mature, Indi.

"I'd consider it if you didn't scream my name every time I made you come. There's also the little matter of you carrying my child."

Heat unfurled low in her belly even as she rolled her eyes at his words. He was playing the asshole card to the hilt. That should make it easier for her to leave.

"Knocking me up is a function of biology, not chemistry."

They didn't have to like each other to make a baby. He'd just needed a Tab A to go into her Slot B.

"But the chemistry made it memorable, didn't it?"

So challenging him in that way had been a mistake. She backtracked.

"This may surprise you but I managed to survive twenty-eight years before I met you."

He pushed away from the wall and breached the room. "And you're happy living that way? Wandering from place to place? Making no connections, establishing no roots?"

"Actually, I am."

"How's that going to work now that you're pregnant?"

"I won't be pregnant forever."

"So you'll just go back to being alone."

"Maybe I like being alone."

"But you don't have to be."

"I know. That's the beauty of being me. I don't *have* to do anything."

He narrowed his eyes. "Except give him away, right? Because that's what you've repeated. You can't possibly raise him by yourself. Or with me."

"You don't know when to quit—"

He shoved his hands into his pockets. "I never have."

"You just keep pushing and pushing." She stuffed her

belongings into her bag with way more force than was required. "You've got some serious control issues."

"Oh, we're flipping the script?"

Yup. "Look at your relationship with Skylar. You controlled that, didn't you? It probably began on your terms. It definitely ended on your terms and you're still getting what you wanted. Is she?"

The muscle in his jaw ticked. "You don't know what you're talking about."

"Adam and Chelsea? You had to get involved in that situation. Adam told you he didn't want help. Chelsea said she wanted to tell him the truth, but you dismissed both of their concerns because you thought you knew better."

"It worked out in the end, didn't it?"

"And you're going to take credit for that?"

"I *did* talk to Adam—"

"So no one can be trusted to make their own decisions without your input?"

"Trust?" He laughed and she flinched from the bitter blowback. "That's rich coming from you."

He couldn't turn this around on her. "What does that mean?"

He pointed at his chest, then at her. "If I have control issues, then you have trust ones. You hold everyone at a distance, like you're waiting for them to disappoint you."

"I didn't have to wait long, did I? From the moment I told you I didn't want to raise the baby, you substituted your judgment for mine. Making me take pictures, consider names, go shopping. All so you could fit our situation into some picture in your mind. Did you ever stop to think how hard it would be for me to do those things? Did it ever occur to you that I might have a good reason for not wanting to raise him?"

"How would I know? I asked you several times and you never answered me. That's what I meant about keeping people at a distance. You'd rather I believed you were some ditz who wanted to travel than tell me the real reason."

"Fine. You want to know why I can't raise him? Because I'm terrified. Terrified that I don't know how. Terrified that I'll make a mistake." She lowered her voice. "Terrified that he'll hate me."

"Why would he hate you? You're his mother. He'll love you."

"My mother didn't love me. I went through countless foster homes and none of them chose to adopt me. Can all of those people be wrong?"

"You don't know your mother didn't love you. Maybe she had a good reason for leaving you. Maybe she thought it was the best decision for you."

"Dropping me off at a hospital?"

"Yes! Think of all the other places she could've left you. She took you someplace she knew they could take care of you."

She shook her head, unable to reexamine a belief she'd clutched tightly for so long.

"What about Chelsea? She loves you."

Indi shrugged. "Maybe she's the exception that proves the rule."

He closed the distance between them, cradled her face between his big, warm hands. "What about me?" He brushed his thumb along her lower lip. "I love you."

She wanted to believe him . . .

"Do you? Or do you want to do the right thing? Maybe you see Nugget and me as a package deal." She moved away from him and his hands fell to his sides. "We aren't."

"I know my own mind."

It's funny, she'd been trying to convince him of the same about her for the past two weeks.

"Are you sure? Because what if I rely on that? And after the baby's born you decide that he was all you wanted after all? I can't take that chance."

She wanted to, but what if he was wrong? She wouldn't survive it if Mike or Nugget realized something was wrong with her. She couldn't bear to watch their love slowly curdle to disgust.

"It's called faith, Indi."

She shook her head. "After twenty-eight years, I'm fresh out of that."

Chapter Twenty-Three

MIKE'S PAIN WAS a raw, throbbing wound that had suffered several direct punches and been jabbed with the red-hot tip of a fire poker.

Overdramatic, but who cares? The feeling was accurate. He discarded his tuxedo jacket across the chair in the corner of his room and plopped down on the bed. He'd gone from blissfully planning the rest of his life with India and Nugget to possibly losing them forever.

No! Fuck this!

He scrubbed a hand down his face and pushed himself to his feet. Being in here, where he'd awakened to find her in his arms yesterday morning, screwed with his mind and ravaged his heart. But he wouldn't act like some college freshman sitting in his dorm nursing a broken heart while listening to Dave Matthews.

He needed a drink to numb the pain. Maybe several.

The house was still, dark. After the spectacle of Adam

and Chelsea's arrival and Indi leaving, no one felt like sitting around and rehashing the night's events. It hadn't taken long for his parents and Morgan to retreat to their rooms. He was grateful for the solitude.

Unlike in his childhood when he could maneuver from one wing to the other with his eyes closed, his mother's renovations, and recent furniture placements, meant he needed to take his time. It would be icing on the cake for him to stub his toe or bang his knee. He navigated through the various seating arrangements and made his way to the kitchen.

It was a popular notion.

His father sat on a bar stool, one foot resting on a lower rung, the other planted on the floor. Only the pendant lights above the island were lit, the soft glow somberly framing Robert's hunched posture and glinting off the quarter-filled cut glass tumbler nestled in his right hand. A bottle of Balvenie fifty-year-old Scotch whiskey—the centerpiece of his father's collection—sat on the counter near his left elbow.

Mike couldn't recall ever seeing his father rumpled and unkempt. Part of that may have been Robert's many years in the public eye, but Mike had always felt a certain formality was probably imprinted on his father's DNA. But with rebellious strands of his hair falling across his forehead, his tie undone, and his cufflinks missing, he possessed the despondent air of a man who'd blown the deal of a lifetime.

Concern for the picture he presented conflicted with the anger simmering beneath the surface.

It wasn't his father's fault. He may not like what

Robert had said or the way he'd treated Indi, but it was Mike's own actions, or lack thereof, that had caused the disintegration of his happiness this evening.

Still, he wasn't in the mood to endure another lecture, and despite their strained interaction, the man deserved a respect that Mike couldn't currently muster. He reversed several steps, intending to backtrack.

"I remember the first time I held you in my arms," Robert said, alerted to his presence though he hadn't raised his head. His voice held no trace of a slur.

Realizing retreat wasn't a viable option, Mike leaned a hip against the counter, crossed his arms, and said, "That was a long time ago."

"Having a child changes your life. You experience a wave of love so strong, it knocks you on your ass, and this baby you love is helpless. If we didn't feed you, you'd starve. If we didn't change your diapers, you'd develop a rash. We had to burp you, because your system hadn't matured enough to do it on your own. And we did it, happily, because we loved and adored you. But what about the people in the world who didn't? One day I wouldn't be there."

Mike slid onto the neighboring stool, drawn to his father's vulnerability.

"The day of the accident . . ." Robert cleared his throat and shook his head. "We got the call that you'd been involved in an accident by the cliffs . . . It was like a sucker punch to the gut. As we raced over there, I promised God that if you were all right, I'd do everything I could to protect you. So when I wasn't there, you could take care of yourself. And I meant it."

Robert finished off the Scotch in his glass and turned exposed eyes on Mike.

"I wanted you to have the best life possible, to never have to deal with sadness, pain, or heartache. I know, it sounds ridiculous and not very practical, but . . ." Robert shrugged. "The irony is in my effort to keep you safe, I pushed you further away."

With that additional piece of information came clarity, a shift in perspective. Suddenly, Robert's actions made sense. His father's lectures on responsibility, his extreme disappointment when Mike declined to participate in the family business and left Barton Point, his interest in and wanting to be a part of Computronix, his push for Skylar Thompson as Mike's wife. A father's misguided attempt to ensure his son's happiness.

Controlling, sure, but well intentioned and from a place of love.

Robert laughed, the sound bittersweet. "You'll know this feeling soon enough."

He fucking hoped so.

"Then you believe Indi that I'm the father?" Mike kept his voice low. It wasn't a challenge; he truly wanted to know his father's opinion.

Robert shook his head. "It doesn't matter whether the baby is biologically yours or not. You've claimed him. That stupefying combo of love, fear, and panic? I felt the same way when I held Morgan all those years ago in that orphanage in South Korea. And I'm making the same mistake with her that I made with you."

"That's different."

"No, it's not. When she told me she wanted to study abroad—in Seoul of all places—I flashed back to the orphanage. I wanted to keep her from there even more now than I did back then. It didn't even occur to me that *my* actions had been causing her pain." Robert exhaled forcefully. "I've been wrong about so many things."

While Mike was grateful for this new understanding of his father—and Robert's own expanding self-awareness—he didn't want the other man to believe their entire childhood had been unacceptable.

He clapped a hand on Robert's shoulder. "Yeah, but you've been right about so many others. We've had a great life. You couldn't keep us from the hurt and pain of growing up, but that's normal. You *did* keep us from the hurts and pains you could control: we had a place to live, food to eat, and parents who cared for and loved us."

Unlike Indi. She'd had to make her own way without the emotional cushion loving parents could provide. And in spite of that—or maybe because of it—she'd turned into a beautiful, courageous, resourceful woman.

As if reading his mind, his father said, "She's a special lady and she has a big heart."

Mike was aware of her compassionate nature. Had seen it in the way she related to people and how they were drawn to her. But how would his father know that?

"Because she'd barely met your sister, yet she cared for her enough to stand up to me," Robert said, when Mike posed the question. "After a disastrous introduction that involved her throwing up in our bushes." A smile quirked the corners of his mouth. "That's a story we'll be telling the grandkids for years to come."

Mike's heart achieved a lightness he hadn't thought possible an hour ago at the promise and acceptance implicit in that statement.

"You're not the only one who confused control with protection and love."

That's what he'd been doing with Indi from the moment she'd come back into his life. He'd been so afraid of losing her, of waking up to find her gone—again!—that he'd done the same thing his father had; he'd pushed and pushed until he'd pushed her away.

But he wasn't done. He loved her and Nugget and he knew she loved him. And like he told her last night, it wasn't in his nature to give up.

Robert stood and rounded the counter to grab another glass from the cabinet. He poured a finger of Scotch into both and lifted his glass, his eyes fixed on Mike's. "In case it's not clear, I'm proud of the man you've become. Congratulations on the new addition to our family. I'm happy for you."

Mike touched his glass to his father's, the clink signaling the dawn of their new relationship. And just in time.

His smile contorted into a grimace. "While I look forward to no more lectures, I have a feeling I'll be calling on you for advice. Often."

Robert finished his drink and sat his glass on the counter. "I can't wait. But despite all the books and all the advice, it'll come down to doing what you think is right. And you'll be great at that."

Chapter Twenty-Four

I NEVER THOUGHT I'd see the day when the adventurous India Shaw would let fear get the best of her.

Even the crisp beautiful morning on the wraparound patio of Adam and Chelsea's apartment in San Francisco couldn't mute Mike's refrain.

And she wanted to. She needed to. She'd spent the past thirty-six hours in a vicious cycle of crying and sleeping, with some occasional vomiting thrown in.

Damn hormones.

She'd awakened a little while ago and instead of rolling over into the fetal position to commence le pity party, part deux, she'd forced herself to shower and get dressed in yoga pants and a T-shirt. She'd grabbed a throw from the sectional in the living room and headed out to enjoy the air and the magnificent view.

The glass door opened and Chelsea stepped out carrying a tray. "Are you feeling better?"

"If you don't count the sand in my eyes, the rocks in my throat, and the slight nausea in my belly, I'm peachy keen."

"I can help with the nausea."

Chelsea sat the tray on the side table and handed her a cup. "It's peppermint tea. And be careful, it's hot. There are saltines if you want to put something in your stomach." Chelsea sat down on the end of the lounger, pulling Indi's feet into her lap. "How about I paint your toenails?"

"Yes, please." Indi wrapped her hands around the warm mug and took a sip of the tea. She wiggled her toes. "Where's Adam?"

"He went for a run. Wanted to give us some privacy."

"That was sweet of him."

Chelsea smiled and the love she felt for her husband illuminated her face. "It was. But he'd tell you sticking to his usual routine helps the body counteract the effects of jet lag."

Yup. Indi could hear him saying that exact statement.

"How far along are you?" Chelsea asked.

"Coming up on sixteen weeks."

"That's the second trimester right? Shouldn't the morning sickness be gone by now?"

"My nausea is a diva. It comes and goes whenever it wants. It cares nothing for labels like morning, afternoon, or evening. But you're right, it should've settled down by now. Mike's mom said when she was pregnant with him, she was sick the entire pregnancy."

"Oh really? 'Mike's mom said'?"

"Shut up!" Indi laughed.

"What?" Chelsea asked, all wide-eyed innocence. She held up two bottles of nail polish. "Which one?"

Indi pointed to the pretty tangerine color in Chelsea's right hand. "Anyway, it makes total sense. Even in the womb, Mike had to control things. He's such a pain in the ass."

"A pain in the ass you love."

Indi shook her head, but she didn't dare respond, not wanting to cry again. She pressed a fist to her mouth.

"Am I wrong?" Chelsea asked. "Because if you don't love him, this situation becomes exponentially easier."

She fought to control her emotions.

"No, I do." Had been halfway to falling in love with him during their first weekend together. "More than I know what to do with or how to handle."

"So what's the problem?"

She exhaled loudly. "He was right; I'm afraid."

"Afraid of what?"

"I was four years old when my mother left me. She didn't give me away when I was baby because she was scared or overwhelmed. I wasn't taken from her because of bad behavior. She kept me for four years and suddenly she decided she didn't want me anymore." The acidic sting of tears burned Indi's eyes and Chelsea's image wavered in front of her. "What could've been so wrong with me that my own mother would reject me?"

"Oh, Indi."

Chelsea set the polish down and gathered her close as Indi succumbed to the sobs wracking her body. She cried for the little girl she'd been, for the years she'd been afraid, and all of the time she'd blamed herself. She even cried for her mother. When she was done, she sagged back against the lounger.

"Until this moment," Chelsea began, "it never occurred to me how much you and Adam have in common."

"Say what now?" Indi tilted her head to the side and eyed the other woman. Seriously? She had something in common with the intense genius Chelsea had married?

"It's true. His mother left him when he was younger, too. He still had his fathers and sister but, for years, he blamed himself. Thought it was his fault. It wasn't his, just like it isn't yours."

"You don't know your mother didn't love you. Maybe she had a good reason for leaving you. Maybe she thought it was the best decision for you."

Indi looked down and fiddled with a clean cotton ball. "I never told you this, but I've been waiting for you to leave, too."

Chelsea's eyes widened. "What?"

"You're married to Adam now and his family became your family. Soon you'll be having your own children—"

"Not that soon," Chelsea inserted, rapping her knuckles on the back of the teak patio lounger.

"—and I thought I was going to lose you, too. It's the reason I've traveled so much. You know, houseguest, fish, and yada yada yada . . ."

"Why didn't you ever tell me?"

"Because I felt petty and selfish. I thought I'd eventually get over it, but everything that's happened forced me to face it."

"You're my sister. I know you. I see you. I love you. Nothing and no one will ever change that, and I'll say it as many times as you need to hear it."

Maybe the tears had shaken something loose in her, maybe it was the experience of being pregnant or spending time with Mike's family, but this time, when Chelsea said the words, Indi focused on the certainty shining in Chelsea's brown eyes and . . . accepted the truth of them.

"I love you, too."

"Now, what are you going to do about the baby?" Chelsea asked, placing a hand against the gentle swell of Indi's belly.

A smile teased one corner of Indi's mouth. "You mean Nugget?"

Chelsea sat up straight and wrinkled her nose. "I refuse to call my unborn niece or nephew Nugget."

"You're making some pretty big assumptions there, Aunt Chels."

Like Indi being involved in Nugget's life or, she swallowed past the boulder that materialized in her throat, actually keeping and raising him herself.

"It's possible. But I have faith in you, India Shaw. You'll do what's right for you and the baby. It'll work out. Whatever you decide, Adam and I are here for you. We can help."

"Thank you. What *won't* be an option is keeping the baby from Mike. Since the beginning he's made it clear that he would be willing to raise Nugget, even when I was convinced that I couldn't. He'll be a great father."

Chelsea hesitated. "And apart from the baby? Do you think there's a chance for the two of you?"

He hadn't called or texted or tried to get in contact with her since she left Barton Point the night before last. "I screwed things up so much. That's the second time I walked out on him. He'll never forgive me."

She wouldn't blame him if he never wanted to speak to her again.

"Of course he'll forgive you, but it's only been a day and a half. Give it some time." Chelsea reached down and grabbed something off the tray. She held up a bottle of sunrise/sunset nail polish and shook it. "Although I'll need more time than that to get over the fact that you and Mike had sex the weekend of our wedding. It was those damn tequila shots, wasn't it? How was he? Wait—" She made fake retching sounds. "I think I threw up a little in my mouth."

Indi wrinkled her nose and placed a hand against her protruding lower belly. "You'll wish you hadn't done that when my real nausea sympathizes with your fake nausea and I vomit all over your pretty outdoor furniture."

They both laughed.

Indi stroked her chin. "And as for Mike, as good as he is—and he's spectacular—I gotta say, he's no Jeremy," she said, referring to the top-of-the-line spa quality shower-head in Chelsea's LA apartment.

"You are so gross," Chelsea said. "I'm going in the house."

"What? What did I say? Chelsea? What about my pedicure?"

INDI PUSHED THE call button for the elevator and checked her reflection in the large mirror on the opposite wall.

"It's going to be down there?" she asked.

It would take her another week before she'd ceased being shocked at the first glimpse of her reflection. When she'd taken her braids down, she'd liked the resulting shoulder-length corkscrew curls, so she'd decided to keep that style. For now.

And at seventeen weeks, in her comfy yoga pants and a tank top, her belly was slightly rounded when she examined her profile.

"Yes," Chelsea insisted, her voice coming through the speakerphone. "Stanley said it was waiting."

Stanley. The doorman who'd had her arrested.

It had been a week since she'd returned from Barton Point and whenever she felt a moment of sadness descending, one of her favorite things to do was to recall the look on Stanley the doorman's face when she'd walked through the lobby with Adam and Chelsea. The first thing they'd done was add Indi's name to the list of approved entrants into Penthouse A.

Indi had told the couple that part of the doorman's reasoning for not granting her access to their penthouse was his belief that Indi had lied when she'd said she was Chelsea's sister because he'd overheard Chelsea telling Adam she didn't have any siblings.

"I remember that day. That's not what I said," Chelsea snapped. "We were coming through the front door and Adam asked if, other than Indi, I had any siblings I'd never mentioned. I said no. And from that statement, he presumes to know me?"

Adam frowned. "So he likes to gather his information from eavesdropping?"

You do not want to anger the wife of a genius. When Adam came through the lobby the following day, he'd called Chelsea on his cell to get her "opinion" on his idea to purchase the Hermitage at Avalon and completely computerize the concierge services.

"Let him worry about the possibility of unemployment," Adam had said, once he'd gotten home.

It wasn't a lie—Adam didn't abide lying—because he'd seriously considered the investment, before discarding it as an overreaction to the situation. And he'd only been slightly discomfited by Indi's hug and kiss of thanks on his cheek. It appeared the number of people she could count on to have her back was growing.

"What're you expecting?" Indi asked Chelsea now. "It's not too big, is it? Maybe Adam should've waited to have this delivered until you guys got back."

She'd finally convinced Chelsea and Adam that she'd be fine here by herself while they went to spend the last few days of their time off in San Mateo. She appreciated their care and consideration but she was grateful for the time alone. Plus, she'd planned to start looking for her own place soon. She'd texted Jill earlier this morning and made a date to check out a few of the available units in the other woman's building. Indi couldn't live at the Hermitage at Avalon. It'd take more than a few ceramic penises to afford a place in this building.

Chelsea laughed. "Too funny. You'll know it when you see it and I'm pretty sure you'll be able to handle it."

She poked out her bottom lip and shrugged. "Okay."

"Call me later."

"I will. I promise. Now don't worry about me. Enjoy the rest of your honeymoon."

Indi ended the call and the elevator touched down on the lobby floor. She pulled at a couple of curls while she waited for the doors to open. Maybe she'd get the tips dyed red? Ooh, maybe a navy blue? Could she use hair dye while she was pregnant?

The doors opened and she strolled out to the concierge desk and froze.

Mike stood there waiting.

Her stomach shifted.

He's here, Nugget. It's really him.

She took in his appearance. He wore a pair of slim-fit pressed khakis and a forest-green V-neck pullover that stretched across his broad chest and hugged his trim waist, an outfit she knew he considered casual. He was so gorgeous, he made her mouth water.

"What are you doing here?"

"I came for you." His blue eyes were fevered. "Did you really think I'd let you go that easily?"

Yeah, she actually had.

He made an encompassing motion around his head. "You changed your hair again. Curls. You look so beautiful. And you're showing more. How are you feeling?"

"Better. My energy is up. But I'm still nauseous."

"My mom said she was nauseous with me the entire pregnancy."

She smiled and ducked her head. "Yeah, I know."

She remembered she was supposed to be looking for a package for Chelsea. She whirled around to face the concierge desk. "Where's Stanley?"

"Who?"

"The doorman."

Mike jerked a thumb over his shoulder. "I sent him on a break. Wait, is he the one who had you arrested?"

She nodded and exhaled. "That would be him."

He actually growled. "I'm going to kick his ass."

"You can't kick anyone's ass in those pants."

"Watch me."

He punched the air a couple of times, executed a couple of moves.

She laughed. "You'd do that for me?"

His entire body seemed to take a deep breath and relax. He moved closer to her. "I'll always take care of you."

"I don't need you to."

"I know. But taking care of you isn't a way to control you, and it doesn't mean I don't think you're capable of taking care of yourself. It just means I care about you and I want you to be safe." He paused. "Because I love you."

It wasn't long ago those words filled her with fear. Now, she reveled in them.

"I'm sorry, I didn't quite catch that. What did you say?"

He closed the distance between them and cupped her face in his hands. "I love you, India Shaw."

She wrapped her arms around his waist. "I love you, too."

"Finally!"

He lowered his head and when their lips touched it felt as if she'd finally found out where she belonged. Her heart pounded and her pulse raced, her soul soared.

When they parted, he swept a thumb over her mouth before leaning in for another kiss. "God, I love that lip," he said, taking the object of his affection between his teeth and tugging on it gently, before laving it with his tongue.

"I'm not perfect, Indi. I'm going to make mistakes. But I need you to have faith in me. Believe that when I say I love you, I mean it. I'm never going to walk away from you."

"I believe you."

"This is about us. We can talk about Nugget later, figure out the baby situation—"

"I think I have. I mean, I'm still terrified, but I want to raise him. I can't give him away."

"Thank God." He hugged her tightly, buried his face in her neck. "You're not just doing this for me, are you?"

"No. I'd already made this decision. And I want you to know, I never would've kept you from him. No matter what happened between us."

"I know." He picked her up and swung her around. "You're going to be a great mom."

She frantically tapped his shoulder. "Are you trying to ruin this moment? Put me down."

He laughed. "Sorry, I forgot." When he put her down,

he pulled her back into his arms, as if he couldn't bear to not touch her somehow. "You're naturally giving and loving. You'll give Nugget everything you always wanted but never received. And between us, my family, Adam and Chelsea, our friends, that baby will never lack for love."

"Thank you."

"I have a proposition for you."

"Isn't that how we got in this mess in the first place?"

He pressed a quick kiss to her lips. "Is sex all you think about? I propose we take some time to get to know one another."

"What did you have a mind?"

"I'm so glad you asked." He pulled out his phone and began flipping through pictures. "How about New York, Barcelona, Athens, Cairo, Dubai, Bangkok, Sydney, Auckland, and then back here? A three-month trip around the world. And we'll return in time for your last trimester. You may not get the chance to travel for a while and this way I get to share it with you. I don't want to change you, I just want to share your life."

Happiness radiated from her heart, through her chest to fill every pore of her being. She loved this incredible man and he actually loved her in return. It was possible that they could get as close as two people could be and he'd still love her.

"I guess there are perks to loving a man whose company made twenty-six billion dollars last quarter."

"I thought you were going to stop bringing that up?"

"Hmmm," she murmured, noncommittally. "It's a

good thing the criminal charges have been dismissed, so I can travel."

The day after they'd returned from Barton Point, Sully, acting on behalf of Chelsea and Adam, and Viv Sutton had gone to the DA with notarized statements confirming Indi's story that she had their permission to be in their residence and none of their belongings had been missing. Without any evidence to the contrary, the DA had no choice but to dismiss the charges.

"I know. I called Adam first thing Monday morning to remind him to take care of it."

"You did?"

"I planned this elaborate vacation. It'd be no fun if I had to go alone." He smiled. "This isn't a marriage proposal, but it doesn't mean I'm not sure. It's the exact opposite. I love you and I want to be with you forever. But I have faith enough to wait. You want us to take our time. I understand that and I'll wait as long as you need."

She hugged him and wasn't surprised to experience the same feelings she'd had the moment she'd awakened in his arms back in Barton Point: safe, protected, loved.

"Just so I'm clear: are *you* the package I'm supposed to get?"

"Do you have to be so crude about it? Yes." He laughed. "I love you. I swear, I've never worked harder for anything in my entire life."

"Really? Then it pains me to tell you it wasn't necessary."

He leaned his upper body away from her and stared

down into her face, grooves carved on either side of his mouth. "It wasn't?"

Oh no. That wouldn't do.

She took her fingers and smoothed away the tension until his face was warm, open, and loving again, sneaking one more kiss for good measure. Then she braced herself against his hold and crossed her hands over his heart. "Nope. I was yours from the moment I stepped off the elevator and saw you standing there."

And two months later, on a small isolated beach in a quiet part of Thailand, surrounded by their family and close friends, Indi made her faith official.

THE END

**Don't miss the next sparkling and
sexy contemporary romance
from Tracey Livesay!
Coming Spring 2017 from Avon Impulse!**

Acknowledgments

I CAN'T BELIEVE I have the privilege of doing this again!

A big hug to my agent Nalini Akolekar of Spencer-hill Associates for always being in my corner and giving me a loving but firm nudge when I need it. My editor, Tessa Woodward, has been such a joy to work with and she even fulfilled my dream of having an editor/author revision meeting just like Jessica Fletcher on *Murder, She Wrote*.

Much gratitude to the two doctors who provided invaluable information to me during the writing of this book: Dr. Imani Williams-Vaughn, one of my best friends for the past twenty-five years & Dr. Barbara Mercado, who delivered two of my children. (Surely that would be reason enough to thank her, right?)

When I had questions about criminal procedure in San Francisco, I turned to Greg Goldman, Deputy Public Defender & Tamara Barak Aparton, Communication and Policy Assistant from the San Francisco Public Defender's office. As a former public defender, I know how hard they work to make sure everyone has access to outstanding legal representation. I want to thank them for taking time out of their busy schedule to speak with me.

To Sharon, Annette, Petra, Ashley, Leigh, Nellie & Chrissy. The LaLas: often imitated, never duplicated. By the time this book is published, I'll be a couple of weeks out from running my first full marathon. And I never would've been able to do it without them. Their support and friendship has meant the world to me. But this is the last one. I mean it . . .

To Mary & Alleyne, my writing crew. They've listened, laughed, plotted, cried, eaten, and drank with me. They've restored my sanity on more than one occasion.

And finally my biggest and best thank you goes to my family: my three beautiful children who expand the boundaries of my heart daily and my husband James, my favorite person on this Earth.

I pledge my faith to you—always.

TL

About the Author

A former criminal defense attorney, **TRACEY LIVESAY** finds crafting believable happily-ever-afters slightly more challenging than protecting our constitutional rights, but she's never regretted following her heart instead of her law degree. She lives in Virginia with her husband—who she met on the very first day of law school—and their three children.

Discover great authors, exclusive offers, and more at hc.com.

Give in to your Impulses . . .
Continue reading for excerpts from
our newest Avon Impulse books.
Available now wherever ebooks are sold.

INTERCEPTING DAISY
A LOVE AND FOOTBALL NOVEL
by Julie Brannagh

MIXING TEMPTATION
A SECOND SHOT NOVEL
by Sara Jane Stone

THE SOLDIER'S SCOUNDREL
by Cat Sebastian

MAKING THE PLAY
A HIDDEN FALLS NOVEL
by T. J. Kline

An Excerpt from

INTERCEPTING DAISY
A Love and Football Novel
By Julie Brannagh

When Daisy Spencer wrote an erotic novella about
the Seattle Sharks' backup quarterback and her
#1 crush, Grant Parker, she never expected it to
become a runaway bestseller. If anyone discovers
she wrote the sexy story, her days as a flight
attendant for the Sharks would be over. But once
she gets to know the real man behind the fantasy,
her heart may be in more danger than her job.

He could have hit the Stop button and kissed her in the elevator, but there was probably a security camera. He didn't really care, but she might not like being the center of attention when the snip of video got leaked to the local press or put up on YouTube. He wasn't letting her drive away without kissing her, though.

She paused in front of her car as she turned to face him.

"I had such a nice time. Thank you so much for dinner," she said. She shuffled her feet a little. He'd observed her so many times while she did her job. She always seemed at ease, even during the turbulence they'd experienced on the last Sharks flight. Maybe she had the same butterflies in her stomach that he had in his.

He moved a little closer to her and slid his arm around her waist. She tipped her head back to look into his eyes. He had to smile at the flush making its way over her cheeks as she licked her lips. Yes, Daisy wanted to kiss him too.

He touched his forehead to hers for a few seconds. Her skin was so soft. He could smell her perfume. He couldn't identify the flowers in it if someone offered him a million dollars, but it was nice. The parking garage was not exactly the backdrop for romance. Next time, he'd say good-bye to her at her front door instead.

"I had a great time too. I'm already looking forward to next Thursday," he said.

"Maybe we could go bungee jumping."

"Sounds perfect," he said. He heard her laugh again. "Right after that, we'll go zip-lining at Sharks Stadium."

He felt her shiver. He wasn't sure if it was the fact she was wearing an almost sleeveless dress, the idea she'd be that far off of the ground and speeding along a relatively slender cable, or that she was as attracted to him as he was to her. He needed to make his move, and he'd better do it before someone came screeching around the corner in search of a parking spot. He reached up to take her face in his hands.

"Maybe we should have a glass of wine in front of a roaring fire instead," he whispered, and he watched her eyelids flutter as they closed. He touched his mouth to hers, adjusted a bit, and kissed her.

She tasted like the wine they'd been drinking with a fresh, honeyed overlay that must have been all her. Her lips were soft and cool beneath his. He felt her arms slide around his waist as he deepened the kiss. He slid his tongue into her mouth, tasting her again. As he felt her tremble, he knew it had nothing to do with the cold. He pulled back a little and laid his cheek against her smoother one.

He wanted to kiss her until they both were breathless. He wanted to spend the rest of the evening with her, and maybe tomorrow too. Mostly, he wanted to figure out how to entice a woman into falling in love with him, and he wondered if he'd been going about it all wrong. The woman who currently regarded him with a soft expression as she reached up to stroke his face deserved more than he'd offered to women before.

"Thursday," he said. "I'll text you."

"Should I get more life insurance?"

"No. We'll have a great time." He pulled back a little and looked into her eyes. "I promise I'll figure something out that doesn't land us both in a body cast."

She dug through her purse, extracted her car keys, and hit the button to unlock her car. He made sure she was safely inside. She started her car, opened the driver's side window, and looked up at him again.

"Thursday," she said.

He watched the taillights of her car vanish around the corner seconds later.

An Excerpt from

MIXING TEMPTATION
A Second Shot Novel
By Sara Jane Stone

After a year spent living in hiding—with no
end in sight—Caroline Andrews wants to
reclaim her life. But the lingering trauma from
her days serving with the marines leaves her
afraid to trust the tempting logger who delivers
friendship and the promise of something more.

Oh hell, she should push him away. A better friend would demand that Josh Summers share his pies with a woman willing to daydream about a place in his picture-perfect future. She shouldn't let him waste his life waiting for her to make up her mind about a first date.

"You should do it," she said firmly. "You should buy the land. What are you waiting for?"

He cocked his head. One red curl fell across his forehead. His hair looked as if he'd rolled out of bed, run his fingers through the loose, wavy locks and prepared to face another day looking like an Irish god who'd somehow landed in rural Oregon. Though that might have something to do with the muscles he'd fine-tuned over the years of felling trees.

But right now she kept her gaze focused on his face, waiting for his answer.

"What if I decide on five bedrooms and the woman I want to share my dream home with thinks it's too much. I might have to settle for three in order to talk her into an outdoor kitchen that I'm thinking about building in addition to the monstrous one in the house."

"As long as you're not planning to turn half the house into some sort of man cave with beer pong tables lining the hallways, I think you'll find someone who will love your dream house," she said. "Of course to meet that special someone you will have to start dating."

And that was as close as she was going to get to kicking him in the butt and demanding that he turn his focus away from her. They could remain friends. But another kiss would just lead to a dead end.

His smile faded. "You think I should ask someone else to be my date to the wedding?"

She forced a brief nod and let her gaze settle on the half-eaten pie.

"No," he said slowly, lingering over the simple word. "I don't think so. But I might put in an offer on that land."

"You should do both," she pointed out despite the relief that threatened to turn to joy. "I can't move into your four- to five-bedroom dream home. Not when I'm still so . . ."

Scared.

Nearly fifteen months had slipped by since she'd run away from the military. She'd pressed pause on her life that day. There had been moments here and there were she'd felt ready to hit play again and move on. Each one revolved around the man standing across the stainless steel counter looking down at his pie.

"A couple of weeks ago you stopped wearing those baggy cargo pants." Josh dug his fork into the dish and glanced up at her. "I like the skinny jeans better."

Me too. And I like the way you look at my legs when you think I'm distracted . . .

"I stood out in the cargo pants and boots," she said with a shrug. "Lily said I'd blend in more if I dressed like the university students. And Josie had some clothes she didn't think would ever fit again even if she lost all the baby weight. She gave these to me."

"You stand out in those jeans too. I'm glad I only have to share the view with the dishwasher." He nodded to the machine. "And not all those young kids from the college."

"You're twenty-eight, Josh. Not that much older than those 'young kids.' Many of them are graduate students."

"More than half would love to have you serve their drinks," he said.

"I like it back here where no one will—"

"Notice you. Yeah, I get that. But my point is, you've changed since you first showed up here looking for Noah." He set down his fork and took a step back. "Who knows what will happen next?"

"Nothing."

I hope. I pray.

Because the only life-changing events she could imagine would land her in trouble. She'd carved out a safe place to hide. She had a cash job and a place to live thanks to her boss. If she lost this—

"Something always happens next." He turned and headed for the door.

She'd touched the hard planes of his chest when she'd kissed him, but the view of his backside left her wanting more. More pies. More conversation. More Josh.

One . . . Two . . . Three . . .

He turned and glanced over his shoulder. And then he

flashed a knowing smile. Oh, she'd seen plenty of hard-bodied men. She'd served alongside soldiers with drool-worthy muscles. There was nothing special about Josh Summers.

Except for his smile.

She was falling for that grin and the man who wielded it like an enticing treat. Tempted to trust in him. Believe in him.

"I'll see you at the wedding," he called and then he walked his delicious smile out the door of the bar's back room.

She abandoned her fork and dipped her fingers in the pie dish. Sugar. She needed a burst of sweetness to take her mind off Josh Summers.

Next time he asks you to lick the whipped cream from your lips, say yes!

Because Josh Summers was right. Something always happened next. And if she wanted to reclaim her life—or at least a small piece of it—if she wished for another chance to land in Josh's arms with his lips pressed to hers, then she needed to find out what happened when she said yes.

An Excerpt from

THE SOLDIER'S SCOUNDREL

By Cat Sebastian

From debut author Cat Sebastian, an
enthralling regency male/male romance about
a former criminal who has never followed
the straight and narrow and a soldier whose
experiences of war have left him determined
to find order in a chaotic world.

Jack could almost feel the heat coming off Rivington's body, almost pick up the scent of whatever eau de cologne the man undoubtedly wore. If he moved half a step closer he'd be standing between Rivington's legs. He knew that would be a bad idea, but at the moment could not seem to recall why.

"What I don't understand"—Rivington tipped his head against the back of Jack's worst chair as if he hadn't just been told to leave—"is why she didn't destroy the letters. If she knew the contents would harm her, why not throw them on the fire?"

Ah, but the ladies never did. Not in Jack's experience, at least. Mothers and governesses ought to spend more time instructing young ladies in the importance of destroying incriminating evidence and less time bothering with good posture and harp lessons and so forth.

Besides, that wasn't the right question to ask. The real wonder was that Mrs. Wraxhall hadn't kept the blackmail letter, the one clue that might lead them to her stolen letters.

Of course, people did all manner of foolish things when they were distressed, but Jack would have thought a woman who had the presence of mind to stay so tidy on such a muddy day wouldn't do something as muddle-headed as flinging a blackmail letter onto the fire.

Jack looked down at Rivington, who still hadn't moved. The man was apparently under the impression that they were going to sit here and discuss the Wraxhall matter, and really Jack ought to waste no time in disabusing him of that notion.

But instead Jack kept looking. A man this handsome was a rare pleasure to admire up close. He was younger than Jack had first thought—somewhere between five-and-twenty and thirty. Perhaps five years younger than Jack himself.

Yet he looked tired. Worn out. For God's sake, his coat was all but falling off him, despite obviously having been well-tailored at one point. "Shouldn't you be home, resting your leg?" Such a question might just be rude enough to send Rivington packing, and besides, Jack couldn't remember the last time he had seen a gentleman in such clear need of sleep and a decent meal.

Rivington opened his mouth as if to say something cutting but then gave a short, unamused huff of laughter. "If only rest worked." He didn't seem offended by Jack's rudeness. He was, Jack realized, likely a good-natured fellow. He had arrived here in a pique of anger—and likely pain—that had since worn off. Now he had the wrung-out look of someone exhausted by an unaccustomed emotion. Jack would guess that Rivington was not a hot-tempered man. And now he was contemplating his walking stick with something that looked like resignation bordering on dread.

"They always keep the letters," Jack said quickly, before he could remind himself that he ought to be ordering this man to go home, not engaging him in conversation.

When Rivington looked up, something flashed across his face that could have passed for relief. "Sentiment, I suppose."

Jack stepped backwards and sat on the edge of his desk to preserve the advantage of height. "I tend to think people hang on to love letters in the event they might choose to blackmail the sender." But then again, he never did quite expect the best from people. Maybe the lady was simply being sentimental, but in Jack's experience of human nature, people were more likely to plot and connive than they were to indulge in sentiment. Jack's experience with humanity was admittedly a trifle skewed, however.

Rivington's eyes opened wide with disbelief. "I knew a man who couldn't bring himself to sell his father's watch, even though he had creditors banging on his door at all hours. But he kept the watch because he couldn't bear to part with it. It may be the same with your Mrs. Wraxhall."

Jack shrugged. "Could be." Never having had a parent who inspired any feelings of tenderness or loyalty, or indeed any sentiment at all beyond a resentment that lingered years after their deaths, Jack mentally substituted his sister for Rivington's example. What if Sarah had a brooch or some other trinket—would Jack hesitate to sell it in the event of a financial emergency? He doubted it. Sarah would be the first person to tell him to sell all her brooches if need be. If she had any, which she did not.

"What will you do to recover the letters?" Rivington stretched one leg before him and started rubbing the outside of his knee.

Jack knew he ought to send the man on his way, but found that he didn't want to. Not quite yet. Maybe it was the dreariness of the day. Maybe it was the fact that this man clearly needed to rest his injured leg. Maybe it was simply that it had been a long time since Jack had been able to discuss his work with anyone. Sarah thought—correctly—that Jack's work was too sordid to be discussed. Georgie never sat still long enough to have an entire conversation. And nobody else in all of London was to be trusted.

Or, hell, maybe he just wanted to spend fifteen bloody minutes enjoying the sight of this man, appreciating the way the slope of his nose achieved the perfect angle, the way his eyes shone a blue so bright they likely made the sky itself look cheap by comparison. How often did Jack get an opportunity to admire anyone half so fine?

He pulled open the top drawer of his desk. "Care for a drink, Captain Rivington?"

An Excerpt from

MAKING THE PLAY
A Hidden Falls Novel
By T. J. Kline

T. J. Kline launches a brand new series with
the charming story of a NFL player who
finds love when he least expects it . . .

"Any day, bro."

Grant McQuaid did a few ballistic stretches and picked up the football he'd brought along with him, tossing it toward Jackson, knowing his brother wouldn't turn down a quick game.

"How's that arm of yours?"

Jackson shrugged. "I guess that depends on your point of reference. I'm no Miles."

He meant Aaron Miles, the starting quarterback for the Mustangs, and the guy who'd rallied the team, taking them to the playoffs last year. The same game where Grant had sustained his last concussion, the one that might have ended his career. He crushed the thought before it sank in. He was *going* to play this season, there was no room for doubt.

"Let's see what you've got." He jogged down field from Jackson, effortlessly catching the ball. Grant had been a decent receiver in high school but his size had made the transition to running back a no-brainer in college.

The two of them played catch for the better part of an hour while Grant tried to ignore the people beginning to crowd under several of the shady trees nearby, watching. It wasn't unusual to see at training camp but here, in his hometown, he hated being a spectacle. He couldn't walk down the street without someone pointing, staring or asking for an autograph. Here he just wanted to be Grant, not Grant McQuaid, starting running back for the Memphis Mustangs.

"Last one," Jackson called, lobbing the ball down the field for a Hail Mary pass.

Grant went long, sprinting to make the catch. He was damned if he was going to look like a fool with this many people watching. It wasn't until the last second he heard the child's yell and the woman's voice calling for him to "Look out!"

"I've got it!" the boy yelled as he reached into the sky, a broad grin plastered across his face.

Grant glanced away from the ball in time to see the little boy run directly into his path.

Bethany couldn't watch. She'd looked away from James for two seconds to find a napkin in her purse to wipe away the ice cream dripping over his hands and the next thing she knew, she was chasing after him as he ran directly into the path of the two men playing catch. She should have known better than to believe James would sit still when someone was playing football.

The man who'd gone out for the pass barely flinched before he leapt over her son's head as if he was no more than a small hurdle, clearing James' outstretched hands by at least six inches.

Holy crap!

James might be small for his age but that was incredible,

to say the least. A few of the other spectators agreed and began to applaud as the man caught the ball and jogged back toward James, tossing it to him gently as he came close. She watched him go to one knee in front of James and place a massive hand on his shoulder. She tried to fight down the overprotective instinct rising up in her. He obviously wasn't going to hurt James after he'd just, miraculously, avoided crashing into him. She caught up to where the pair were chatting like old friends.

"I'm so sorry." She gasped for breath, cursing the sandals she'd worn and her lack of aerobic exercise since moving to town. "I looked away and he'd taken off." She squatted down to James and grasped his shoulders. "What in the world were you thinking? You could have been hurt, badly. If this man hadn't seen you—"

"It's no problem, ma'am. He's just keeping me on my toes and prepared for anything." He smiled at James and gave him a wink before turning his deep chocolate brown gaze on her.

He rose slowly, unfolding his tall frame, to tower above her, leaving her eye level with his bared, sweaty chest. Bethany felt her mouth go dry, unable to speak even if she was able to get her brain functioning again, which it didn't seem inclined to do.